# BEHIND THE SHADOWS

## SARA JORDAN-HEINTZ

Inkd
Publishing

# BEHIND THE SHADOWS

# CONTENTS

# INTRODUCTION

It seems since the beginning of time, humankind has relished fear and the rush of adrenaline that accompanies it. We like to be scared by movies, games, amusement park rides, and, dear reader, let us not forget literary works, such as those by Edgar Allan Poe, Bram Stoker, Mary Shelley, Shirley Jackson, H.P. Lovecraft, Stephen King and so many others. Perhaps our primal fight or flight response is to blame for this natural inclination. And some, more than others, may even find comfort in what haunts us because it is familiar.

The fifteen stories in this anthology, penned by tremendously talented authors of varying backgrounds, all center on the theme of horror. These individuals have crafted stories of humanoid beings living (and plotting) among us, creatures of folklore lurking just beyond reach—some more familiar than others, and a few that are only one of many.

These stories, chosen through blind reads, were penned by a mixture of authors whose work has appeared in earlier Inkd Publishing anthologies, while others are not only new to the roster, but are cutting their teeth in the horror genre with this book. Eight of the fifteen writers identify as female, a positive thing in what can be a male-dominated genre.

You'll witness the dead come back to life and meet the people who must "round them up"; learn the dangers of playing with magic; see the hunters become the hunted; take the road less traveled and see its disastrous consequences; and learn first-hand how there's nothing more powerful than a mother's love.

But these tales chill the bones not just because of their fantastical settings and plots; but because we know at an innate level that we're never more than one phone call, one decision, one set back or one split second away from entering a world of fear.

Can you put the lid back on Pandora's box once it's been opened?

Will you see through a cultist's trickery before it's too late?

The storytelling ability of the authors in this book is impressive. You'll accompany richly developed characters as they tempt fate, battle forces of evil, seek vigilante justice, grapple with loneliness, get bogged down by self-doubt, stir up trouble in the metaphorical pot, seek the wrong acquaintances and do anything to ensure survival.

Our protagonists can be impulsive; other times, cunning. Occasionally, when a lesson is learned (or not), it has eternal consequences. In other cases, when reality becomes too difficult, all you have to do is change the movie reel or take that first step through the vortex.

You'll find between the covers of this book dystopian worlds, glimpses of the future, echoes of the past, monsters within us and those that lurk behind the shadows.

Sara Jordan-Heintz, editor

Sara Jordan-Heintz is an award-winning journalist, editor and historian. She is the author of the biographies Going Hollywood: Midwesterners in Movieland and The Incredible Life & Mysterious Death of Dorothy Kilgallen. She has written hundreds of articles for newspapers and magazines, many republished through the Associated Press and USA Today Network.

Her novella "A Day Saved is a Day Earned" was published in Rod Serling Books' inaugural anthology Submitted For Your Approval edited by Anne Serling.

Her fictional stories, heavily inspired by film noir, The Twilight Zone and everyday observations, have appeared in: 101 Words, Red Planet, 365 Tomorrows, Friday Flash Fiction, Blink Ink, The Mambo Academy of Kitty Wang, Better Than Starbucks, Potato Soup Journal and Shady Grove Literary.

Her work was published in the Brilliant Flash Fiction anthology Branching Out, in Inkd Publishing's debut anthology Hidden Villains and in Savage Realms' horror anthology Symphony of the Damned.

She most enjoys writing speculative fiction, human interest stories and pieces meant to provoke deep feelings and opinions in its readers. She lives in Iowa with her husband Andy Heintz, also a writer, their baby daughter Louisa and tuxedo cat Madeline.

# FAMILIAR MONSTERS

## HEIDI HUNTER

"*L*ast call!"

"Care for another?"

"No, thank you." Why can't a girl have a drink in a bar without someone trying to pick her up? Shannon thought.

Charles seemed to be a nice man, but they all seemed to be at first. Perched on the stool next to her, he made non-threatening small talk throughout the evening. Shannon looked him over. His suit fit tight as if he had recently put weight on a former athlete's body. And sadly for Charles, he was losing the battle with the hair gods. Why had he chosen her?

This pub dissatisfied Shannon, as did most of this Podunk little village miles from vibrant London. It was a dive but the only pub for miles, and she so needed those drinks after the dreary journey south on the train. British travel at its worst; the train was late and wheezed along like an old geezer on a golf course.

Shannon was down from London for a job interview she hoped would be a fresh start. No more being followed home by someone she turned down for a date, texting friends to let them know where she was, walking home from the tube with keys interlaced between her fingers. All part of being a young woman in London, she thought.

Lately, though, it seemed Shannon had one persistent "admirer." The phone calls from an unknown number with threatening messages, disgusting notes slipped through the mail slot, and texted photos of her around town. Then a girl disappeared a few blocks from Shannon's flat, found strangled later in a nearby park.

And now Shannon was here. With Charles. Was there nowhere she could go to escape unwanted attention?

"I should get back to my hotel." Suddenly weary, Shannon picked up her bright green peacoat from the stool on her other side. Charles helped her shrug it on.

"Need a ride home?" Shannon had feared this overture. She had done nothing to lead him into thinking they would continue their impromptu date at her hotel, had she? Was her responding to his chatter all the impetuous he needed? The dim shadows made his expression appear more leering sleaze than hopeful puppy dog. "It's not safe here on a night like this."

"I'll be ok. It's not far. Just a couple of blocks." It was more than that, but she didn't want him to know where she was staying.

Charles persisted. "You don't want to walk alone on a night like this."

"No, you don't." The bartender agreed as he returned with another pint of Charles's brew.

"Why not?" Were they working together?

"The Shalgaree comes out on a night like this," Charles said.

"The what?"

"Shalgaree." Charles jerked his head to the left. "Lives out on the marshes west of here. He only comes out when the conditions are right, like tonight—unseasonably cool, overcast, the darkest night of the moon. But it's the wind changing direction, blowing in from the sea, carrying the smell of the salty air and human flesh toward the marshes that draws him into town to feed."

Shannon snorted. Seriously, this guy would say anything to take her home. Marsh monster?

"Charles is right." The bartender, of course, supported his mate. "There are stories of the Shalgaree going back to when this pub first opened several hundred years ago."

"Who was the last that got snatched?" Charles asked him.

The bartender scratched his head. "Been a couple years since a night like this. Couple of people disappeared then. Never saw them again."

"Could they have gotten so plastered they fell into the sea and drowned?" That seemed the most likely scenario, as there was nothing else to do in this town but drink.

"I think the first was a seaman from one of the ships in port. Left here and never reached the docks. But the second was Esme Reynolds," the bartender continued. "Walking home from her boyfriend Thomas' flat after a date. Not far from here."

Charles nodded as if his memory had been refreshed.

Another missing woman, could Shannon not escape them anywhere? "Well, what does this Shalgaree look like so I can avoid him?"

"No one knows. No one has ever seen it, leastwise anyone alive. And you won't see it either 'til it's on ye."

Shannon had had enough. She didn't want to hear about made-up monsters when her life was full of real ones. She was exhausted and just wanted a good night's sleep.

"Well, thanks for the drinks and the story, but I'll be on my way now."

Charles' face fell. Guess he got his hopes up. Shannon's heart clenched a little witnessing his dejection, and the politeness instilled in her since childhood took over. "But thank you for the evening. I enjoyed myself."

Charles flashed Shannon a troubled smile. "Don't let the Shalgaree get you!" His voice held a note of warning, which caused Shannon to glance back at him. The low light of the pub bathed Charles' face in shadows, making him appear slightly devilish. She bit her lip, a tad concerned, as she exited the pub.

Shannon halted as the pub door eased shut behind her, cutting off the murmur of voices and the odor of greasy fish and chips. Charles was a nice guy, but his persistence had irritated her. Shannon had been hoping for a quiet drink after a draining train ride south, not a pick-up. And that absurd story about a shal-what?

The street before her was desolate, the Victorian-style streetlamps distant and dim, barely casting a glow on the uneven stone sidewalk. Worse, the cobblestone street was deserted, all shops having shuttered long before last call. The soft bong of the church bell heralded the one o'clock hour.

But Shannon should be safe to walk alone here. This wasn't London.

Cold wind tore through her, causing Shannon to shiver and pull her peacoat more tightly around her. She traversed the narrow sidewalk; the sharp uneven stones caused her to stumble like a drunk. She walked east toward the sea, the breeze blowing directly in her face, bringing with it the briny smell of the saltwater. Leaves scuttled around her feet.

The town was silent but for the wind and the soft tap of her heels on the stone. When the gusts briefly abated, another faint noise took its place. *Clop. Clop. Clop.* A horse? Shannon glanced over her shoulder but couldn't see one on the cobblestones behind her. Shrugging, she continued toward the inn.

*Clop. Clop. Clop.* There it was again. Matching Shannon's pace. A little louder, echoing off the limestone buildings on the narrow street. That's what it was—just an echo of her own footsteps. *Don't start hearing things that aren't there*, she warned herself.

She walked on, shoulders back, trying to appear confident to anyone watching.

*Clop. Clop. Clop.*

Shannon immediately halted. Another *clop* followed, then silence. Not an echo. Was Charles following her? To scare her into letting him escort her back to the inn? What a nutter.

Determined to give him a piece of her mind, Shannon spun around.

"Charles, is that you?" Squinting into the shadows, she tried to spot her follower. But the night was too dark with no moon, no stars, the streetlamps too far apart. No one was there.

The wind kicked up again, loosening several strands of hair from her tired up-do, which she tucked behind her ears with more force than necessary. "Charles, if you're there, show yourself." Tapping her toe, she waited for Charles to appear. The street remained deserted. "This isn't funny." Her voice trembled.

A door slammed behind her, causing Shannon to jump and spin around, nearly losing her footing on the uneven walkway. Hasty footsteps hurried off to the right, down an alley. A girlish giggle faded in the distance.

Well, at least she wasn't alone out here. Had she gotten to where she saw danger around every corner? She cursed Charles and his stupid tale of the Shalgaree for igniting her imagination.

Stiff-legged and straight-backed, Shannon accelerated her pace. If Charles were behind her, she would not let him see how much he had scared her.

Her shoes clicked in haste but didn't drown out the footsteps of her pursuer. *Tap-tap-tap-tap. Clop-clop-clop-clop.* Louder. Closer.

Other, darker thoughts began to fill her mind. Had her stalker followed her from London? Is that who was behind her? Shannon wracked her brain, trying to remember anyone suspicious on the train ride down. There was that guy who seemed to be staring at her every time she turned around...but she didn't think they had gotten off at the same stop. Maybe he doubled back?

The persistent *Clop-clop-clop-clop* sounded closer. Louder.

A foghorn hailed her from the docks. *Just what I need, to get lost in the fog and fall into the sea.*

Heart quickening, clutching her handbag tighter, Shannon hurried onward. How far could the inn be? Four more blocks? It was taking forever.

*Could Charles be her London stalker?* The thought rose unbidden in her mind. He had fixated on her at the pub almost from the time she arrived. If so, she'd never clapped eyes on him in her life. Where would they have ever crossed paths? Shannon shook her head as if to toss the thought from her brain. No, that can't be right. He was from here. He knew the bartender and the legend of the Shalgaree.

Shannon's head swiveled from left to right, alert for possible attackers leaping out from doorways and alleys. The bleak stone buildings with their dark, empty windows seemed hostile, as if blaming her for her own predicament.

And it was her fault; she should never have been out this late.

Not much farther.

The trailing footsteps continued, louder, closer. Shannon

dared to cast another peek over her shoulder, but the street was deserted.

Flinching when a garbage can clanged nearby, Shannon took off at a swifter pace, nearly jogging. Her stalker trotted behind her. *Clop-clop-clop-clop.* Catching up. How can that be when no one was there?

A dark form darted out of a doorway to her right, accompanied by the pounding of feet. Her stalker had come for her! Shannon froze, a scream welling up in her throat. Something brushed by her, knocking into her leg, panting. Her eyes tracked the shape as it raced to the other side of the street. Would he return for a second attack? The figure ran under a streetlight, revealing it to be a dog. Shannon exhaled a long, shaky breath. Just a dog. *Get a grip.*

She took one step, a phantom step echoing behind her. Shannon swung around, but still, the street was empty. *Maybe this story of an invisible monster is true after all.*

The sidewalk was so narrow Shannon's wobbly leg accidentally stepped off the curb, turning an ankle. *What else could go wrong?* She rubbed her sore foot, using a streetlight for support. The streetlamp buzzed above her and flickered. She turned around, her face pale and shiny with sweat, her eyes wide.

"Who's there?" her shrill voice rang out.

A disembodied laugh came out of nowhere. Shannon screeched and clung to the streetlight, eyes squeezed shut against the impending attack.

When none came and no footsteps approached her, Shannon opened her eyes, darting them around. There, on the top floor of the building, two doors up. An open window with the soft light from a telly spilling out. Help was close at hand; the laugh probably came from up there.

Shannon tentatively tested her ankle, found it tender but

useable, and limped to the door. "Help!" she yelled, pounding on it.

She cupped her eyes and peered through the dark window, hoping to see movement inside of someone coming to her aid.

She pounded on the door again. "Please, let me in!"

The lower level remained dark and silent. No one came.

Above her, the window whooshed shut. The light also extinguished, leaving Shannon in the dark once again.

Was this what that poor murdered girl in London felt like before she was caught? Alone, terrified, with no one coming to her aid?

Shannon sagged against the door, covering her face with her hands, willing herself not to cry. How she wished she had never gone to the pub at all!

The street remained hushed. Had her stalker given up? Feeling somewhat hidden in the doorway, Shannon forced herself to creep back onto the sidewalk. Immediately, an echoing step answered her from nearby. Nope, her pursuer was still there, in the shadows, waiting.

*If I don't move, will it just stay where it is?* Maybe if she just waited there until morning, she'd survive.

A crash and screech from a nearby alley caused Shannon to scream and flee.

Shannon gasped for air. Blood pounded in her ears but didn't drown out the sounds of her pursuer, so close she almost felt its breath on the back of her neck. Her hair came loose from its restraint and tumbled around her shoulders. Bumping into a streetlight, the bag flew from her hand into the gutter. She hesitated, then left it behind and dashed on.

*Don't look back.*

The footsteps seemed to multiply and surround her.

*Faster. You're almost there.*

The warm glow from the building's windows up ahead,

lighting up the sky, signaled the end of the chase. Her inn! Shannon sobbed and stumbled toward the safety of the lobby.

Movement flashed in the corner of her left eye. Hair? Something sharp reaching toward her.

What—?

A hand seized her right arm. Shannon released a blood-chilling scream and struck out at her attacker with her free hand.

"Whoa! Whoa!" The man before her dropped her arm and held up a hand in supplication.

The man looked threatening, stockily built, tweed flat cap pulled low over his eyes. However, his brow wrinkled in confusion rather than menace.

It took Shannon a second to realize it was Charles.

"Charles! Why are you following me?" Anger teemed from every pore in Shannon's body, and her hands clenched, ready to do battle. "Why didn't you respond when I called out to you earlier? Were you deliberately trying to scare me because I wouldn't let you bring me home?" She practically vibrated with rage.

"I'm sorry. I didn't mean to startle you. I told you it's dangerous on a night like this. I wanted to make sure you got home safely." He held out her handbag. "You dropped this."

Shannon's shoulders sagged. Had she overreacted? Was Charles just a Good Samaritan? She felt as if her judgment about men was failing her. "Thanks." She took her bag from him.

Charles touched the brim of his tweed flat cap and turned toward the docks.

"Hey!" she called. "Did you, um, see anyone else behind me just now?"

He looked over her shoulder, frowning, then shook his

head. "No one else out here on a night like this." He whistled as he walked toward the docks.

Shannon hobbled up the steps into the inn, her ankle throbbing from her flight. The brightly-lit lobby blinded her after the murkiness of the street. She felt foolish about her fright and flight. Her stalker had not pursued her here, no invisible monster had trailed her, and if Charles had not followed her home, she would have lost her purse.

Charles. Was he just a nice guy? Maybe she should track him down in the morning and apologize for her behavior? But then she remembered how he tried to scare her with that stupid story of an invisible creature. How could she have fallen for that? Charles must have had a good laugh watching her panic as she fled from an imaginary monster.

But then Shannon recalled her fleeting glimpse of something else. Hairy, sharp. Could it have been...? No, it had been Charles she saw; she was certain.

But the lingering dread would not go away. Her sore ankle later in the morning reminded Shannon of her terror from the night before. Feeling knackered, she dragged herself from the bed and went in search of breakfast.

No one was staffing the desk when she reached the lobby. A small crowd gathered outside, pointing at something on the sidewalk. Shannon joined them.

A housekeeper sobbed.

"The Shalgaree..." someone else murmured.

Shannon's heart seized, and she pushed between a couple of the inn's staff. A spatter of blood covered the sidewalk, and a trail of blood drops led away from the sea. In the blood was—Shannon bent closer to see—a chunk of flesh? Shannon's stomach revolted. She nearly collapsed from numb legs when she saw what was lying next to the blood: a blue, tweed flat cap.

"Got his next victim, he did," the desk clerk said.

Shannon's head swam, and tremors overtook her body. Charles hadn't been having a laugh at her expense last night. Was the Shalgaree real? Had it, in fact, stalked her last night? And Charles paid the price for her foolish disregard of his warning. Shannon mourned his unintended sacrifice on her behalf.

Eager to get to the train station and return to the safety of London, Shannon fled to her room and grabbed her suitcase. She dropped her key at the front desk and strode toward the railway station.

"On your way home, Miss?" the desk clerk called after her.

"Yes." Shannon grimaced at her thought that London was safer than the coast. There are all kinds of monsters. Some of them are more familiar than others.

*HEIDI HUNTER now pursues her passion of writing short stories with mystery and horror themes. Her stories have appeared in anthologies such as Wrong Turn, A-Z of Horror: I is for Internet and Halloween Horror Volume 3 as well as e-zines such as Flash Bang Mysteries and Mysterical-E. She's a member of Sisters In Crime and the Horror Writers Association. Her website is https:// wanderwoman376.wordpress.com/.*

# POTASHE PRESERVE

## CE ALBANESE

*T*he sign read Private Property. No Trespassing. It hung sideways from the arm of the barrier gate, the metal clips on the left side rusted and broken.

Russ cut the engine of the aging Ford F-150, then killed the lights, plunging everything into darkness. "We're here," he announced.

Eddie squinted out of the passenger-side window. No longer illuminated by the truck's high beams, the wall of trees and bushes on either side of the narrow dirt road had dissolved into a single, blacker-than-black, shadowy blob.

And where exactly is *here,* he thought as he looked down at his phone. He slid his finger across the screen till he found a globe-shaped icon. He pressed it, and the screen blinked then became a map. Eddie focused on the blue dot in the middle. He zoomed out. The otherwise invisible border between New York and Pennsylvania came into view.

Russ turned to his son. "Looks like we go on foot from here," he said, shoving open the driver-side door.

The interior dome light burst to life. A gust of late-November air, tinged with snow, rushed into the cabin. It bit at Eddie's exposed hands and face and neck and sent a shock to his brain, warning him the outside wasn't safe.

Russ stepped out of the truck. He pulled his jacket tight and said, "Put your phone away and grab the packs on the back seat. I'll get the guns." He slammed the door shut.

Eddie rolled his eyes. Guns. Backpacks. Hiking. This wasn't exactly how he envisioned spending his Thanksgiving college break. He glanced down at his phone. Opening the messenger app, he selected the thread with Sarah—a new love interest back at school—and started typing.

*My dad has literally taken me to the middle of nowhere. I can already hear the banjo music. Do me a favor, if you don't hear from me by the end of the day, call search and rescue. LOL. TTYL.*

Knowing that Sarah wouldn't be awake for at least another couple of hours, Eddie didn't wait for a reply. He shoved his phone back into his jacket. Then, donning his gloves, snatched the backpacks off the back seat and exited the vehicle. He met his father at the rear of the pickup truck.

Russ had flipped down the tailgate and was hovering over a pair of hard shell rifle cases. He flicked open the lid of the nearest case, revealing a Ruger American Predator rifle with a black scope mounted above the frame. "Remember this?" he asked as he held up the weapon.

Eddie tossed his backpack over his shoulder and took the vaguely familiar-looking rifle from his father. He ran his hand down the lightly tapered barrel and moss-green composite stock. "Is this—"

"The rifle I gave to you on your fifteenth birthday? Yup," said Russ with a smile.

"How? I thought Mom made you return it the next day."

Russ grabbed an identical-looking rifle from the second case. Slipping his right arm through the shoulder strap, he said, "She did. But I couldn't bring myself to do it, so I left it and the one I bought myself, at Uncle Bobby's house. They've been sitting inside his gun safe ever since." Russ took a deep breath. "Even though your mother never really warmed to the idea, I thought one day she'd let me take you hunting. I just never thought it would take three years and your mother's...."

Russ's jaw went rigid, and his voice trailed off like a whisper in the wind. Closing the tailgate with a thud, he trudged off, the newly fallen snow crunching under his boots.

Eddie lingered at the rear of the truck, his limbs frozen by a wave of bitter-tasting grief. Although six months had passed, his mother's death still felt raw. He swallowed hard, but the gloomy feeling clung to the pit of his stomach like the light snow falling from the sky clung to his wool hat and jacket.

A shrill caw pierced the silence.

The harsh and sudden noise shook Eddie from his thoughts. He straightened his back and pulled a flashlight from his pocket. Flicking it on, he pointed it in the direction he heard the sound. A pair of beady eyes reflected in the light.

And then he felt it, a tingle in the center of his back. It crept up his spine like a spider inching toward a fly caught in its web, the uncomfortable sensation growing stronger with each passing second.

*The crow wasn't the only one watching.*

Eddie swept his flashlight up and down the trees and bushes.

Nothing.

He pivoted and shone the light across to the other side of the road.

"You coming, or what?" yelled Russ.

Eddie flicked the light off. He shook the jitters from his

limbs. *Just my nerves*, he thought, then joined his father standing in front of the truck near the barrier gate.

Using a knife-hand gesture, Russ pointed down the road. "It shouldn't be more than a fifteen-minute walk to the meadow."

Eddie reached for the sign hanging from the arm of the barrier, his eyes locked on the words No Trespassing. "Are you sure we're even allowed to be here?" he asked.

Russ shrugged. "Stratton said this was where he saw Houdini."

"Yeah, I know, you told me like a thousand times on the drive out here. But did *Sheriff* Stratton mention it was OK for us to trespass on private property?"

Russ answered by swinging his leg over the barrier and hopping over to the other side.

Eddie sighed. He glanced down at the heavy lock and chain securing the swing arm to the concrete post, then up at his father.

Gone was the clean-cut, by-the-book, Marine turned community college professor. The man now standing before Eddie sported a shaggy salt and pepper beard, a recent full-sleeve tattoo—a roaring lion with lilac flowers, Mom's favorite—and apparently now believed the words "No Trespassing" were only a suggestion.

The one-hundred-eighty-degree change in character not only shocked Eddie, it frightened him.

"Let's move with a purpose," said Russ with a wave of his hand.

As Eddie scrambled over the gate, he stepped on something metallic—a small square-shaped sign. He bent down, picked it up, and wiped away a thin layer of snow, revealing a two-word inscription. "Hold up a second, Dad." Eddie's voice was tight, and he spoke quickly. "Are you kidding me? You brought us to Potashe Preserve—*the* Potashe Preserve?"

Russ halted. He turned. "You say that like it's supposed to mean something."

"You seriously never heard of this place?" Eddie rubbed the back of his neck as he looked over his shoulder toward the pickup.

Russ cocked his head to the right. "What gives, Eddie?"

Eddie clenched his jaw. His voice cracked. "This place is home to devil worshipers."

Russ stared into his son's dark brown eyes, then doubled over in laughter.

Eddie pressed his gloved hands against his hips and waited for his father to stop.

Russ finally caught his breath. "You had me there for a second, son. You really did." He straightened. "C'mon," he said as he pivoted on his heel, "let's get moving. I want to find the meadow before the sun comes up." He started fast-walking down the left side of the rutted dirt road.

Eddie gave the metal sign one last look before dropping it and running after his father. "I'm serious, Dad." His words came out in a puff of condensation. "In high school, Sean told me how he overheard his mom and dad talking one night about a group of people who used an old abandoned chapel up here for Satanic rituals. Said they'd hang pieces of aborted babies from the rafters as they performed sacrifices. Just thinking about it scares the literal shit out of me."

"Watch your language, Eddie. And you heard this ridiculous story from Sean? The pimply-faced kid who dropped out of college, lives in his parents' basement, and cuts grass for a living? That Sean?"

"He's still cutting grass?"

Russ rolled his eyes and picked up his pace.

For the next twenty minutes, father and son walked side-by-side in silence. They followed the unlit dirt road as it zigged and zagged between the slender pines and towering hardwoods and plum thickets.

Eddie kept his head on a swivel, and like a little boy, his imagination ran wild. He saw horned monsters behind every shadowy tree trunk and hunched and disfigured witches lurking inside every darkened bush.

And then there was the flutter of wings.

The carrion bird kept its distance but every so often called out—a taunt, a threat, maybe a warning. Eddie couldn't tell the difference. But every caw made his stomach twist like an eel trapped in a net.

Russ led them farther down the road.

Through a break in the trees, Eddie noticed yellowish-orange rays of light creeping above the horizon. He was about to ask his father how much longer when the road split. To the right, the road continued on; to the left, it emptied into a wide-open grassy field, dotted with short shrubs and ringed by an innumerable number of tall pines and mostly leaf-less hardwoods.

"Looks like we found the meadow," said Eddie. "So, can we go now?"

A deep frown entrenched itself in Russ' wrinkled fore-head. "No," he said, "now we wait for Houdini to appear."

Eddie's shoulders slumped forward. He was cold and tired and hadn't checked his phone for at least thirty minutes, which was probably some kind of record. "Great," he said. "Let me know when he shows up." Retrieving his phone from his jacket, he trudged over to a nearby fallen pine tree and plopped down.

Russ moved a couple of feet away to a shadow-filled spot near the edge of the tree line. He un-slung his rifle. Peering through the scope, he scanned the wind-swept meadow and then the wood line, looking for movement. Halfway to the other side, he noticed a blur of brown between two dead pines.

He held his breath as a whitetail deer stepped into view. The doe inched her way into the meadow. A second and third doe followed, their noses turned up, sniffing the air for danger.

And then a buck emerged, a massive rack of antlers adorned its head. Russ counted the points, then lowered his weapon and glanced over his shoulder. "Son," he said with an ear-to-ear grin, "we've found him."

Eddie looked up from his phone. "Houdini?" He was surprised by the excitement in his voice.

Russ motioned to the far side of the meadow. "Straight out. About a hundred yards. Near those two dead pines."

Eddie jumped to his feet. He brought up his rifle and pointed it in the direction. Looking through his scope, he quickly made the three does, and then he saw Houdini—the legendary whitetail buck with fifteen points, who showed up in the summer only to disappear during hunting season. At least, that was the story Stratton apparently told his father.

"I want you to take the shot," whispered Russ.

Eddie blinked. He dipped the barrel of his rifle.

"You can do it," said Russ keeping his voice low as he placed an assuring hand on his son's shoulder. "Just ease your grip and bend your knees a bit. And aim for the broadside of the deer, just behind the crease of his shoulder and slightly below the centerline of his chest."

Eddie inhaled. He pressed the butt of the rifle into the pocket of his right shoulder. Besides playing paintball with his friends and going to the indoor shooting range a few times with his father, he didn't possess much experience shooting guns, and he had zero experience killing something as majestic-looking as Houdini. Yet here he stood, his index finger inside of the trigger guard, moments away from becoming its reaper. His pulse raced. His hands started to tremble.

The crow cawed.

"Take the shot before he disappears," hissed Russ.

Eddie silently counted down from five. He didn't remember squeezing the trigger.

The crack of the bullet echoed across the meadow.

"You hit him!" shouted Russ.

Eddie nearly threw up.

"Hurry. Let's get to him," said Russ, who quickly slung his rifle over his shoulder and bounded off across the snow-covered meadow.

It took a minute for the ringing inside of Eddie's ears to subside and another for him to regain his composure. Then, with his head hung low, he stepped from the shadows and walked as slow as possible to the kill site. When he finally reached the other side, he found his father standing over a small pool of blood.

Russ pointed down at a set of tracks in the snow that led back toward the two dead pines. "He stumbled off," he said, eyes wide with excitement. "But he can't have gone far."

Eddie fixated on the red-stained snow. Regardless of how the day ended, he knew at that moment it wouldn't include any happy memories, at least not for him.

Russ slapped his son on the back then started walking toward the forest.

Eddie glanced across the meadow. He could leave now and make for the truck.

"C'mon," yelled Russ over his shoulder.

Eddie closed his eyes. But this adventure wasn't about him. He dipped his chin. "I'm coming," he mumbled as he turned and shuffled off after his father.

Although the trail of blood was clearly visible in the snow-filled meadow, it all but disappeared on the forest floor, the canopy above shielding the ground from the recent snow. It made following Houdini's death walk almost impossible, and forced Russ and Eddie to double back several times to reacquire it.

The minutes ticked past, and Eddie began to think he'd only grazed Houdini. "I think Houdini pulled a Houdini," he said aloud.

Russ turned around. A look of frustration replaced the one earlier of exuberance. He made an inches sign with his fingers. "We're this close to bagging an epic buck, and you want to turn back now?"

"No," Eddie lied. He leaned against a nearby tree. His legs ached. His stomach grumbled. "I just need a break."

"Fine," groaned Russ, "but only for a minute."

Eddie unzipped his backpack and retrieved a water bottle. As he twisted off the cap and brought the bottle to his lips, he froze like a pointing dog. The bottle dropped from his hands.

"What's wrong now?" said Russ, his voice tinged with frustration.

Eddie pointed. "What the fuck is that?"

"Jesus Christ, Eddie, your mouth," said Russ as he turned to look.

Rising above the tops of a nearby grove of snow-covered pine trees was a narrow dilapidated concrete chimney. Near the top, a hand-painted white eye glared down at them. And sitting motionless on the capstone was the crow.

Eddie felt his pulse thumping in his neck. "Let's get the hell out of here, Dad," he said. His voice cracked. "Like now."

"Calm down, Eddie. It's probably just an old abandoned hunter's cabin."

"With a white eye painted on it?"

Russ crouched to inspect a speck of red at his feet. "Eye or no eye," he said, gesturing toward the chimney, "Houdini went that way. So, that's the way we are going too." He stood and started purposefully walking.

An uncontrollable tremor crept up Eddie's leg. He stomped his foot to quell the sensation.

"Start moving with a purpose, Eddie," shouted Russ. "Because the sooner we find Houdini, the sooner we can leave."

Eddie didn't care about Houdini, not before, and definitely not now. *Screw that stupid deer,* he thought. *And that crow. And screw Potashe Preserve!* He looked back the way they'd come. Every fiber of his being begged, pleaded with him, to turn and run, to put as much distance between himself and that white-eyed chimney. And yet, he pushed himself off the tree, squeezed the rifle tight in his hands and mustered the will to march after his father.

The chimney was attached to a small windowless stone-covered structure, no larger than a two-car garage. Four decaying concrete steps led up to a thin, pitted metal door that hung loosely on a pair of rusted hinges.

A cold, stiff wind blew through the small grove, swirling snow and bending the treetops. The gust caught the inside of the door and flung it wide open.

Eddie felt the clang of metal against stone in his teeth. But that wasn't the only thing he felt emanating from that building. "Do you feel that, Dad?" The words croaked from his dry lips.

Russ nodded, his face expressionless, his focus drawn to the doorway. He took a step toward the building. "Stay here," he said.

Eddie didn't need to be told twice. He kept to the edge of the clearing, his feet rooted to the ground, his hands wrapped tight around the stock of his rifle.

Russ slinked toward the structure like a fox approaching a chicken. He produced a flashlight as he climbed the four steps. At the top, he hesitated, then poked his head inside of the doorway.

Eddie was twelve years old the last time he heard his father curse. Then it was funny; now it made him almost piss his pants.

Russ lurched back and stumbled down the steps. Steadying himself, he scrambled over to his son. He held out his hand. "Phone. Now!"

Eddie's fingers couldn't move quickly enough. He unzipped his pocket, retrieved his iPhone, and handed it to his father. A thousand questions rushed through his mind, but the words wouldn't form in his mouth.

Russ dialed. He brought the phone to his ear.

"Stratton," he said when the call was answered, "It's Russ. You have to come up to Potashe Preserve A-SAP...Huh? Yeah, we were up here hunting Houdini, you know the... Who's with me? Just me and Eddie. We... Stratton, shut the hell up for a second and listen to me. We came across this old stone building with a white eye painted on the chimney, and inside of it was a—" Russ paused. He looked at Eddie. "—a body hanging from the ceiling...No, this isn't a joke. I'm as serious as...Yeah, of course, I have one. Let me get it out of my bag."

Russ reached into his backpack to retrieve his GPS unit. Powering it on, he read the coordinates aloud. "OK. We'll see you soon."

Russ pocketed Eddie's phone. "He said he'll be here in less than twenty minutes."

Eddie looked past his father toward the door of the building. "Why can't we wait for him back at the truck?"

Russ un-slung his rifle and chambered a round. He kept the weapon at the low ready. He scanned the forest. "Because he said to wait here for him. So, we're waiting here. Now, shut your mouth and keep your eyes open."

Less than ten minutes later, Eddie heard the rev of an engine. Then, he saw an ATV through the trees, driven by a man dressed in an olive-drab uniform.

Deputy Sheriff Steve Stratton parked the Arctic Cat four-wheeler near the edge of the grove and hopped off. He peeled off his goggles and wool hat, revealing a clean-shaven face and bald head. His long legs covered the distance to Russ and Eddie in six quick strides. The deputy stood a foot taller than Russ and was twice as wide.

The two men shook hands.

"That was fast," said Russ. "I thought you said at least twenty minutes."

"Yeah, well, I was already on my way up here after the alarm tripped," said Stratton. "I guess that was you."

"The sheriff's department responds to alarms out here?" asked Eddie.

Stratton's glare made Eddie take a step back. He scanned the area. "Is there anyone else up here?"

"I told you, it's just us," said Eddie.

"All right. Good. Now, why don't you show me what you think you saw?"

Russ pointed to the building. "It's in there." He glanced at his son. "You wait here."

Russ led Stratton to the concrete steps. A second later, the two men disappeared through the doorway.

Eddie found the courage to inch forward, and before he knew it, he was standing at the bottom step. He heard Stratton and his father speaking in hushed tones. Leaning forward, he strained to listen.

"His skin is translucent," said Russ, "like his blood had been drained out. And those are precision cuts on his neck and collar. And his eyes—"

"Ray Ray was in the wrong place at the wrong time."

"Jesus, you know who this is?" asked Russ.

"He was a local dope dealer, a shitbird that no one is gonna miss."

"Damn, Stratton, we saw some heinous stuff when we deployed to Iraq, but nothing like this. You know, I laughed when my son told me there were devil worshipers up here. But after seeing this..."

Stratton took a deep breath. "I thought I told you not to come up here."

"I know. Sorry. I wanted to do something special with Eddie. And when you told me about Houdini...I thought it would be the perfect opportunity to make some new, happy memories with him. Those have been in short supply since Liz passed."

"Yeah, but you and Eddie being up here and seeing this puts me in a tight spot, Russ. Dammit, I liked you better when Liz was alive."

"What the heck is that supposed to mean?" asked Russ, his voice tight.

"It means the old Russ knew how to follow my orders, especially when I told him to stay out of Potashe Preserve. And that same old Russ wouldn't have snooped around in places he shouldn't be—"

Eddie heard Stratton's voice trail off, then the swish of a jacket and the snap of a button.

"And that old Russ would still be breathing."

Eddie jumped when he heard the gunshot. It took his brain half a second to recognize what it meant, and then he was leaping up the steps.

"Dad!" he yelled as he crossed the threshold. He caught a glimpse of a naked man hanging from a rope tied to the ceiling and then of his father's unmoving body crumpled on the floor in front of the deputy.

Stratton aimed his pistol at Eddie.

Eddie stumbled backward. He instinctively twisted sideways.

Stratton pumped the trigger twice.

The bullets shredded the thin fabric of Eddie's backpack before lodging themselves in the guts of the emergency hand-crank radio his father made him pack.

Eddie lost his grip on his rifle as he raced down the steps and into the grove. His legs were a blur of denim as he shed his backpack and dashed for the tree line.

He heard several loud pops, then felt something whiz over his head.

Ducking behind the wide trunk of a massive oak tree, Eddie pirouetted ninety degrees to his right, put his head down, pumped his arms, and took off at a sprint.

Not far off, he heard the whine of an engine.

Eddie willed his legs to move faster. His lungs burned, his muscles ached, yet he pushed himself harder. He burst through a sticker bush, the thorns grabbing and ripping his clothes, and stumbled onto a narrow dirt road.

In front of him, he saw the headlights of a small pickup truck speeding up the road; behind him, the sound of the four-wheeler.

Eddie sucked air like a sprinter who'd crossed the finish line. But Eddie was nowhere near the finish line, and he knew there was no scenario in which he'd be able to outrun the sheriff or hide from him. The pickup truck and whoever was driving was his only option. He broke for it, quickly closing the distance.

Eddie waved his hands high in the air.

The pickup truck slid to a halt.

Eddie peered through the windshield and nearly fainted when he saw the pockmarked face of the driver.

"Sean!" he yelled, then scrambled to the passenger side, yanked open the door, and jumped in. "He just shot my dad,

Sean! He just fucking shot my dad! We need to get out of here! Hurry, put it in reverse!"

Sean stared at Eddie wide-eyed.

"Put it in reverse, Sean! Go. Go. Go!"

Sean locked the doors. He slammed on the gas. The truck sped down the road in the direction Eddie had come from.

"The other way, Sean! Go the other way!"

The cell phone sitting in the center console cup holder rang. Sean looked down at the screen then calmly answered the call. "Yeah," he said, his voice emotionless, his eyes burrowing into Eddie. "I got him."

It took Eddie less than a heartbeat to figure out who was on the other end of the call. His body tightened. He clenched his gut. A guttural scream erupted from his mouth like a pyroclastic stream of searing hot ash and gas. Then he lunged.

Sean dropped the phone and raised his arm to fend off Eddie's vicious onslaught. He pinned the gas pedal to the floorboard.

"You mother—" Eddie leaned forward, curled his left forearm tight to his bicep, and swung his arm backward toward Sean's face. The devastating elbow strike landed with a satisfying crunch.

Blood burst from Sean's nose and mouth. He let go of the steering wheel and reached for something on the left side of his seat.

A second later, Eddie was staring down the barrel of an all-black pistol. Without thinking, he grabbed the weapon with both hands and twisted.

Sean squeezed the trigger.

A single nine-millimeter bullet punched a dime-size hole through the windshield, and then another and another, till the glass was fractured in half a dozen different places.

Eddie planted his feet, went up on his toes, and

summoning every last ounce of strength he possessed, pushed the handgun toward Sean's chest.

The pimple-scarred youth barred his teeth and grunted as the weapon slowly turned inward, his index finger no longer on the trigger.

Eddie pushed harder.

The barrel was now pointing directly at Sean.

As Sean struggled to regain control of his weapon, his thumb slipped inside of the trigger guard and onto the trigger—a fatal mistake. The hollow-point round sliced through the center of Sean's chest.

The truck lurched to the right. Sean's foot was still jammed on the gas pedal. The front tires caught the side of the deep rut in the road and launched the truck sideways into the air. The wheels spun wildly, and the engine growled.

Out of the corner of his eye, Eddie caught a glimpse of a massive tree trunk. He braced himself.

The front end of the pickup slammed into the base of a towering maple tree. The hood crumbled like a sheet of tin foil, and both airbags deployed with a bang.

Acrid smoke, like cheap Chinese firecrackers, swirled past Eddie's nose. And a hiss emanating from the front of the pickup filled his ears. Dazed, but conscious, Eddie lifted his head from the quickly deflating white bag.

*I need to get out of here.*

The primal urge to put as much distance between him and the truck overwhelmed Eddie. He shifted his weight. A sharp and intense pain lanced through both of his thighs and he looked down. His legs were trapped between the dashboard and floorboard. He wasn't going anywhere without help.

The crow landed on the hood, its dark beady eyes peering through the windshield.

Eddie held his breath.

The menacing bird cocked its head to the side and cawed twice. This time, there was no doubting the meaning of its call.

Not far off in the distance, Eddie heard the whine of the deputy's four-wheeler.

Even if he could somehow free his legs, he knew the time for running and hiding had passed. He flexed his fingers around the grips of Sean's pistol. There was only one way he was going to survive.

The crow cawed one last time, then flapped its wings and leaped into the sky.

Eddie pressed the magazine ejection button and caught the sleek double-stacked cylinder as it slid from the pistol. Counting the remaining bullets, he thought of his mother's pretty face and infectious smile and then of his father's motionless body lying in front of the deputy. Eddie rammed the magazine into the handgun, his anger and resolve grew with each passing second.

The sound of the four-wheeler drew closer.

Through the driver's side window, Eddie saw the deputy's ATV skid to a stop several feet away. The tall, square-shouldered officer rose like a periscope from his seat and surveyed the crash.

It was now or never.

Eddie leaned across Sean's still body, and as he brought the pistol to eye level, he heard his father's voice whispering in his ear:

*Ease your shoulders. Aim center mass. Kill that bastard.*

Eddie placed the front sights on the golden badge pinned to the deputy's olive-drab jacket. *Don't worry, Dad,* he thought as he squeezed the trigger.

*He's no Houdini. He's just a man.*

. . .

*C.E. ALBANESE IS a former U.S. Secret Service special agent with over twenty years of law enforcement experience. His manuscript Drone Kings earned the prestigious Grandmaster award in the 2021 Clive Cussler Adventure Writers Competition, while his short story, "Actual Stop," appeared in The Mystery Magazine.*

*He has contributed to CareerAuthors.com and serves as a board member of the Virginia Writers Club. Additionally, C.E. Albanese is the co-creator and co-host of The Crew Reviews podcast, a highly regarded weekly show that attracts over 12,000 unique monthly viewers across multiple platforms and showcases renowned thriller and crime authors.*

*A graduate of Rutgers University, he resides in Northern Virginia with his wife, who is also a special agent for the U.S. Secret Service, and their two children. For more information about C.E. Albanese, please visit www.cealbanese.com.*

# GIVE ME MY WORLD

## KELLEE R. KRANENDONK

*S*un filtered through the trees and glinted off the tiny crests of water in a burbling brook. Nearby on a large, flat stone, Ian Swan lay on his back, relaxing. A gentle breeze brushed over him as he reveled in the quiet of the forest.

The company he worked for was razing the trees to make way for apartment buildings for another company. He didn't relish the idea, but it was a way to earn a paycheck.

*Soak this in while I can.*

The gurgles of the brook changed suddenly. Ian opened his eyes and rolled to his side. Sun-diamonds appeared to bounce off the water. "Not possible." He closed his eyes. Opened them again. The diamonds were grouping and breaking, then regrouping, forming images and patterns. "What the—"

"Those are my creatures." A feminine voice came from behind him.

As he turned, he tried to clamber to his feet. Losing his footing he fell onto the stone and slid into the brook. The diamonds in the air surrounded him, but when the owner of the voice came close, they backed off, allowing her to reach him. She held out a helping hand.

"She" appeared to be a child with a grown-up's face. Barely bigger than Ian's twelve-year-old daughter, her mature face displayed a wisdom accrued over many years. Her only clothing was her own long chestnut curls in which was scattered a variety of colored leaves. Twigs wreathed her head and a little brown bird sat preening on her shoulder. Ian noticed her skin was a strange shade of green-brown.

He clasped her hand. A sort of dull electricity passed between them. Not like a shock, but Ian wasn't sure how to describe it.

"You're different," she said as he stood and towered over her. Her voice was deep and raspy, yet still feminine.

"Who are you?"

"My name is Ondeya. This is my realm. These—" she indicated the shining spots around them—"are my fairies. This is their home that your people are about to destroy."

"How—" he started to ask, but there was no need. The noisy machinery, weapons of mass destruction, Ian liked to call them, the felled trees and barren landscape, were all enough clues for anyone to understand what was happening here.

"You're not happy with it either," Ondeya stated. "Make it stop."

"I can't make it stop. I don't own this company." Ian looked into her eyes and saw one was a golden green, the other a soft brown with flecks of green. She looked confused at his words. The bird stopped preening to look at him as well.

"Make them go away. Stop working."

"I can't," Ian insisted. "It doesn't work that way."

She smiled, but there was little mirth in it. "Come with me." She took his hand and led him deeper into the forest.

As they went, the trees thickened and the sunlight waned. Unnerving shadows began crawling across the ground. Fairies darted in and out of those shadows, forming and unforming shapes.

"Where are we going? Look, I've got work to do. The guys will be back from lunch soon—"

"You did not go with them. Because you are different. You don't like this either, Ian. I know I have chosen correctly."

Wait! How did she know his name? And what was she talking about?

"I don't understand. How—"

She cut him off yet again. "You will soon enough."

As the trees thickened and the darkness grew, Ian heard whisperings, as if the shadows spoke.

"You will take this message back to those who need to hear it," Ondeya said, and then she was gone. The little flecks of light disappeared also, but the whispering remained. Ian couldn't see a hand in front of his face. The darkness pressed in, soft and cold on his skin. The sound of leaves skittering were all around him, competing with the rush of blood in his ears, the pounding of his heart. The taste of mushrooms and mud and decaying leaves filled his mouth.

Ian put out his hands and turned in every direction, but everywhere he turned, his palms and fingers met strands of sticky wetness, like a spider's web covered in dew.

Something skittered across his shoulders, something the size of a housecat, but with pointed feet that pricked and burned as they touched the skin on his neck. He reached around and his fingers came away wet. "Hey!" he called.

His response was a rattle, like that of a rattlesnake. The whispering grew louder and he could pick out words.

"…You'll die…death…punishment…you should not be

here...death awaits them...go away...get out...GO AWAY! GET OUT!"

Ian ran, breaking through the sticky strands, the wetness soaking his clothes. His face, hands and eyes all became covered with little sticky hairs. Tiny legs skittered across the pain in his neck, and into his hair. Something shaggy crawled in his mouth. He spat it out, but it left behind a vile taste that ran down his throat and slithered up into his nose bringing the smell of rotten eggs. Ian stopped running, gagging on the taste and smell.

An image flashed before his eyes. Something bloody and dead. Ian dropped to his knees, spat again. Another image flashed, this one lasting a little longer. Dead, bloody bodies lying on the flat ground that would soon be a parking lot.

Something in the darkness caressed him, like stroking hands. "Death will be yours. Or theirs. Or no one's," a deep, gravelly voice hissed in his ear, each word prickling like the branches of a pine tree. "Watch!"

More images flashed just long enough for Ian to understand them. Grass and trees growing over the bodies, worms and insects crawling in and out of orifices. Tree roots wrapping around arms, legs and skulls. Screams echoing out of the vision and into the blackness around him.

"Make it stop!" Ian yelled, panic enveloping him.

Immediately a face appeared in front of him. Ondeya! Except this time the leaves in her hair were dead and crumbling and the twigs had become writhing snakes. The bird was gone. One of her eyes was an opaque white, the other dead black. "This is what I have asked of you," she said, touching Ian's cheeks with rough, cold fingers, yet slimy like fish.

Even after she disappeared and the blackness lightened to gray, Ian could feel the slime on his face. No matter how much he tried to wipe it off, it remained. The stench was like dead fish in the sunlight.

In the grayness, Ian found himself in a forest of dead, fire-blackened trees. A river ran nearby, foam frothed at its edge, stones of white beneath its surface.

But as Ian cautiously approached it, he found they were not stones at all but bloated, rotting creatures, bones and skulls littering the riverbed. Dotted along the shore were more carcasses, writhing with maggots. Across the river in a fallow field, black smoke rose into the air.

"What is this place?" Ian muttered. "Ondeya?"

No response. No sound except for the crackle of some unseen fire.

Then Ian saw a bridge, rickety and made of bones and twine. Ian approached it, tested his weight, and only then did he realize the twine was actually spider silk. He crossed and made his way toward the smoke.

*What am I doing? Why am I here? Where is here?*

Before he could reach the smoke—he never really seemed to be getting any closer anyway—a great gust of wind slammed the smoky wall aside. Although it barely ruffled Ian's hair, he suddenly found himself at the edge of an abyss. The chasm stretched beneath him like a glass floor. Walls of dirty gray smoke encircled him and only now did he smell the acrid stench of it.

Under his feet hoards of people swarmed like ants, trying to build a structure, but never quite finishing because it kept falling like a weak sand castle. They started screaming at one another, though Ian was unable to hear the voices. Then the weapons came out and the people began killing each other, bodies stacking up, blood flowing freely, carving a river in the earth. Too terrified of what might happen if he took even one step, Ian stood frozen, unable to take his eyes off the chaos.

"Do you see?"

Ian jumped, turned and fell. The ground beneath him cracked like ice, a big jagged split zigzagging halfway across the hole, tiny veins splintering off either side.

Ondeya was back, her diamond-flash fairies accompanying her in rolling waves. Her little bird flew from her shoulder to Ian's, its tiny claws digging through his shirt and into his skin, prickling like needles.

"What?" screamed Ian. "What do you want?"

"My world. Give me my world and I'll take this all away."

"How can I give you the world?" Ian had no idea what she was asking. He was certain he was going to die here. Tears ran down his cheeks.

"Not your world, mine."

"What are you talking about?"

Once again, the fairy queen pulled him to his feet. "Come with me."

As she led him away, the cracked glass disappeared along with the smoke. Even the bridge and the river were gone, leaving everything gray and barren, the charred remains of trees and scattered, blackened bones all that dotted the land.

After walking for some time, Ondeya put out her arm and swung it to one side as if she were opening a curtain. She took another step, pulling Ian with her. They were back in the land of the living, near the stream where Ian had rested and eaten his lunch. Ondeya turned to him. "You know what you have to do."

Then she was gone along with the brown bird.

The brook continued to sparkle like diamonds, but were those just sun glints, or were they fairies?

Ian wasn't exactly sure what she was talking about. What was he supposed to do? But there was only one thought in his head.

"Hey, it's Swan," called one of the other men as Ian

stepped out of the forest and onto the work site. "Where you been? It's just about quittin' time."

"Yeah, where'd you wander off to?" asked his supervisor. "What's wrong with your neck? Is that blood? And why the hell are your clothes wet?"

"I fell asleep by the brook."

"No you didn't. We checked, you weren't there."

Having no idea what to say, Ian blurted, "We have to stop work."

"What?" shouted his supervisor.

"We can't build this here." It was as if someone else were controlling his tongue, his voice.

"Says who?" The supervisor started laughing. The other men joined in.

"Go home, Swan, have a good night's sleep and we'll see you here tomorrow. And take care of that mess on your neck."

"No."

"No what?" Supervisor was beginning to get angry. "What the hell you on about?"

"I quit." Ian turned to walk to his truck, ignoring the angry slurs coming from behind him.

\* \* \*

TWO DAYS LATER, his wife Misti called him to the living room while the news was on. He'd told her he quit, and had tried to explain what had happened, but it had already become foggy in his head. She hadn't quite understood—Ian barely did— but she supported his decision, if indeed it had even been his.

"Listen to this," she said and turned up the television.

"...Explosion last night at the construction site in Ferry Brook. Construction had only begun a few weeks before and no structures had been erected. It's believed that an underground gas chamber may have been disturbed during construction. There have been several deaths..."

Misti turned the sound down. "What's going on? Gas chamber? Ian, people died—"

"I have no clue," said Ian, just as confused as she was, emotion swirling inside. He could have been among them. He continued watching the images run behind the news anchor, subconsciously rubbing his neck. Most of the wounds had healed already. "Hey, wait! Can you rewind?"

Misti went back frame by frame. "How far?"

After a few more frames, Ian stopped her. "There. Pause. Look, do you see that?" He pointed at sparkles in the plume of smoke.

"Yeah, what is that?"

"It's what caused the fire."

"That woman?"

"What are you talking about? What woman?"

Misti pointed. There in the lower corner of the television, half hidden by the big brown cloud, was a woman with a child's face, naked except for her leaf-laden hair and a tiny brown bird on her shoulder.

*KELLEE KRANENDONK HAS SPENT a lifetime writing. According to her late grandfather, she was born with a pen in one hand and paper in the other. She's certain that these days he would have claimed she was born clutching a laptop.*

*She's had over a hundred published stories, poems and non-fiction pieces. Her work has received honorable mentions, been shortlisted; she's been a spotlight author and some of her pieces were to appear in a school book project, though that didn't pan out. Kellee has been an editor, has managed online writing groups and one of her stories appeared in a best selling anthology. She lives in a brand-new merged municipality in New Brunswick, Canada. You can find her here:*

*https://www.facebook.com/EclecticAuthor*
*https://twitter.com/MaritmeK1K*
*https://www.instagram.com/k2j2t1/?hl=en*

# THE IRON SIGH

## J.E. PITTMAN

*T*he box was cursed, though that detail hadn't been in the listing. Brady Flowers only found that part out later.

He'd felt drawn to the ornate embellishments of the black iron against which gold leaf accents popped. The artful metalwork seemed to call to him.

It was only later that he noticed the skulls buried among the gold leaf. The gravestone corners had been pointed out by his brother.

"Lot number seventy-five. Decorative metal box," the auctioneer had called. "Done in Art Nouveau style. Provenance unknown, but family legend has it that this box seals within an evil spirit captured during the War." This last he said lightly, with a bemused expression, corners of his mouth upturned as he looked over his spectacles. "Opening bid, ten dollars."

Down the aisle, Glasses Guy with a long beard raised a hand. Then a pink scarfed lady in the corner. Brady jumped in on the action when it quickly hit seventy-five, fighting his way between the two other bidders. The crowd surrounding them quietened—no further bidders joined—simply watching the frenzied trio.

Brady just had to have it. The thought of this piece of art going home with someone else made his stomach turn. The iron box called to him, a hushed whisper, a sigh of pleasure as the bid rose to one-fifty and the other two dropped out.

Glasses glared and Pinky Lady puckered like she'd eaten a lemon. In return, Brady smiled at his win. Relief edged out satisfaction in his mind. He'd *needed* to win.

"Thank you for your purchase Mr. Flowers," the auctioneer told him when he'd picked up his purchase. "One thing," his face darkened slightly, leaning close to Brady. "The family left a message for the winner."

"Yeah?" Brady arched a brow, excited to learn more about his prize.

"Yes." The auctioneer met Brady's eyes, holding the box out. "This box has an old darkness about it. Do not let it out."

Brady laughed at the ominous face the auctioneer made. He moved to take the box, but the hands gripping it held a second longer before breaking the gaze.

"Okay, okay," Brady finally acknowledged. "Don't open the box. Got it."

Message delivered, his duty discharged, the man let go, wiping his hands on his pants. The auctioneer was certainly glad to be rid of the dread weight.

* * *

"YOU PAID how much for that hunk of junk?" Brady's girlfriend Rylee did not share his enthusiasm over the win.

"It's not junk!" Anger flashed across Brady's face. "It's cool! I've never seen anything like it," Brady smiled, turning the gilt box around on the table.

"That thing is super-creepy. Is that skeleton blowing bubbles?" She looked at it out of the corner of her eye. She flicked through movies to stream, unable to look at it directly.

"See? It's wistful and fun." Brady held it closer to her, hoping his enthusiasm would be contagious. She cringed and pulled away.

"Get rid of it." She quickly slid off the couch with a muttered excuse of popcorn, stubbing her toe on the table as she went. "OW! Son of a..."

"See, karma," Brady grinned. "Shouldn't have bad mouthed my box."

"Ugh, get rid of it!" Rylee limped off.

"What's her problem?" Brady ran his fingers over the reliefs carved into the iron, sighing with pleasure. "How *do* you open it?"

"Brady, come give me a hand," Rylee called from the kitchen.

There were no seams apparent, no buttons to push or hinges visible top, bottom or on the sides. The box itself was taller than it was wide, only a few inches deep. Like a miniature cabinet. Except, sealed shut.

"Brady?" Again.

"There has to be a way." Brady shook it gingerly, hearing a rattle from inside. "Or they wouldn't have told me not to."

"Brady!" Rylee'd run out of patience.

"Coming!" He got up from the couch and put his precious box on the mantle.

The cursed box settled into its new place with a sigh.

\* \* \*

"IT'S BROKEN." Rylee's toe had turned purple overnight. She'd gone to the doctor after waking up that morning, crying from the throbbing pain.

"Shouldn't have kicked the table," Brady joked.

"Not funny, jerk," she threw a pillow at her boyfriend. "I thought I said get rid of that." Rylee hobbled over to the mantle, big toe splinted up. "Eww."

"What now? Are there skeletons boning?"

"No, it's leaking." Rylee gagged at the sight. Black liquid had pooled around the bottom, dripping off the mantle's edge. "Gross."

"Well damn, it sure is," Brady picked the box up, the sides sticky with sludge. He looked closer to see where it was coming from, trying to find a seam to open. "I'll get a rag," he said, putting the box back in its puddle.

"Hurry, it's dripping," Rylee plaintively called behind him, totally disgusted.

Brady went through the kitchen out to the garage where he kept a bag of old t-shirts. He grabbed one, lingering a second to rummage around for a flathead to pry open the leaking seam.

Rylee's scream ripped through the house. Brady's heart clenched as he ran back inside, flathead forgotten.

"Rylee?" Brady burst through the door to see her bleeding on the floor. "Rylee!" He dropped to the ground and cradled her, pressing the rag against the head wound. "What happened? Did you trip?"

Rylee made some vague sounds, waving toward the doorway.

"Hang on, don't move," Brady panicked, trying to pull his phone out. "Shit, shit. 911? We need help. My girlfriend fell, she's bleeding bad. Hold on Rylee." Words tumbled from his mouth so fast he barely noticed she was trying to mouth the words *it's out*.

* * *

"She's going to be okay, Dav." Brady switched ears as he told his brother what happened. "Just a nasty bonk to the head and a lot of blood." He was trying to scrounge a late dinner after they'd kicked him out of the hospital. Family only.

Not that she'd asked him to stay.

After she woke, Rylee kept staring at the black smears on his fingers where he'd touched the goo before she fell. Her blood had washed off easy enough, but the inky stains remained.

"They're keeping her for the night in case there's internal bleeding or something." Brady had the feeling Rylee wouldn't be coming back to his place. She'd looked terrified.

"Probably thought I did it," Brady said. The way they'd looked at him said it all. "Hey look, I'm going to let you go, Dav, need two hands for this." He'd fumbled the phone several times while trying to assemble all the ingredients for cereal. "Yeah, sure thing."

"Milk," Brady said to himself in the dim kitchen light. He hadn't bothered to cut all the lights on. "Milk," he repeated, light from the fridge spilling over his face. "Where...there you are." Brady pulled the jug from the back, taking his prize to the counter.

Bowl—acquired. Spoon—located. Box of sugary goodness —yes please. He'd only lacked the milk.

Brady flipped open the box top and pulled open the bag, pouring it with that satisfying clinking sound as the cereal fell into the bowl, ruined handily by the roach that skittered out of the cascade of golden puffs. Brady jumped back, swatting at the lightning quick bug, unable to kill it before it made its escape.

"Goddamn it," he threw the tainted box down into the trash. "What the hell?" Brady shuddered, stomach suddenly queasy. But he was still hungry. It'd been a long time since breakfast.

"Guess I'll just have a swig," Brady grabbed the milk jug with his stained fingers. Sniff check.

Failed.

Brady gagged as putrid egg smell flooded his nose to the point his eyes watered. He jerked the jug away, splashing a little out as he did, sending more sulfurous stench into the air.

"Are you shitting me?" He upended the milk jug into the sink, holding his nose as thick curdles glugged out. "I just bought that!" He ran water, trying to force the sludge down the drain, moving the gleaming faucet head side to side. Something dark moved in its reflection, startling Brady.

He turned to find nothing behind him. Just an empty kitchen.

"You're losing it, Brady," he said to himself. The stench and startle had driven all thoughts of hunger away. "Just go to bed. Things will be better in the morning."

That night, he dreamed of a shadow darkening his doorway as he slept.

\* \* \*

THE NEXT MORNING, Brady went downstairs to clean up the mess from the day before. Whatever ooky goo had leaked from his auction find had probably crusted and dried. Maybe he could do something about it. He grabbed some more rags and spray cleaners, heading for the living room.

The black sludge, though, was gone.

The box sat upright on the mantle. No puddles. No stains. No sticky bits. Nothing. Clean as could be.

Brady looked at his fingers. Not clean. The stained spots

that wouldn't wash away were the only evidence the black sludge had existed.

He picked up the box, trying to find any sign of the goo or the opening it had come from.

"Well I'll be damned." Brady set the box back on the mantle, sorting his thoughts as he sat down to stare at the gilt iron vessel, wondering what to make of it.

CLANG!

Distracted by his thoughts, Brady hadn't noticed the box shift forward on the mantle, tipping over—end over end—to land on the stone hearth below.

Brady popped up, inspecting the box for damage. He let out a sigh of relief when he spotted none.

The box clicked as he held it, opening ever so slightly. Just enough for Brady to work a fingernail into, then a finger. The iron sighed softly as it revealed its secrets.

Inside he found a small silver plate, a sharp knife, and a thimble stained black.

"Is that what spilled?" Brady picked the thimble up, turning it over between his fingers. "Too small," he said. It was an ordinary thimble, but it appeared to have been used as a cup.

A shadow flickered out the corner of Brady's eye, causing him to jerk his head around. At the same time, he heard a loud crack behind him as a rock flew into his window, fracturing the pane. Next door, he heard the vrum of a lawnmower.

"Come on, Jacobs." Brady stalked to the door, thimble still in hand, to give his neighbor a piece of his mind.

Jacobs was bobbing his head, dancing about with headphones on, as he pushed his old mower—a shoddy POS that barely worked and was held together mostly by duct tape. And not the good kind—while his dog lazed about in the sun.

"Hey!" Brady flagged him down as he neared the chain link fence. "Hey Jacobs!" Bile built in his gut.

"Oh, hey Brady!" Jacobs smiled, killing the mower and pulling off the headphones. "How ya doin' bud?" He walked up to the fence, his dog in tow.

"Man," Brady skipped the niceties, "how many times have I asked you to fix your damn lawnmower?"

Jacobs' dog growled low, lip starting to curl.

"Whoa man," Jacobs said. "What's with the negative vibes?" He squatted to calm his dog.

"You cracked my window with that rock-slinging junker!" Brady curled his fingers around the thimble and pointed back at his house. Sick blackness filled the pit of his stomach as his temper rose.

The dog lunged at the fence, barking. Brady flinched, stepping back.

"Sasha, quiet!" Jacobs grabbed the dog's collar. "Down. Dude, I'm sorry man," he said, his attention divided. "Look, I'll help you fix it. Sasha!"

Sasha the dog kept barking at Brady, going wild. Teeth bared in a vicious snarl. His mouth ran dry as he stood there.

"I don't know what's gotten into her dude," Jacobs said, now working twice as hard to restrain his dog. "She's usually super chill."

Brady felt a shadow come over him as he gripped the thimble, like a cloud blocking the sun for a moment. Sasha yelped and ran, breaking free of Jacobs' grip.

The pair stared after her, not saying a word until she'd hid herself under the porch.

"So yeah," Jacobs began. "Sorry about the window dude. Like I said, I'll help you fix it."

"Appreciate," Brady nodded, going back to his house.

Once inside, he put the thimble back in the box and shut it with a sigh.

\* \* \*

THAT NIGHT, Brady dreamed again. This time of an old woman.

They were standing on a dusty farm—drought stricken, overwhelming desolation—when a mortar shell went off nearby. It was being bombed.

The old woman pointed and shouted but her words were lost to him. There was no sound, despite the raining debris from the bombs.

Brady came close in an effort to hear the woman, her eyes frightened, pleading. He took her hand as she urgently tried to tell him something, but too late.

Black goo consumed her, rising up from the dust over her kerchiefed head, running down the length of her outstretched arm and onto Brady.

The last thing Brady saw of her was her eyes. Haunted and wide. Terrified she'd failed to give him the message.

Brady awoke, paralyzed with fear as he saw shadow gathered in the doorway. He wanted to scream, but his throat clenched. His eyes burned as he struggled to draw breath— pinned beneath the blankets by the figure's vacant gaze, unable to break free. The shadow loomed closer by the second, bending over Brady as he lay there helpless in the night.

He whimpered as the blackness brushed against his stricken face.

Brady bolted upright in his bed, cold sweat pouring from his brow. Confusion addled his reason. Unsure if he had just then awoken, or had simply been released from his paralytic bindings.

Another twinge at the corner of sight drew his eye.

The shadows had moved.

* * *

DAYS, this went on. Horrible nightmares of engulfing darkness and abject desolation—but never again the woman desperate to warn him.

Brady no longer slept. At least not at night. During the day, at least, the sunlight kept the shadows at bay for a few moments of fractured rest.

But even in daylight, the shadows twitched and moved. Things would break inexplicably and all the food in Brady's house went bad as soon as it came through his kitchen door. The stain on his fingers had grown larger than before. Everything they touched turned to rot.

Rylee had been discharged from the hospital, but refused to see Brady. Refused to even speak to him or about what had happened to her, but he had his suspicions.

And then one day, seven or eight later—Brady could no longer keep track—a knock at the door.

"Doc said the eyes burning is from ammonia exposure," Brady told his brother on the other end of the phone. "And the swelling and pain in my foot is gout. Gout! At my age!" The last few days had proved unpleasant for Brady, myriad ailments popping up all at once.

The knock came again.

"One second!" Squick, squick, Brady walked across the carpet. His downstairs bath had flooded in the night, soaking everything through.

"So I think the doc was full of it, Dav." Brady cast one burning eye at the box as he passed. It sat there, quietly waiting. "Had no idea what's wrong and just said something to get me out of there."

The knock came a third time, snapping his trance.

"Hang on!" Brady undid the bolt and turned the knob.

"Dav, I'm going to have to let you go," he said. "There's a Rabbi at the door."

On the other side of the doorknocker stood Glasses Guy with the long beard from the auction. The one Brady'd beaten for the cursed box.

"You opened the box," Glasses said. No preamble, no introduction. He just took one look at Brady and knew.

"It kinda opened itself," Brady said in defense. The accusatory tone Glasses opened with put Brady on edge. "It fell."

"Dr. Isaac Hamer," Glasses said. "Not a Rabbi." Hamer made to shake hands—shifting an old school doctor's bag to his off hand—but stopped short, seeing Brady's stained fingers. "You touched it?" He looked dismayed.

"I don't see as how I had a choice," Brady stiffened, "since it oozed out on me while I was holding it. Made a damn mess of things, too."

"Oh? The cursed box holding an evil spirit that thralled you into releasing it," Dr. Hamer paused, "quote 'made a damn mess' you say? Shocking." The man in glasses pushed Brady aside with the small doctor's bag—careful not to get near the stain—and invited himself in.

"Just a second, pal," Brady squicked after. "I didn't say you could come in."

"Look," Dr. Hamer said, "I'm trying to help you here. Now, where's the Dybbuk Box?"

"The what?"

"That," the doctor pointed to the iron box on the mantle.

"Is it toxic?" Brady looked down at his stained hand. "Is that why the other doctor couldn't figure it out? Some kind of radiation poisoning," he asked, tallying his sudden ailments.

"I'm an occult philosopher, not a medical doctor," Hamer

clarified. "And your doctor couldn't pinpoint the cause because, frankly, you're cursed, Mr. Flowers."

"Now just a minute," Brady started. "That's bullshit. Cursed? There's no such thing."

"Oh really?" Dr. Hamer looked Brady square in his red, swollen eyes. "Tell me, have any nightmares lately? Ones that follow you when you wake?" The occultist stepped forward, squelching the carpet. "Or how about freak accidents?" Squelch. Squelch. "Ringing any bells yet?"

"How did..." Brady stared, stunned.

"Food spoils as you touch it," Hamer gestured to Brady's stained fingers. "People, animals avoid you? Need I go on?"

"What the hell is it?" Brady admitted, finally, what he'd known deep inside. The box was evil. He needed help.

"Dybbuk," Dr. Hamer said. "Spirits of the malevolent dead, called to protect. Now set free upon the world. Restless. We need to..."

The lights flickered and the doctor screamed. Brady flew back, hitting his head on the banister, his body tingled. Darkness plunged into the room. Brady smelled hair burning, then all was dark.

* * *

"IT KILLED HIM, DAV." Brady clicked around the internet as he talked, looking for a way out. "The damn thing electrocuted him!" And caught his house on fire in the process. He'd come to wearing an oxygen mask on a stretcher watching firemen bust out his already broken window to get a hose in.

"My throat's better now, was all scratchy from the smoke." Brady clicked a video on exorcisms. "S'why I haven't called," he coughed, belying his improvement. "I know."

Brady listened to his big brother Davin, gone out to California, lecture him for a bit half-heartedly, his focus drifting toward his research.

"Look Dav," Brady interrupted. "I'm going to try to fix this tonight, but I wanted to tell you I love you. Just in case."

From his research, Brady'd cobbled together a plan from bits of Jewish and Catholic tradition, a smidge of modern witchcraft and whatever hadn't burned in Dr. Hamer's bag—salt, mostly. The candles had melted, and Brady couldn't read the words on the scroll he'd found in a metal tube, but he didn't think he'd need to. Just stick it in with the box.

"I'll be fine," Brady lied. He doubted he'd ever be *fine* again. But hopefully he'd at least be *free.* His eyes lingered on the cold iron box, taunting him, unburned upon the mantle. "Let me let you go, Dav."

Brady hung up on his brother then silenced his phone. He didn't need any spam texts distracting him at a pivotal moment.

Down into the basement he went. He'd spent the last three sleepless nights digging a pit back into the foundation, lining the bottom, top and sides with welded steel plates. At every step of the way the darkness whispered.

On these plates he drew all sorts of signs and circles he'd found online—most variations on a pentagram or a star—sealing them with his blood as the sites told him to. The shadows cringed.

Brady lit candles at the five points of the star on the bottom plate on which the cursed box sat, its doors opened. A broken circle of salt surrounded it, waiting to trap the Dybbuk back in its prison.

"I make this offering of spirit." Brady took the ritual knife from the box and cut a lock of his hair, placing it on the silver plate. The candles flickered in the windless basement, shadows dancing on the wall. He had its attention.

"And blood." He cut his palm with the knife, pouring the

welled blood into the thimble—feeling violently ill as he did. More blood flowed than was needed to fill the cup, spilling over the lip and into the box below, vanishing with a hiss of smoke.

The exposed timbers of the basement groaned and the house above rattled. Darkness grew deeper, rushing past Brady to lap at the blood. The hair plated up for the spirit burst into flame. All was consumed, blackening the inside of the now hot iron.

"To bind you," Brady forced out the words. Fighting for every syllable. "My will..." intense pressure built in his head, feeling as if it might explode. "...be..." He reached for the stout iron doors, forcing them closed. "...done." With a sigh, the iron sealed shut again. Once more seamless.

Brady felt the darkness fill the box. The malevolent dead gathered within. His own soul less leaden, poison drawn from the wound.

Panting for breath, Brady completed the circle of salt to seal the spirit in the box, saying prayers to God, Jesus, Allah, Buddha, Hecate and any other deity who may listen. He repeated this litany as he placed Hamer's scroll across the opening of his steel box and welded the final panel in place.

Exhausted, Brady crawled his way upstairs to the bath.

Part of the ritual, he'd read, had been the cleansing bath that followed. That sounded heavenly right then.

Hollow eyes regarded Brady in the mirror as he stripped, unrecognizable as his own. His body gaunt from the festering food, ribs showed as he slid into the bath he'd prepared according to the Pink Lady's videos.

Brady had been surprised to find out the other bidder had a rather popular modern witchcraft channel online that offered practical advice. The herbal bath was one of them and it felt heavenly as he scalded his skin clean of evil.

"Wash the face not seen in dream," he said ritualistically, cupping his hands, letting the water flow over him.

He sighed, closing his eyes, luxuriating in the warmth.

Searing pain stabbed into his stomach, causing Brady to convulse.

"Oh God," he cried, thrashing in the bath, steaming herbal water splashing everywhere. "Noooo," he spasmed and seized, arching his back. The pain overwhelmed Brady, his mind going blank.

He coughed up a mouthful of vile blackness. Again and again, gurgling for breath. His eyes bulged, rolling wildly as he heaved torrents of sludge into the tub.

No delightful herbals could cover the putrescence. Bile rose in his throat and then...

It was gone. All trace of the vitriolic malice consuming his life vanished.

Brady felt cleansed for the first time in weeks. Felt whole again. Light. He regained his senses.

His throat no longer burned, his eyes no longer red and bloodshot. The pain in his foot and joints was miraculously gone. As quickly as the maladies plaguing him manifested, they now disappeared.

Brady smiled at himself in the mirror. He was free. He could live again. He felt reborn.

Distracted as he was by this blissful lack of illness, Brady did not notice the stain lingering on his fingers.

Did not see the deep shadow looming behind him.

Did not hear the whisper of iron locked away.

Did not feel the hand grab his hair.

Until it was too late.

Sigh.

. . .

*J.E. PITTMAN IS AN EMERGING author dabbling in many speculative worlds. He blurs the borders between genre and crafts salient lies to tell a measure of truth. His work has been described as: capriciously chimeric, dreamlike, and a vivid enigma with indelible images stamped on your brain. He's currently published in the Hidden Villains Arise anthology and independently publishes his urban fantasy series: Felix Chance. Discover more of his words on www.halfacrepond.com*

# ALL WRAPPED UP IN POE

## ROBERT KOSTANCZUK

*T*he night to settle in had arrived.

This time, there would be a glorious opportunity to read in his den throughout the full length and breadth of the deep, dark atmosphere of a tantalizing Tuesday.

It had taken months to reach this perfect confluence of conditions that allowed for a perfect, and warmly embracing, environment for classic horror literature. In the past year, there always seemed to be one or two impediments that interfered with the contented mood needed to truly enjoy hunkering down with spine-tingling tales, such as the seemingly chronic edginess that vexed him.

Tonight was different, though. A relaxed mentality encased him.

Outside, December sheathed the arched window by his high-back leather armchair in crystalline splotches of frost.

Methodius intended to get lost in the works of Edgar Allan Poe.

The literary style of Poe was elaborate, nineteenth century...even flowery—and that very much suited Methodius because he could dive into it, escape into it.

His hectic week of crime reporting for an urban newspaper had left him spent, but with a mellow, placid sense of accomplishment.

He often worked nights and weekends, so free periods for leisure were hard to come by.

Methodius needed them because his job was a high-pressure one that routinely left him in an agitated, unsettled state. High blood pressure was a medical condition that came with the territory.

He had recently covered a beheading. It was unreal. A drunk, psychotic ex-boyfriend had lopped off the head of his former girlfriend with an ax, in his backyard, after he had knocked her unconscious.

Methodius managed to uncover that he was a stalker. The restraining order issued by the court had done no good. The ghoul planted her head on a pointed, wooded fence post.

The elderly lady next door nearly fainted when she saw the ungodly sight while leaving her home to get some basil from an herb garden. The eyelids of the unfortunate young lady made it appear as if the left eye was winking at the neighbor.

Methodius hated covering that story. It was too intense.

He loved reading terror yarns, but always approached them with a this-is-entertainment attitude.

Poe's writings were a way to get a rush of excitement without actually having to inhabit the crazed world that many of the author's fiction pieces were set in.

The decapitation shook Methodius for weeks. It added to his overall, persistent anxiety.

Methodius was stout, with average looks and chubby fingers that he hated. Social skills were also lacking—he yearned for the companionship of women, but was clumsy around them.

It made him tense that he was thirty-three, with little prospects for a steady girlfriend, much less marriage.

However, this particular evening was intended to serve as something akin to a soothing balm, and all things appeared to be lining up nicely. Below-zero weather lent a frigid stillness to the outdoor world, accommodating dark literary pursuits.

The house was all his, in all its Victorian splendor and shadowy nuances. Leafing through a handsome bound volume of Poe's *Complete Works* he made it a point to mentally run through examples of the author's edginess, which defined his psyche.

There was animal cruelty in "The Black Cat"...gruesome dental desecration in "Berenice"...simian savagery in "The Murders in the Rue Morgue"...a vengeful jester in "Hop-Frog"...

Even the manic alliteration in the poem "The Bells" tingled with an odd, icy sensation.

And "The Raven" wasn't particularly scary, but the poetic classic did indeed create a closed-in realm that plopped the reader into the middle of the visit by the winged intruder.

The swath of literary imagination was deliciously diabolical in the eyes of Methodius.

There was no end to Poe's fevered, pioneering genius in the realm of horror.

* * *

RESTING the open book on his lap, Methodius smiled, took a sip of coffee and then flipped to "The Masque of the Red Death."

The blood-colored tone of the tale mesmerized him.

Hues spoke to Methodius: He donned a turtleneck, cardigan, sweatpants and thick socks—all crimson.

Methodius ran his fingers along the golden-gilded edges of the pages, which next offered up "The Tell-Tale Heart."

Methodius savored how the master of the macabre described the killer's panicked detection of "a low, dull, quick sound" akin to what a watch makes when "enveloped in cotton."

Gradually, and with focused acuteness, Methodius became aware of a muffled, rhythmic beating that strangely emanated from the hardwood floor on the side of his large and opulent chair.

How could this be? He shook his head in wonder.

Leaning an ear downward, he determined that the firm, repetitive thuds seemed rooted beneath the floor.

Taking a deep breath, he stayed silent for a few seconds, and listened again.

The heart-like beating was still there.

Methodius grew increasingly concerned.

"I don't need any weird stuff now," he said to himself through gritted teeth. Mere agitation suddenly shot to near panic.

Usually, Methodius did not mind his solitary life.

Living alone in his grand and stately house was often a font of rich and enveloping tranquility.

Yet, the slightest disturbance or annoyance that rattled his regular routine was a monster that could spiral him into a state of flux and tingling unease.

He was obsessive about order, about controlling his environment—especially when it came to personal time.

This particular unearthly moment—with its incomprehensible sounds of cardiac palpitations—was one of those instances that shattered the serenity. Panic began to worm its way into his fragile being.

\* \* \*

DESPERATE TO CHANGE THE ATMOSPHERE, Methodius turned to "The Premature Burial."

For a minute, the words transported him away from the unpleasant reality: "I feel that I am not awaking from ordinary sleep...I writhed, and made spasmodic exertions to force open the lid..."

Methodius tried to race through the passages in an effort to drown and kill the assault on his ears.

However, his state of mind could not prevent the intrusive return of the torturous cacophony.

Methodius scrambled onto his knees, placing an ear to the floor.

Scratching beneath the floorboards could be heard.

Methodius cringed. A distressed wailing also was discernible, if ever so slightly.

It rose from the depths.

He placed his ear to the floorboards again, not breathing in order to accommodate total silence. A sharp, insistent tapping at the window jolted him, diverting his attention.

Methodius lunged his head toward the sound, glimpsing something fluttering on the window ledge. It was feathery... the color of coal.

Transfixed, Methodius stared as the creature glided into the deep, expansive sky.

It was a bird—a different kind of bird.

He both shuddered and beamed at the thought that it could actually be a raven.

Emotionally wound up, Methodius headed to his nearby parlor for a change of atmosphere, and to gather his senses.

The curtains were thick and richly purple.

This was his self-decreed, other-worldly room.

At the entrance—on a finely crafted pine nightstand—was a small model of the deathly, slowly-descending, crescent-shaped blade from Poe's "The Pit and the Pendulum"—it was stainless steel, about four inches long, and swung from an A-shaped frame made of cherry wood.

Unlike the spine-tingling Poe work that told of heightened torture, there was no replication of a bound victim under the swinging instrument of slicing, which could be rocked side to side with a flick of the finger.

Methodius noticed several dark spots—resembling drops—at the bottom of the pendulum.

They stood out on the surface of the nightstand.

After a minute or so of studying the sight, Methodius came to the conclusion that they resembled blood.

He laughed an uncomfortable laugh.

No, he scowled, that could NOT be real blood directly under the blade.

In any event, Methodius was in too much of a shaken state to really probe the true composition of the mysterious little stains.

Exhausted, he headed back to his reading room that was rimmed with lofty bookcases.

There, he eased into the den's opulent chair, with the intention of resuming his reading.

But mentally, Methodius was spent. He laid back his head, and ever so slowly, drifted into the fog of fatigue.

Stillness reigned.

Then came the piercing of sharp chimes that darted from the stately grandfather clock, which loomed in front of him, along a wall of mahogany.

It was midnight.

Methodius wondered where the time had gone.

Did he drift off to sleep for a while?

Methodius didn't know.

Confused, and battling a growing sense of fear, Methodius gazed blankly at the clock.

Inexplicably, something moved across the open doorway

of the den. Methodius caught sight of it in his peripheral vision. For a few seconds, nothing could be seen in the doorway.

But then, a figure appeared outside of it, standing motionless in the hallway adjacent to the den. A small lamp on an end table next to the entrance barely illuminated the tattered shroud-like raiment worn by the intruder.

An all-encompassing cloak draped over the shoulders, but remained slightly open in front, exposing shredded, dingy garb that flowed downward, hiding the feet.

The cloak's hood draped over the head of the unfathomable threat.

Everything worn appeared to be saturated in a concentrated scarlet color. Methodius could not make out any facial features, but something dripped from the area of the visitor's face. All his instincts told him he was witnessing the dripping of some kind of bodily gore, perhaps thick blood.

Words from Poe sliced into the head of Methodius: "... and the Red Death held illimitable dominion over all."

Methodius closed his eyes tightly and shook his head in an effort to clear thoughts and put a fresh sheen on the situation.

Start over, he thought to himself; maybe this is a bad dream.

Slowly opening his eyes, Methodius could no longer see the figure in the hallway.

However, a warmth could be felt right next to him.

He methodically turned his gaze upward and slightly to the rear of the armchair.

Hovering above was the cloaked head of that unholy thing which had crept into his home.

Blackness swallowed everything around the eyes.

But there was a glint from splotchy, rotted teeth, which

were exposed when a hellish grin started to stretch across the dreadful visage.

The invader then admonished Methodius in a guttural, croaking tone: "When you delve into Poe, expect an in-kind response."

The breath of the uninvited was rancid. The air in the room seemed somehow humid and heavy, with an oppressive weight.

Methodius hurriedly turned away, quickly feeling the tight, vise-like squeeze of a hand on his shoulder, which brought stabbing pain and churning fear. Methodius jerked his head back toward the assailant.

The deathly specter was gone.

Still, Methodius knew in his soul that an unwanted world had been stirred up. It was now part of *his* world, forever.

There would no longer be peace. Fate had spoken about the possibility of future contentment...nevermore.

* * *

THE GLINT of morning sunlight through a window gently poked at Methodius' closed eyes. Ever so slowly, he awoke from fitful sleep in his armchair.

Cautiously, warily, Methodius scanned the den. He simultaneously repeated a couple of prayers in his mind in an attempt to subdue his rising blood pressure.

All was silent, normal.

There were no creepy cardiac murmurs, no repugnant rappings on glass, no shrill clamor of pain from beneath the floor, and no ghostly vision hovering around him. It was all a bad dream! That was the conclusion that elicited a physical sigh of relief.

As Methodius sank down in his chair with every intention of relaxing, he noticed his open Poe book on the antique reading-lamp table to the left.

Wedged in between the pages of the morose "Morella" was a pearly white, satin-ribbon bookmark. The vertical strip of stiffened fabric stuck up sideways in the air, showing off some rather eloquent, cursive writing on one side that had not been there previously.

Methodius, who was stirred out of his blissful state, read it with heightened apprehension.

The brief message jumped out at him like a coiled serpent.

It said: *This was all frightfully enjoyable ~ E.A. Poe.*

A COUPLE OF WEEKS LATER, the salutation from the grave became a treasured keepsake for Methodius. His initial feelings of revulsion and disbelief gradually gave way to appreciative acceptance.

The world is strange; life is unfathomable, unexplainable, he thought. Sometimes the supernatural happens; forces beyond our control intervene.

That was his take. He had to embrace the bizarre greeting on the bookmark as actually having come from Edgar Allan Poe.

There was no other explanation. There could be no other explanation.

ON ANOTHER WINTER'S NIGHT—THAT preceded a day off from work—Methodius again settled in with his book of Poe's works.

It was two days before Christmas.

Things had gotten away from Methodius this holiday season...he forgot to put up any yuletide decorations. Usually, he sprinkled his vast, cavernous house with them.

The atmosphere was always lonely this time of year, but knowing Poe had recently acknowledged him eased the hurt.

The den also didn't seem nearly as gloomy and foreboding as holidays past.

Clad in a particularly cushy bathrobe that was complemented by equally soft house slippers, Methodius smiled to himself as he gazed down at the yet-unopened volume of Poe masterpieces.

His mood quickly changed. Dread moved in.

At the top of the book, scratched irregularly in the gold-gilded edges of the pages, was writing that seared the sensibilities:

*That was not Poe...Best regards, Beelzebub.*

At the exact moment when the weight of the words started to sink in, Methodius heard a rustling directly behind his grand, high-back chair.

He didn't dare turn around. But Methodius did slowly rise and walk ever so calmly to his upstairs bedroom to gather himself.

He heard no noises going up the stairs, for which he was very thankful. Sitting down on the mattress—at the foot of the bed—he quietly put the Poe book down next to him.

What just happened? He thought to himself.

This can't be real, came the next thought.

Just then, he felt a slight sinking in the bed, as if someone —something—was sitting down next to him.

But he saw nothing, just a depression in the bed.

The reckoning was here, he reluctantly admitted; the visitant had followed him.

*Robert Kostanczuk is a former full-time entertainment/features reporter for the Post-Tribune daily newspaper of northwest Indiana.*

*He won first place for "Best Personality Profile" in a 1992 competition sponsored by the Society of Professional Journalists, Indianapolis chapter.*

*His fiction piece "Safe Haven For Nathan" was published in Homicide Lullabies: A Collection of Adult Horror Stories (2016: Severance Publications Ltd.).*

*Robert's horror-themed "I Eat Anything" was included in Shocking Stories (2018), a collection from Rainfall Publishing Company of the United Kingdom.*

*In 2019, his beastly yarn, "A Stirring in the Woodland," was published by Schlock! Webzine of the United Kingdom.*

*Robert's "Lizzie Borden Versus Belle Gunness" appeared in the Spring 2020 issue of Suspense Magazine, while Burial Day Books published his supernatural piece "Fatsy Noodles" in 2021.*

*Robert's flash fiction "Coming Along Swimmingly" appeared in Beyond Words international literary magazine (Issue 13; April 2021): Beyond Words Publishing House; Berlin, Germany.*

*Twisted affection was the subject matter of his chiller "Steve Loved Her to Pieces," published online by The Chamber Magazine in February 2022.*

*Robert lives in Indiana.*

*Twitter: https://twitter.com/hoosierkos*

# ONLY ONE OF MANY

## L.A. SELBY

*E*scape, by nature, is a desperate and lonely act, which is why I go alone to the cheap theater on Eastman.

My name is Tithonus, Tito for short and "Tits" when I'm passing in the same city for a few years, after the cops and splatter techs get to know me. Nothing to do with my looks —it's just too good a joke for them to pass up. *Tits*. For a seven-foot, long haired guy. My parents named me before English was a thing. Doesn't bother me. People with crazy nicknames have access to lots of places other people don't.

I like the three-dollar movie night and the frequent oldies. The floor is only moderately sticky under my leather boots, the sagging seat cushions make me seem closer to normal height, and no one looks too closely at anyone else. The whole place smells like old popcorn, burned grease and stale nachos. Conversations are mutters and the ceiling is made of those white plastic tiles, the preformed ones that always seem to be cracked. There are so many flies up there, those cracks could be moving. Buzz, buzz.

In a world where most all the flies are dead, no one

understands why the last ones swarmed to Phoenix. Why thousands picked today to plague this old movie theater.

It's me.

They're here because I'm here—which the guy three rows up from me wouldn't appreciate. He's never going to zone out enough for a movie if he has to keep flapping his hands around and cursing like that.

I'm sitting in back. Even with pictures on the screen it's dark enough that my oversized duster is just another shadow. Arizona heat means a jacket like mine stands out, but it can't be helped. The jacket stays on when I'm off duty. It hides how my skin writhes over my chest better than my park ranger uniform. I don't have easy answers for all the questions when people notice something happening under my skin. Learned that a few centuries ago. So, I wear the jacket, and when the locals aren't calling me Tits, they're calling me nuts. I get it.

I'm breathing a little fast now, I know. A little shallow. It's the anticipation—and not for the movie. Today is another live run of SWTRS: the Screen-Weave Tasing Room Separator. The idea started with those electrified tennis rackets, the neon green ones that fit in your hand and zap flies in the air. But here we are in 2035—and this adaptation—it's really something.

SWTRS is a mass extermination device. And I need it to work. It may be a way to kill the last of the flies, and I'm pretty sure until they're all dead, I won't be. Then again, I hurt because *they* hurt, so who am I really here for? Me or them?

A twitch begins under my skin, along the left side of my jaw. I clench my teeth and it stops. My control over this body is getting weaker. Didn't used to have to do anything physical to get it to quiet down. The more of them that die, the weaker I get, and I can't afford to get so weak I can't use the machine when I'm ready.

SWTRS attaches to walls—walls like the one about thirty feet away from me. Electric walls sound dangerous but they're not—for people. Floor-to-ceiling rubberized bars are too close together even for little kids to stick their hands through. It's fine. I might not be so excited if children were poking their hands in there. I'm a cynic—more properly a nihilist—but I hate to see kids in trouble, and I've seen them hurt a lot in my current line of work. Kind of makes me sick. Which is ironic, when I think about it.

Below the mesh is the moat, a six-inch tall pheromone reservoir. That's where the bodies will fall, and that's where they'll be vacuumed out later. Piles of rotten meat might have been a more powerful draw than synthetic pheromones, but we know that's not going to happen.

I'm guessing once the flies are all gone some genius will find another use for this system. I've seen things like that happen before. I bet the inventor thought of that too. Dollar signs.

All that matters to me now is the inventor got permission to get this electrified wall installed in one dark, fly-infested theater inside the last fly-infested city in the world.

It's fly-infested because I've been a park ranger near Phoenix a long time. The work suits me. Suits my children. I find bodies a lot. People don't think finding bodies is a part of being a ranger, but it can be, and I'm really good at it. Animal bodies, people bodies. Lots of things die in national parks, and they used to sit out longer than bodies in the city. Anyway, it's the difference between feeding my children junk food or whole food. It was never really a question. I've always done the best I could.

There are tiny, hairy feet crawling up the back of my neck. I don't mind. It won't last long.

Problem is, I can't save them from ghastly deaths and I can't escape the screaming. There are so many of them. Feeling them die is like peeling the blister off a third-degree burn. Sure, after centuries I can think and talk and live around it, but still. Regrets are a plague, like the flies.

I did try to get away before.

I had myself tied to a block and dropped at sea. Why wouldn't that work? I can't live down there. That was, what, a thousand years ago? But the fish gnawed at me, and then they died and floated, and then parts of me came back and, well, it's gross.

Then I found that serial killer—the one who buried people alive. I was sure if he buried me really, *really* far down—but I only slept for seventeen years. When the temperature hit sixty-five—*bam*—I tunneled up before I knew what I was doing. Damned cicadas. They're the whole reason I'm an immortal god, and why should I have thought I could be buried without coming back? But I'm way past cicadas now.

And I can't kill them myself. It has to be something else, like SWTRS. There should be an initial zap prior to the movie. I saw it on the internet. It makes sense not to have everybody sit through a movie with flies landing on them.

Commercials are still playing onscreen. Fifteen minutes is an unacceptable amount of time for commercials. Sometimes new movies seem like one big commercial. Another reason I like oldies.

"Welcome to the Weisbart Theater on Eastman. Please stand by for SWTRS." The recorded female voice pronounced it "swatters," over the PA, which I appreciate. "You will hear a popping noise. The system is activated for your movie-going comfort. Thank you."

There's still the one fly on the back of my neck and now two crawling on my left hand. Usually, I've got at least ten flies somewhere on my skin when I go out. Three means the moat pheromones might be working.

I'd wondered if I'd be bothered by the pheromones, but I'm not. Too big for that sort of thing, though I admit I'm a little creepy crawly under the skin.

The two flies on my hand just took off. They could have stuck with me and they didn't. This was happening. It was real.

The theater is full. I can't tell if it's packed for the classic movie or for death. Maybe both. Swatters.

Someone brought up the house lights. That doesn't make sense. You can't see the mesh through the protective bars. But this is a theater. Maybe someone is being theatrical?

There's a change in the ever-present buzzing. It's concentrated at the edges of the room. Mostly. Lots of people are standing up. About a hundred heads turn toward the electrified wall. I'm not sure what they expect; the bars are too close together for a good view. I feel twitchy. This is it.

*Crack!*

People gasp. I figure the electric death of thousands is louder than the audience expects.

I'm sure I'm the only one who heard the split-second screams.

There's a small pause, then clapping, more clapping, and then louder clapping. Laughter, hooting, hugging all around the room. The movie screen is still empty. It gives the audience time for just this reaction. Ghoulish. My mouth tastes sour.

It's getting quieter. They're hearing what I heard, even before the clapping stopped: the sizzle of one stuck fly keeping the system active. It can't free itself and it can't fall in the moat. People are looking that way. They can't see what's happening but it's mesmerizing, the cracking and popping. The suffering. I smell the body, the sour of burning hairs mixed with the clean bite of ozone. If someone doesn't clear the body from the wires, audiences won't go for this. Maybe I should go over there just in case I can—

It stops. Maybe it disintegrated in there. I settle back. People are sitting but there are a lot of little conversations. It's not suffering any more. That's the goal. That's the point. My children.

The movie is starting. Silly music and silly images quiet the swarms in my brain. *It worked.* Thousands dead. Just like that. I'm thinking it's time to watch the movie but I'm keyed up. Sure, I'd hoped, but I hadn't really believed. Once the movie is over, I'll sneak into the Swatters control room.

*What's that?* Sounds like a scuffle or some kind of racket by the back doors. Just behind me.

Even twisting as best I can—not easy from a slouch—I can't quite see what's going on. It's not just my eyes, it's dark and the noises are coming from behind the entrance panel, the part that separates the two doors. The general loudness rises. Everyone realizes we have company. I'm not the only one trying to figure this out.

Looks like twenty or thirty college kids in a disorganized mass. Full of vim. Young, like nymphs, except without the compound eyes.

"Stop the Murder!" they're chanting. "Stop the Murder!" and "We're all connected!" and "If they go, we go! If they go, we go!"

I didn't see that coming. I stretch one arm across my chest and then another. What's inside my shoulder doesn't pop; it crackles like week-old crispies. The lights are up again and the screen is gray. I guess no movie.

"Stop Swatters! Stop the murder!" More like that. They want to stop it, but I'm not going to let them. I'm not sure what they think chanting is going to do. Even after three thousand years, I can still have questions. It occurs to me I won't have time to find out any answers.

The moviegoers could have panicked but they seemed to have caught on pretty quick. It's just noise. The mood went from worry to annoyance. Booing and twittering.

How long will it take the police to get here? I'm guessing not long. This is no good. I was counting on slipping to the back, checking out the Swatters system, then getting to the control room to pull the lever as many times as I had to. Swarm after swarm.

I don't want to have to hurt these kids to get to the control room first. They've spread themselves around the theater. Maybe they're picking likely allies? At least they're in here. Not looking for the control room. Not yet. They're not doing any damage here but the control room would be sensitive. They might decide to smash it. They might get to the control room before I did.

This body doesn't sweat, but I figure if it could, I'd start sweating now. I'm so close to the end—and now this.

One of the younger ones marches toward me—if marches is the right word. She has to squeeze between seat backs and seat cushions, but the look on her face and the chanting make me think marching. I've seen a lot of marching in a few thousand years. She's on one side of me and there are at least three of them in the aisle on the other side between me and the doors. It would be too easy to reach out and grab—

"Swatters is murder! Don't you want to stop murder, Sir?"

*Sir.*

Her strident voice from three feet away appeals to me for some reason. Points to her for approaching me, an unknown man with an over-built body, in sort of a confined space. That's commitment. I respect that. A few moments until I am free. I can give it, for that kind of courage.

"Murder only applies to human beings." Sometimes I argue so I can get my own thoughts out. It helps me think.

I guess she's going to sit here beside me.

The fact that her head is well below my shoulder hasn't been a deterrent. Her faded pink tank top is droopy, like a used trash bag over her flat chest. It covers most of her equally faded shorts. She's wearing sandals. Considering the floor, she gets points for bravery there, too. Twisting to look me in the face, she punctuates her sentences with gestures. Her skinny fingers almost poke me in the breastbone.

"No! It is murder!" She stabs a finger toward me. "Our insects are dying! Flies are the foundation of our ecosystem!"

Big words. "You think so?"

"I know so! We can do this!"

"Do what?"

"You can join us! Stand up for the little guys! Help us shut down Swatters before it's too late!" Her eyes search my face for a response.

I wonder if my eyes give her that. "People kill flies every day, one by one. A single fly is nothing anyone cares about. It's only one of many. An electrified wall gets the same result, only faster. Hurts less."

"Every life is precious!"

"The flies are already dying out." I hope no part of my face is twitching a way she wouldn't expect. "They're almost gone now, except here. Some place had to be the last, and here we are." If I weren't a ranger, I'd have grown a beard.

Her lips twist down and she leans forward.

I hold up my hand in that special way teenagers love during arguments. "There are no more carcasses for them to feed on. No innards to hatch inside. No piles of waste. Drones hover up the dead in a grid pattern throughout the wild, to be rendered for fuel. We don't need flies."

"They're essential to the chain of life." She continues over my headshaking. "They are! Birds eat them. Reptiles and other insects eat them. Without them, we're doomed."

I'm trying not to smile. "Wrong. There aren't enough birds and reptiles and insects left to matter. The food chain is synthetic. As for that big electrified wall over there—there are worse ways to go than being swatted, wouldn't you agree?"

"No." She's got that look humans get when they want to say two important things at once. Vacant and urgent at the same time.

The chanting got sporadic while we were talking. Not enough reaction to feed it. These things tend to fade without an audience, but the police will probably show up soon. I imagine that'll get the energy up again.

"So, tell me," I ask her, "if you discovered you were a useless, pointless creature serving no function, a creature destined to die a brutal death having accomplished nothing, would you want to prolong your despair?" I wasn't really asking her. Just thinking out loud.

I get up slow—a big man trying not to look scary. It's habit. Her bright, white face tilts up at me. Not afraid, not relaxed either. I wonder if she thinks that twitching by my eyebrow is nerves.

Time's up. I'm not here for her. I'm here for the others.

The flies are back, jerking and slipping between us like little mad things. They settle in the wrinkles of my jacket. Their hum fills my ears. The first group has died, but new legions infiltrate through every possible door, duct and window. The pheromones draw them, but so do I. No choice.

Her eyes flicker. Hard not to with flies buzzing around your face, isn't it? I don't say it out loud. One of her hands is lifting, as if to swat a helpless victim. Her eyes are dilated with concentration. I bet I know what that's about. If she hits that fly, she's a liar.

She stands. Sidles a foot away from me.

"Murderer!" It wasn't aimed at me. She calls that out to the indifferent room. I appreciate her attempt to put some *oomph* into it. She checks to see what the others are doing. I'd describe this moment as "a diminishing trickle of outrage."

One young gentleman eyes the doorway, presumably awaiting the authorities. That's always the best time to rouse things up. If I were anyone else but me, on any other day but this, I'd be all about admiration.

Looks like she's had enough of me. She's backing through the seats. Uncomfortable.

Did I embarrass her? I hope not. Passion like hers should be encouraged. I'd had tremendous passion, when I was her age. I'd wanted to love Eos forever. Big mistake. Asking the gods for eternity to love her, forgetting to ask for eternal youth.

I wrap my duster closer. Time to go. More flies head for the pheromones, but the mesh is off. It's not set up for continuous automation—a safety thing. It still takes pressing a lever, and that takes a hand to press it.

I did my homework before I came. Directions for these sorts of things are always online. I just need to find the right door. Get to the control panel.

"Deirdre!" A young man is calling out to her. Interrupts my thoughts. "What are you doing? We have to form a chain in front of the wall! We have to show solidarity, a united front! I hear them—they're coming!"

There's a lot of eagerness in the room. Some moviegoers are still around, plus the chanters.

Too late. Every part of this body strains from the pressure inside. Cops are here. I'm the tallest guy in the room. If they're going to confront anyone, it's going to be me.

I'm gangly but I move fast. Even with the kids around, it's easy out through the doors. The hallway has bright posters all over. Distracting even for me. The carpet is hideous, like multicolored spaghetti. Everything seems odd under pale blue lights. Horizontal red and blue stripes lead down the hall and burnt popcorn smell is everywhere. Someone will get in trouble for that.

The door to the stairs I need is labeled "Staff Only." Of course, it's not locked. Not a lot of caring going on here.

There must be five hundred flies in that hallway with more on the stairs. I shake my head. They have no sense of survival. I take the steps two at a time. The door creaks open behind me, I turn and look.

"Wait," Deirdre says, moving up lightly behind me. "Where are you going?"

"Taking care of something."

"I don't know what that means."

My boots are coated in sticky soda residue. For every one of my steps, I hear two slaps of her sandals. If she follows, can she really stop me? One kid. But others might see us, get the same idea. I walk faster.

Hallway doors are conveniently labeled. There's the door I need: the one the Swatters manual said there had to be. It's covered in neatly placed red warning signs.

The door is not locked.

Inside the control room there are more flies. Even there. Wingbeats fill the room with a rising and falling hum. At least twenty or thirty flies have found their way under my shirt.

The power system is designed as a walk-in closet with room for only one body. There are two levers at eye-height for me, clearly marked. The innocuous beige lever on the right, two inches longer, activates the voltage through the wires, downing my children into the moat.

"What are you doing? Are you—wait—you're going to destroy the Swatters!"

I didn't expect her to trust me. She shouldn't trust me. It makes me ache and I don't want to ache. I have to finish. Today. I can't go on. They hurt too much.

"I want to help." Eagerness. "Let me smash it. Let me." She lifts an arm to swat a fly. Stops herself. She wants destruction and she wants to swat flies. She can't help it. No one can.

I could imagine how that would be for her. To destroy the machine itself. To save all those lives. To do something *real*. But if she gets her moment, I lose mine. I could imagine how that would be for her. To destroy the machine itself. To save all those lives. To tell her friends she did something *real*.

But if she gets her moment, I lose mine. If the protests worked, if Swatters got shut down before they were all gone—

Squawking radio sounds come up from below. Above that, the high-pitched humming gets louder.

I face her, my back to the lever. Shielding it. "Serving a cause bigger than yourself, are you?"

She nods, her gaze flickering. Beneath her shallow patience I wonder if that's an anxious anticipation for destruction, but very unlike my own.

The flies are landing on levers, darting in and out of the room, sitting on the ceiling, attaching to the side of my boots. If I stay, they'll bury every possible surface, including us, several inches deep.

But Deirdre doesn't know that. Looks like she's trying not to slap her forehead. There's a fly crawling across it.

It's going to head for the salty sweat on her nose.

There. Another fly at the corner of her lips. She can't help it and brushes it away. Its wings are damaged. Pain slices through my shoulders. I bet her cheeks are flushed from more than adrenaline.

Some people have said humans and flies are meant to work together; I disagree. One has to outdo the other. Inevitable. Because what has to be is what is, and here we are. Swatters.

"Did you plan this all along? You knew just where to go."

"Your name is Deirdre?"

She nods. "You?"

"Tito."

Human bodies are covered in tiny hairs. All of mine are vibrating. It's because there are at least a million flies inside the theater now. My whole body knows they're here. Knows who they are. Even with the pheromones downstairs, even as weak as I've become, some followed me. More will come.

It would be nice if one person understood me, here at the end. "Used to be a million flies in an area the size of this theater would have been nothing." I snap my fingers. "Used to be seventeen million flies for every person on Earth. That means seventeen million flies just for you. Seventeen million for your friend out there. Seventeen million for the tech who was back here a few minutes ago, pulling the lever. Now even one million are remarkable, even in an infested city like this."

"I know! We have to save them! Let me"—she slapped at her hair—"rip that lever out of the wall!"

The layer of flies on the floor has reached at least an inch deep. They've covered her feet. Already more than those on the ceiling. A river of flies.

I shake my head at her. Flies crawl behind my ears. "*Diptera* are mine. My creatures, my subjects, my children. It's not the moat that brings them. It's me. My presence draws them here to die."

People bounce on their feet when they're impatient but her feet writhe one at a time now in those sandals because of what crawls between her toes. Maybe she'll remember later what I said.

I keep myself between her and that lever.

"My *children*. A million—maybe later today another million—they can't stop themselves from finding me. I'm talking to you but I'm hearing them at the same time. I always do. Bottom of the ocean, I hear them. Six feet underground, I hear them. They're praying to me. Asking to find food. To escape traps. For the scraps of a life. And they cry to me when they hurt. Every wing pulled off; I feel it. The darkness when human hands smash out life, I see it. The drownings, being burned alive—it's in me. I feel it now. And I'm tired, Deirdre. I've had enough."

A fly crawls up her nose. I applaud her effort to extract it without harm, but that never works. Noses are tricky. She bites her lip as if that helps. The fly on her upper lip moves just in time.

"I'm sorry." I guess the way I said *sorry* made something click inside her; she realized I wasn't there to take out Swatters.

When she lunges, I don't have to try to stop her.

She slides on two thick inches of winged bodies. Collapses hard on top of thousands, their entrails a slippery soup. Her face twists with perfectly understandable disgust. Her hands crush more bodies in her futile attempts to get back on her feet. I feel their deaths like third-degree burns from the soles of my feet to the roof of my mouth. Flies blanket her tightly-pressed lips and her wrinkled nose. They smother her breath.

She claws at her own skin, and I get it. Being smothered. It hurts.

I've got something else to worry about. Sharp pangs in my sides. A set of barbed legs, like steel rods, penetrates the thorax region of my meat suit. Punch through the jacket. I really loved that jacket.

Chunks of flesh and dark blood land on top of my shoes and Deirdre.

If my body didn't feel pain, I couldn't control it. I quiver on what remains of my legs. I hadn't realized as I lost followers, I'd lose some of that fine motor control. Be less of a god. The buzzing in the hallway changes. The pheromones have started to draw my children more than I do. They'll leave me soon. Not soon enough for Deirdre.

I swallow hard around the burning in my throat. *Poor Deirdre.*

"The problem," I whisper as she thrashes on the floor, "is that although I'm more a consciousness of energy than a thing, it takes being a *thing* to get things *done*. Thus"—I gesture at myself, at the remnants of the park ranger—"this face. This body."

She clutches her throat. She's brave. Worth saving. Maybe I have time to save her and still stop their pain, but I might be wrong. It wouldn't be the first time.

My fractured gaze is darkening. The colors are leaving me. I hadn't expected that.

"When the last fly has escaped from this horror, I can rest." Which is how I ended up in the Eastman theater, watching movies.

She isn't moving—dead. My children already squirm under her skin. Wings and legs cover even her eyes. So much bravery. Passion.

I push the lever down.

She is, after all, only one of many.

*L.A. SELBY PURSUES stories under Roman amphitheaters, inside Egyptian pyramids and atop the battlements of ruined French citadels. She is grateful that her knees still allow the search. After more than two decades of trauma psychology practice, she draws from the dark side of reality to offer the shadows of human feeling through the weird, the wild and the uncanny, whether it hides at home or abroad. www.LASelby.com*

# LIGHT AND SHADOW ON A SCREEN

## MEG CANDELARIA

*A* t 11 p.m. the Metro shut down and I had to find somewhere else to go. I got off where I had to, the end of some line, somewhere I had never been before. The burbs or the next best thing. Crap. Just the sort of place where they'd call the neighborhood watch as soon as they saw me. No benefit of the doubt for strangers in a place like this: the residents would call and I'd be shot. By the watch. Or maybe they'd just shoot me themselves.

At least, if I were lucky, I'd be shot. If I were unlucky, I'd be arrested and taken to a Center.

I walked briskly, purposefully down the street—a person with a place to go and wanting to get there quickly given how late it was getting. Covertly, I started looking for somewhere, anywhere, to hide: a bush, a ditch, a pothole, anything as long as it would hide me so that no one saw me or my shadow moving on the street at a time when the street should be empty. Curfew would start in half an hour.

I had been walking aimlessly for fifteen or twenty minutes and was starting to panic when I saw lights in the distance. Perhaps there was some sort of shopping district.

Maybe they'd have an overnight business where I could stay. I had a little money, maybe enough to buy a cup of coffee, which would allow me to hang out at an overnight cafe.

I couldn't run without attracting unwanted attention, but I walked as quickly as I dared towards the light. Soon it looked to be just around the next corner. Maybe.

I turned the corner and blinked. In front of me was a building half a block long lit up from one end to the other with neon lights and what looked like old-fashioned incandescent bulbs—thousands of them. Incandescent bulbs were making a comeback, part of the Jobs Program, but they were still expensive—and costly to run. Surely this was a fake. LEDs, just pretending. A marquee stretched across the front. It read: "Interactive Movie Theater" in large letters. Underneath, it said: "Special Midnight Movie Marathon. Movies from midnight to dawn! Discounts! Free popcorn! Come one, come all! If you dare!"

A movie theater. No one would notice in a movie theater if I dozed off and if they did notice, I could claim I just got bored with this particular movie. They'd have a bathroom too. I could go inside and clean myself a little in the sink. Plus popcorn! Any food that didn't come out of the dumpster is good, but I remembered popcorn, fresh popped popcorn, especially fondly.

If I could afford it. Well, no harm in trying anyway.

I walked casually up to the ticket booth. A woman sat behind the counter. She was older, gray haired, and wearing thick glasses on her pale brown eyes, but she had a sweet smile and laugh wrinkles around her eyes. Her name tag read "Eve."

"Hey," I said.

"Good evening, young lady," the woman in the booth replied, her pleasant smile unchanged and her voice expressing cheer, as though she did not notice my smell or torn and stained clothing. I wasn't going to complain.

"How much is a ticket to the midnight show?" I asked.

"Twenty dollars," she answered.

Crap. Way beyond my means. I had a crumbled dollar bill. What was I thinking, trying to get into a movie?

"Or a coin," the woman went on. "We love coins!"

"What sort of coin?" I asked, thinking perhaps she meant a gold Presidential twenty-dollar coin or something similar.

"Any coin," she said. "They're so rare these days. No one bothers with coins anymore except for those silly gaudy new ones, but we love them here at the Interactive Movie Theater. So much more traditional than this paper nonsense."

As it happened, I had a penny. I had pried it up out of the street where it had become stuck and probably sat for a decade or more. No one has cared about pennies this century, but for some reason we haven't given them up. I pulled it out. "Like this coin?" I asked, dubiously.

"Perfect!" the woman said, happily. She took the penny and gave me a ticket in return. "The previews start in fifteen minutes. The interactive portion of the show starts promptly at midnight. First theater on the right, past the concession stand. Don't forget to pick up your free popcorn!" She cocked her head and considered me for a moment. "Tell Lil that Eve said to give you a free drink too. Since you gave us this excellent coin."

I didn't know what to make of that. Either she knew who —or rather more to the point—what I was and was trying to give me charity without sacrificing my dignity, or I'd just given away a rare coin worth millions. I wasn't going to complain about the first and was in no condition to do anything about the second, so I just took the ticket and went inside.

My first stop was the restroom. It was better than I ever could have hoped! Clean toilets, large basined sinks where I could wash my whole forearms and rinse off my hair, actual towels to dry off with. I was tempted to stay there. But I had popcorn and a drink waiting for me plus a movie. Heck, I might even watch the movie instead of just sleeping. At least the first one.

It occurred to me then that I had never asked what was playing. Whatever. I'd find out.

I had settled in with my bag of popcorn and an orange soda when the previews started. I finished my popcorn and considered whether to go back for a second bag. I hadn't really felt full since I left home, but knew from unfortunate experience that eating too much would result in stomach cramps, diarrhea and vomiting. Maybe towards the end of the show, after I digested this a little.

"The main feature will now commence," the speaker said. I wondered what it would be.

I smiled as a classic horror show theme played through the speakers. The franchise had been made into a TV series three or four times, a movie at least twice, and a flix miniseries once. I'd seen them all. This looked, if I could judge by the opening credits, like the first movie version, the twentieth century one. Not the most popular, but one of my favorites. I would enjoy the next two hours.

I watched as the opening scene started. A car drove down a small town street and stopped at what was probably the town's only light. Funny, I hadn't remembered this part. I thought the movie had started with the car on a deserted country road.

Somewhere, a clock struck midnight. Part of the film?

"The interactive portion will now begin," the speaker said and with no further warning, I found myself on the corner where the car had stopped, looking into the car.

I laughed. I'd heard rumors about the new 3D technology, but this was the first time I had experienced it. It was better than I ever imagined it could be. I could not only see the car in intimate detail, I could feel the wind, see the sunset, practically smell the car exhaust. These were really great special effects!

"Whoa," I said out loud. "When they said, 'interactive,' they meant it. This is incredible!"

The driver of the car turned and looked at me. "Hey there, cutie, want a ride?" He opened the car door and gestured.

"Sure," I said, still laughing. What would happen if I tried to step in? Was there a platform to maintain the illusion or would I fall right through the hologram? I decided to go for it. I slid into the seat. Inside the "car" was warmer than the outside and smelled of cigarettes and bad beer. If this were a real car I'd be worried about the driver's sobriety. Or maybe I wouldn't be. What did I have to lose, after all?

"Where to honey?" the driver asked.

"I'll just go with you," I said, playing along. "Let me off when it's convenient."

"Sure babe," he said, leering. "I'll take you all the way."

"Oh, right. This guy's a sleaze ball. I'd somehow forgotten," I said to myself softly, not loud enough to disturb the other moviegoers. Where were the others, anyway? Did they see me or were they in their own private effects world, stepping into the car themselves?

From the back seat came a snort. "She's got you down all right," a voice said.

The driver turned red. "Oh, you're one of those politically correct social justice warrior types, aren't you?" he said.

Wait, what? Why did he say that? It was like they were responding to me personally, not just to a generic moviegoer inserted into the film. Worse, while "politically correct" was an old, old term, I was pretty sure they didn't use the phrase "social justice warrior" in the twentieth century.

"This is getting weird," I said. "You're not real, at least not really here. Not any more. Just light and shadow on a screen."

"You think so?" the man in the back seat said. "Are you sure?"

A famous actor from that era played him, one whose work I had liked as a kid. Dead for decades, only his image left. And yet, here he was, asking me if I were sure he was only an image. He was also going to turn into a monster soon, if I remembered how this bit of the movie went properly. I wasn't sure which thought was more disturbing: that I was talking to a long-dead actor or that the character would turn into a monster soon. I looked around. The car had four sides. We were moving down a road, not in front of a green screen. I couldn't see any camera. On the whole, the monster might be the more immediate problem.

"Maybe not," I said. Or was I falling for some trick? Oh, well, all part of the entertainment. "Or maybe so. I'm not exactly up on the latest technology, as may be obvious."

"What do you mean?" the driver asked.

I gestured to myself: my stained and torn clothing. My hair that hadn't been properly washed in half a year. My smell of old sweat and fear.

"Hey, going through a rough patch, kid?" the driver asked. "Don't let it get you down. Things are tough all over. You'll get through it."

"Thanks for the vote of confidence," I said, smiling weakly. Maybe he wasn't so bad. Maybe I should accept his advances: it might get me a bed for the night and he'd probably buy me breakfast. I smiled at him directly. Just in case.

Of course, if the plot went the way it should, he was about to get eaten. Should I warn him?

"How did you end up here?" the man in the back seat asked. "What led you to the interactive movie theater?"

Okay, so I must have fallen asleep as the movie started. This was an interesting dream. And vivid! I wondered if there was something in the popcorn or if maybe that apple core I found in the trash earlier this evening was fermented. If this were a dream, I could tell them, right? On the other hand, maybe it was some sort of trap. Who knows what can be done with VR? Maybe this was real, a real trap to get people to say something bad about the wealthy and get them put in a Center.

"I turned eighteen," I said simply.

"Eighteen, huh?" the driver said. "Legal."

He turned and leered at me. "Do you like scary things?" he asked. "Dares? Scary movies?"

"No," I said, worried about what he had in mind.

"Oh, come on," he said. "I don't believe that. You're here, after all. What would you be doing here if you didn't like scary movies?"

I didn't know what to say to that.

"Oh, no! The lights have failed!" the driver said, turning off the headlights. "Is that scary?" he asked, leering at me. "Want to hang on to me to be safe?"

"Turn the lights on!" I snapped.

"Scared?" he asked.

"Yes!" I said.

"Come over here," he said, with a wink. "I'll protect you."

I moved as far away from him as I could.

"Let me out!" I yelled. "I don't want to be part of the interactive theater any more. I'm just the audience. STOP!" I yanked at the car door handle. The door did not open.

"Oh, for—just stop the car," the man in the back seat said, sounding exasperated.

"Don't be such a spoilsport," the driver said. "It's just a little fun."

"Scaring this poor kid to death is fun?" the passenger asked, angrily.

"Ah, she's fine, aren't you babe? She likes scary movies. She can't deny it!"

I huddled as close to the door as I could, trying to make myself as small and inconspicuous as possible, and closed my eyes.

"You want to see something scary? Stop the car and I'll show you something really scary," the passenger said.

I knew that line. Crap.

"I can see something scary while driving," the driver said.

*No, no you can't,* I thought. Should I say something? What? I should try to save him, shouldn't I? He might be a jerk, but he was a person.

No, he wasn't. He was just an image. Light and shadow on a screen. The actor had gone home and had dinner himself after being "eaten." There was no real danger.

"Pull over," the passenger said. "This isn't something you can see while driving."

"Okay," he said, looking dubiously at me.

"And open the door!" I said. "Let me out."

"Don't worry," the passenger said. "Just stay there. It'll be all right."

The driver smirked and pulled over. "Glad you finally see the light," he said.

The passenger turned his face away into the shadows. Shit. Well, maybe this was a better ending than some I could have endured.

I closed my eyes and waited. I heard a roar and a scream. The scream grew more and more high pitched and then stopped abruptly. The sharp metallic smell of blood permeated the air, overwhelming even the reek of beer. I waited. Nothing more happened. I opened my eyes.

The passenger had his human face back on, but there was blood all over the lower half of it, covering his cheeks, chin and the tip of his nose, dripping off his lips. He was looking at me.

I stared back at him, sure that I was about to become dessert, but he just smiled at me. I should have been horrified. I wasn't. I should have been terrified. I wasn't. I had just seen a straight white man, one with a car and probably a job, the ultimate apex predator, become prey. It was the sight I'd never allowed myself to admit that I wanted more than anything else to see. I was not horrified. I was elated. And I was aroused, almost painfully aroused. The passenger, the monster, the avenger, looked like he was too.

It had to be a test. Or a dream. I could be wary, sensible and live another day. Or I could do what I wanted to do, one last time.

I reached into the back seat, pulled him towards me, and kissed him. He tasted of iron and desire.

He reached back and pulled me towards him as well. We kissed passionately for a few minutes and then I whispered in his ear, "Let's get out of here."

"Good idea," he said.

We exited the car and looked around. The night was dark and brisk, invigorating and empty. There was a field to the side of the road, full of half grown corn. It would do. We held hands and ran out into the corn together.

We had to take our clothes off. That surprised me a little. If this was a movie, even a twentieth century movie, made before the Freedom of Speech Department was founded, surely we wouldn't be permitted to take our clothing off, and if it was a dream, we shouldn't need to. And yet we had to remove every bit of constricting, hiding, restricting clothing before we were released to be together body to body.

We came together and fucked. Is the term offensive? I don't know how else to describe it. It wasn't making love. It was enjoyable and friendly, but only in the manner of two friends splitting a hot fudge sundae with each other. Nothing as profound as love. Screwing would be too twisty a word and copulating too clinical for our straightforward, earthy act. So, fucking is the best I can do.

"Why are you really here?" he whispered to me as we lay together afterwards, cuddling in the field and looking up at the stars.

"I don't know," I admitted.

"Tell me about your life," he continued. "Maybe I'll know."

I shrugged a little, but started, "When I turned eighteen two years ago, I had to leave home. A new law had been passed—just my luck. I didn't have any money to buy a job—"

"'Buy a job?'" he interrupted incredulously. "Why would you need to buy a job?"

"To get a job, you have to either pay some up front money to get hired or work for free for a two month 'internship.' It's supposed to be fairer to the employer: they don't have to pay you until you demonstrate that you're worth paying or you put up some money so that they aren't out money if you don't work out. At the end of the two months, they're supposed to hire you if you do a satisfactory job, but almost no one ever does."

"Why not?"

"It's cheaper to get a new free intern. Or buy prison labor. Usually both."

"Sounds like a problematic situation."

I snorted. "You could say that," I said. "And not just for people looking for jobs. Can you imagine trying to run a business with only beginners and slaves forever? Nothing ever works well. But it's cheap in the short term so the CEOs like it."

"Huh," was all he said.

"They do have to give you lunch, which means one meal a day, but that's it: twelve hours of work for one meal for the first two months. Well, a meal and a certificate of employment which protects you from arrest as long as you're inside by curfew."

He frowned. "Curfew?"

"Yeah, you can't be out from 11:30 p.m. to 6 a.m. You have to be either at an all night business or at home. I don't have any home to go to or money to go to most businesses."

But here I was in an all-night movie festival. What was this place, really? I put the thought aside.

"Your parents won't let you live with them until you find a place?"

"They can't. It's illegal."

"College?"

"I'm not college material."

"What do you mean? You're clearly smart as a whip."

"Huh. Thanks! But that doesn't have anything to do with it. Men go to college if they're rich, to build connections. Women go if they're beautiful and the sort of person a rich man might want to marry, which usually means rich as well, although occasionally a really good looking poor girl will get admitted out of charity or something. They go to meet the rich men."

"What do you do then?"

"I go to places that are open all night and will let me stay —all night coffee shops, bars," I smiled. "Movie theaters—"

"Heh," my friend snorted.

"Or find a place to hide outside: a hole, a bush, anything that can hide me until morning. It's worked so far." I frowned at the stars. Some of them are probably dead by now, super-novae burning bright for an eye blink of astronomical time and then dying and leaving a beautiful "corpse" visible over light years of space and millennia of time. Lucky SOBs.

"What happens if it doesn't work?" he asked, a little reluctantly.

"I get arrested," I said, with a shrug. "Then I go to prison and work for free for the rest of my life. Same as if I don't find a job, a permanent job, by twenty-one."

I fought back panic. I was almost twenty now. I only had a little more than a year and no reason to think I'd find a job in that time. I didn't know anyone who did. And even at my best, I wasn't someone who would be picked by a wealthy man for marriage. Just as well: from what I'd heard, that was not always an easier life than the streets.

The man—my lover—whose name I didn't even know yet, sat up on one elbow and looked down directly at me. "You could just stay here," he said.

"Stay here?" I asked, not quite understanding what he meant.

"In the theater," he said. "You've obviously got the talent to do so or you would never have found it. You don't sound like you have anything keeping you in that world. You'd fit in well here."

I smiled. "Thanks," I said. "But this is just a dream. Movies are not real. They're only pictures taken long ago. Just light and shadow on a screen. I can only stay here until I wake up or come down off my high or...whatever." *Until the VR is turned off and I get arrested for unlawful telling of the facts*, I thought but didn't say.

He looked at me sadly. "I'm sorry," I said. "I wish I could, but I can't change physics. Reality is what it is and it won't change for us, no matter how much we want to believe our own personal alternative facts."

The man didn't say anything for a moment. He simply frowned in concentration. At last, he said, "Did dark energy exist before the twentieth century?"

I blinked. What sort of question was that? "Sure," I said.

"Did anyone know about it before then?"

"I'm not sure..." I said, unsure where this was going. Was this a test? I was likely to fail. I had no idea when dark energy was discovered.

"How about quantum physics. Did anyone understand quantum physics before the twentieth century?"

"I don't think so," I said, though I wasn't really too sure when quantum physics was discovered either. Girls weren't encouraged to look into science too closely at school. Nor were boys, I realized irrelevantly.

"And yet quantum physics existed and when it was discovered it could be used to do all sorts of odd and bizarre things like building computers," he persisted.

"So?"

"So maybe the universe is even weirder than you ever thought possible. Maybe that weirdness can be used to produce interesting new technologies. Maybe those new technologies can be used to right wrongs."

"Maybe," I said, with a skeptical snort. "And maybe there's an invisible teapot rotating around the moon. Can't prove there's not."

"Ah, but I can give you my teapot to hold and drink from," he said. "Try it. The tea will be hot and tasty—as long as you keep the pot filled. You'll never find the edge of the virtual reality. It's not virtual. This is the real world." He stopped for a minute then added, "A real world. Part of it, anyway. The world you came from is real too, more's the pity by the sounds of it."

"Fine," I said. "I'm game to take this, real or illusion, as far as I can go."

"Good," he said. He wrapped his arms around me and we slept together, in the field of corn, under the stars. Other cars passed, but no one minded us. The sun rose in the morning over an ordinary landscape. Alas, we were both still stained with blood and foul smelling. The car was not some place I wanted to be either. Overnight, flies had found it and maggots were hatching.

"Now what?" I asked.

"Now," he said. "I think it's time to change the reel."

"'Change the reel?'" I asked. "I thought you said this was reality."

He shrugged. "It's an analogy. I don't pretend to understand how it all really works either. But we can move into another 'movie' and use it. Have you ever heard of *They Came Over the Wall?*

Huh. Had I! It was the story of an alien invasion with aliens who looked like snakes disguised as humans slipping over the border walls, especially the Mexican wall, to invade and the strong leader who defeated them with the help of the invincible US military. It had come out when I was eight and been shown in school every year since then. And spawned a dozen sequels due to its popularity or maybe "popularity." Even as an eight year old I had rolled my eyes at it—but only after the lights had been dimmed. Showing open disrespect to state or corporate art was illegal and every eight year old knew that.

"Terrible movie and worse sequels, don't you think?" my lover, my friend, this stranger I had met only a few hours ago, said. Some day maybe I'd ask his name and he'd ask mine. Or maybe our names changed with the reel. I looked forward to finding out. I smiled at the thought of looking forward to anything. It had been a long time.

"They could use some editing," I said. "And perhaps a little reinterpretation. A new ending."

"Exactly," he said with a sharp fanged smile.

As the sun rose, we walked into the next town. There was a small appliance store with old-fashioned TVs in the window. One was on and showed a group of obviously wealthy young men entering the interactive movie theater for the all-night showing of *They Came Over the Wall*, parts one through ten. I smiled as I slipped out of my human skin, ran my forked tongue over my fangs, and slithered to my hiding place. There, I, the monster, the villain, the hero of another story, waited in a world of light and shadows and shades of gray.

This was going to be fun.

*Meg Candelaria was born in Louisiana and has lived variously in Texas, Chicago, Iowa, New York and Baden-Württemburg. It all made sense at the time. Her thus far unfulfilled ambition as a horror author is to write something more terrifying than the average story in the current events section of the newspaper. Her work has appeared online and in print in Daily Science Fiction, 99 Tiny Terrors, Nothing Without Us Too and other venues.*

# ONE OF THOSE LADIES

## ANDREA L. STAUM

The whip slashed across his back in rhythm to the inquisitor's questions.

"Who helped you?"

*Crack*

"Where did she escape to?"

*Crack*

"When did she approach you?"

*Crack*

After a few anticipatory moments waiting for the next slash came a snarl and the sound of the coiled leather hitting the ground. "He won't talk."

"Are your arms growing tired?" sneered the priest to the inquisitor. "No worries, a few more nights should convince him."

"Why bother? He's a fool from a forgotten house trying to impress a daughter from a mediocre family. There isn't more to it than that. Some status is better than none."

The air crackled around him as he could feel the familiar warmth of the web's power.

"That," the priest stated, "is for speaking out of turn,

inquisitor. The Caphaxaths were a mighty house once. One built on treachery like that of which he assisted in against House Cidress."

Sylthane choked on the blood in his mouth to keep from laughing. House Caphaxath had fallen from favor when he was a babe. His eldest sister had taken control while their mother was in her birthing bed delivering him. Had his sister followed through with ceremony all would have been fine, but Natix was denied her due and the goddess could not stand by and watch an unsacrificed third son prosper. Eventually his mere existence brought disgrace on the family. If his connection to the magic web hadn't been so complete, he would have met his siblings' fate at the hands of the executioner. The goddess had an odd sense of favoring those who she despised.

Sylthane's arms were released from the ceiling shackles and his body collapsed to the frosted stone floor. He had lost count of the number of sessions he had gone through by this time. He thought they had captured him a week ago but in the dark of the caves it could have been months. He no longer fought the lash. Not that he had done well at the start. It was easier to relax beneath each blow.

Calloused hands dug into his worn, bloodied wrists. They didn't bother to shackle him anymore as they dragged him back to the fissure that served as his cell. He didn't bother to turn his head to see who had brought him back. There was a rotation of at least three inquisitors and countless priests of the goddess Natix that had questioned him. A moldy crust of bread had been left for him.

"If you tell them where the Cidress heretic daughter ran to, they will give you quick death," whispered the inquisitor as he crouched to dip a ladle into the cleansing salve for Sylthane's back.

It was a lie he had heard every night when they brought

him back. The priests never gave quick deaths to heretics. He couldn't answer their questions anyway. He had no idea where Kethryllia had escaped to or if she had even escaped. There was no way to discern truth from lie within the shelves that constituted the dungeons of the Webstryder caves deep in the heart of their mountain.

Sylthane gritted his teeth as the hot liquid ran down his sides and hissed on the cold rock beneath him. Steam soon filled his small cell, barely tall enough for him to roll from front to back, not that he wanted to after the first night of torture. He turned his head to look out but the inquisitor was already gone and the shimmer of the prayer incantation that locked him in was in place.

There were moans coming from other cells. He resisted the urge to shake his head in pity for the occupants because he knew what would come next for them. He had learned it the hard way the first day. Noise attracted the ice weavers faster than the smell of blood would. A spasm caused him to bite his lip to keep any noise from escaping. He could hear the tapping of clawed legs as weavers skittered through the rocks around him. There was no way to escape them in the small cells. Even if the inquisitors hadn't applied the lash or their other implements, the weavers would come. Heat attracted them. After the interrogations, blood would attract them. If any sort of noise were added, they would swarm, crawling out of the cracks in a shimmering blue and white wave to feast.

It was an unspoken device of the priests. After one night of the ice weavers biting and licking most would confess to anything to avoid another night of the shelves. Those foolish enough not to speak, like Sylthane, would spend hours in the dark being eaten alive. The cleansing salve helped heal the wounds and kept the toxins from the bites at bay, so the first night was usually the worst.

The fevered dream that had come that night gave him hope that he was not forgotten here. He let his mind return to it as he waited for the weavers to find him.

Closing his eyes, he saw the woman standing there. At first he thought the dark form Kethryllia, tall, proud, untouchable. She stood at a distance, her features obscured by a mist that hung around both of them. He moved forward and mist seemed to grab and pull at him, keeping him from getting closer to her.

"Keth," he called.

She made no reply.

"I'm sorry Keth," he whispered both aloud and in the dream. "I really thought we had something."

Before the vibrations had stopped within his throat, he felt the piercing of eight skittering legs along his arm. Within moments, the ice weavers swarmed him. He tried to ignore them as their teeth ripped into the fresh tears on his back. Squeezing his eyes shut, he tried to find the woman once more in his dreams.

Warmth spread over him, pulling him from the emptiness of his exhausted mind. He figured he had wet himself again. There was no point in waiting to be taken to the privy. That luxury was granted only if information was given. The acrid stench of the cleansing salve struck him and caused his body to heave. There was nothing but bile left in his stomach and he spat it out over the edge of his cell onto the worn leather boots of a new inquisitor. He turned his head to look at a masked face.

"Interrogator?" he rasped, his voice foreign to him after so many weeks of silence.

The figure nodded and grabbed his shoulder, dragging his bare chest against the stone. He wondered how he still had skin left to scrape and bleed as he saw droplets of red on the floor. The interrogator gave him a moment to get his feet beneath him and allowed him to shakily walk to the room. He had heard that when the masked ones arrived, it was the end of their patience.

Three high priests of Natix sat in high-backed chairs across from the chains. A fourth was piling fruit and other food on a plate from a table behind them. Sylthane smirked. His torture was becoming a dinner entertainment for the priests. Whatever was in store for him today he doubted they intended for him to survive.

The interrogator clamped the shackles into place and pulled the chain higher so Sylthane's toes barely touched the damp stones. Water droplets ran down the chains and down his arms, creating rivers of cold against his skin. He thought maybe he truly was fevered as relief from the dampness washed over him.

"Sylthane Caphaxath," the priest in the middle of the seated three said as he stood. "You stand before us the perpetrator of heresy and treason. You have already been found guilty as your position so close to Lady Kethryllia Cidriss, the betrayer of House Cidriss, and your confession last night, have shown. We are giving you very generous leeway in allowing you to purge yourself of your guilt so the glorious Weaver Mother looks on you sparingly."

Sylthane kept his head up and stared blankly at the priest. He had barely whispered the words last night and they were not a confession of guilt. He had spent unknown nights pondering what had happened and how Kethryllia had used his attraction to her against him. He did not believe in her cause or words, but he had believed she would achieve whatever she set her mind to and had foolishly thought she wanted him at her side. He understood now that she wanted only his ability to tap into the magic web.

He did not see the priest incline his head. The whip

slashed across his back, jarring him from his self-reproach for foolishly speaking in the dark.

"Who helped you?"

It had been an entire network of unsatisfied servants taken in by Keth's lies of better treatment. Her younger siblings also vied for a place within the family that would be denied to them should they not act. It wasn't that what they did was against any of the societal norms, they just hadn't done it well and been caught.

*Crack*

"Where did Kethryllia escape to?"

Sylthane wasn't sure. He had lost sight of her during the melee. He had cast some diversion spells and tried to give cover. It had worked in that Kethryllia and her kin snuck away unscathed, leaving only those considered expendable behind. At first he had thought he had been left because he needed to maintain the spell and buy more time. He had foolishly thought his co-conspirators would somehow divert his transfer to the dungeons and rescue him. Now, he realized he had always been expendable to her. Not that he would tell the priest that. He at least would be loyal.

*Crack*

"When did she approach you?"

When indeed? He had been brought in as her tutor after she expressed interest in her studies. He should have known then it was a ruse. He had met her when his previous student introduced them at a social event. He had forgotten which one since every one after Keth had sought him out until they all blended together. She had chosen him from the onset for this task. He had just been too blind to see it. Was she really worth his suffering?

*Crack*

"When will you give us the answers?"

His lips parted for the first time since they had brought him to this chamber. He choked, "Never."

He looked behind the High Priest at the mist rising up from a crevice to his left. He watched as a woman's form took shape, her face drawn tight in concern at him. He felt her gaze despite there being no true eyes looking out from her features. Her mouth opened but no sound came out, yet he heard her in his mind. "Rest, Sylthane."

The pain from the gashes on his back eased and the room grew dark around him. Still he saw the woman's form, this time unmasked, her true beauty no longer hidden by mist or shadow. How he had ever mistaken her for Kethryllia he was unsure. Keth was everything that could be found in cave darkness and the woman before him seemed to be made of what he imagined sunlight must be like. Her golden hair flowed around her like a gown, covering more than the thin ivory slip that clung to her slight figure. Indigo eyes glowed from a pale face and her impossibly berry red lips twisted as she raised a slim arm with long, delicate fingers before her face. "Interesting that this is how you would imagine me."

"Who are you?" Sylthane asked.

"That is none of your concern," the priest snapped. His voice distant as darkness filled the space.

The woman reached her hand forward, offering it to the bound Sylthane. "I am Molena."

"Are you here to take me to the hells?"

The priest let out a low growl. "If you refuse to provide information there will be no other place for you. Natix will not even deem you worthy of feeding her children."

Sylthane continued to stare at the woman and ignored the priest.

Molena shook her head. "I will take you from here, but I will require your service."

"What of Kethryllia?"

"We will find her and she will pay for her insurrection. Her matron is even willing to forgive her and allow her to remain within the house as a model of contrition."

"He lies. They already captured her. They are trying to break you to find out more of those who go against Natix's directive."

"They have her?"

The priest's words faltered. Sylthane hadn't realized he had still been speaking.

Molena's face softened as she looked at him. "Yes and she has already bowed to their will. She named you the instigator. You will never leave this chamber without my help."

"Then I am yours."

"Finally!" shouted the priest. "Apply it."

Sylthane's throat opened in an agonized scream as a burst of red flashed through his mind and he jolted awake. The smell of burning flesh came to his nose as the brand sizzled against his back between his shoulder blades. He felt the skin melt and mold to the metal so it tore as the brand was pulled away.

The priest was grinning above him, but Sylthane's attention was on the beautiful goddess behind him. She was no longer just a figment of his dreams.

The priest's cold hand gripped his chin to force him to meet his gaze. "You are a traitor and now your corpse will tell that to all who look upon you."

"I think not," replied Molena as she wrapped an arm around the standing priest.

The priest turned. The fair woman was replaced by a twisted old crone with patches of missing gray hair a missing lower jaw. The delicate fingers were talons as she gripped the priest's throat. Her other hand forced his mouth open, pinning his tongue so he couldn't muster a proper scream. The mist poured down the priest's throat, choking him.

When the standing priest fell, Sylthane shifted his head as the three seated priests began gurgling the dense mist, drowning as air refused to find their lungs. A different woman stood behind each of them—a crone similar to the one that took the first priest, except she was blind and her mouth grinned mirthlessly; an acolyte with light gray skin and unusually black hair whose lips were torn from where thread had sewn them shut; and a distortion of woman mated with an ice weaver. In death, only one of the four priests saw his goddess taking hold of him.

The interrogator fell to the floor twitching beside Sylthane. The whip handle had been forced down his throat while it had been wrapped tight around his neck.

The shackles on his wrists fell away and he collapsed to his knees and he crawled to the fracture and followed the mists down to an underground river, which swept his body through the caverns and out into the icy plains of the tundra. Cold and pain entwined with the sound of roaring water. It overwhelmed Sylthane but he gave himself something to focus on and remain in the realm of the living.

"What we have here?" a gruff voice broke through the darkness of his consciousness. "Dead?" A sharp pain struck Sylthane's side. "Nope, still breathing, bit more blue than gray though. Welp, best load him up." He felt his body lifted from the cold wetness that lapped at his legs and he felt soft hides beneath him and furs around him. "All right ya mutts, back home."

A crack of a whip made Sylthane flinch but the ground beneath him jerked and he felt movement and heard dogs barking excitedly so he let himself fall once more into darkness. There he felt Molena guiding him to rest, her whispers lulling him deeper to rest even though he could not figure out the words. He felt the power from the web lapping over him and a new strength coming with each word.

The scents of roasting meat and burnt tobacco brought him back again. The ground had stopped moving. His eyes peeled open. He looked around the rustic cabin around him. He was wrapped in a bear hide on the floor. An old man sat near his feet staring at him, a long pipe dangling from his teeth.

The man stood and ladled some broth into a bowl. "Bout time you woke up. Been near five days. Can't complain too much though. Just took up space without eating me out of supplies."

Sylthane tried to sit up but the pain shooting through his back stopped him.

"Don't be movin'. Spent good coin to bring a healer in who would be willing to treat the likes of you. Most would say good riddance to one less Web Worshipper."

"Why bother?" Sylthane asked. The taste of iron dripped into his mouth from his cracked lips.

"Welp, for the cave dwellers to brand one of their own a traitor must mean you have a story to tell."

"You saved me for a tale?" He tried to roll to his side and gave up as shooting pain caused his vision to turn red.

"No, I gave you a chance. Pulled you half drowned from the water on the tundra, can't say you're really all that saved. Not many will appreciate you walkin' about."

"Who are you?"

"Glasom IceBasher. You?"

"Sylthane Caphaxath."

Glasom nodded and blew smoke into his face. "The healer couldn't fix the scars. Said the cold had set them hard."

Moving his arms, Sylthane groaned as pain radiated throughout his torso. "More than my back hurts."

"Welp, that isn't the smoothest of rivers upstream. Wouldn't doubt you bashed against a few rocks and maybe over a few falls on the way out of the caves."

Sylthane watched his lady's form dancing in the smoke floating above him, causing a warmth to radiate through him. His body relaxed and he forgot the pain. His stomach growled, breaking his concentration on the smoke.

"Get some broth in you. Been awhile since you've eaten, given the state of you," Glasom said as he poked at Sylthane's ribs. "They had you for a time before dumping you."

"They didn't dump me. My Lady saved me."

"Your Lady?" he laughed. "No one was around you so she left you."

Sylthane raised his hand and rested it over his heart. His fingers traced a welted triangle he didn't recall being there. "She is always with me. She made sure someone would find me."

Glasom nodded and chewed the end of his pipe. "Ah, one of those *Ladies*. Don't hold much stock in them, but if you say so."

*Andrea L. Staum is the author of the Dragonchild Lore series, The Attic's Secret, Rogue's Kiss and has contributed to several anthologies. In order to avoid the mundane, she creates worlds and destroys empires in her mind and eventually translates them to the page. She lives in south central Wisconsin with her husband, children, and their overlords...err...cats.*

# LIFE WAS A DREAM

## TYLER CLARK

he coil tattoo machine buzzed, dragging lines of pain across Simone's skin like a cat's claw. Simone focused on the pain—breathed through it. The skin of her forearm had been through a lot. Self-harm scars scaled the inside of her arm like lines of latitude. Damage from a troubled youth.

"How's your mom?" Amber asked, shading in an area of the tattoo. Simone and Amber had known each other since they were kids. Amber saw some of the uglier bits of Simone's adolescence: her father's sudden passing, the substance abuse and the fights. It seemed fitting that Amber would be the one to give her this tattoo. Amber was always there, the kind of friend that stepped up when shit hit the fan. Amber was Simone's very own Virgil in hell; a guide and a witness.

"She's fine, I guess? I don't know. We don't communicate very well."

"Mhm. It's like I said. You and your mom are very different people who grieve in very different ways."

"For real."

"She still at the same place downtown?"

"Yeah."

"Really? I didn't see her sign last time I drove by."

Simone's mother, Veronica Pérez, worked as a psychic. A large, hand-painted sign, faded and weathered from the elements, advertised her business.

"Her sign keeps falling down. We've fixed it so many times, but it's always falling apart. It's crazy to me that she still gets work. You'd think people wouldn't pay for tarot readings or palmistry anymore."

"Well, for some people, it's a novelty, you know? They don't really believe in all that stuff, they just think it's entertaining. I swear I've done a million tarot card tattoos and astrology tattoos just 'cause it looks cool. Some people are actually into it though. People will pay you a lot of money to tell them what they want to hear."

"But what if it's bad news?" Simone laughed.

"Hey, some people like bad news. As long as it means there's something more to life, you know?"

"I guess so. I just don't understand how anyone would continue to believe in any supernatural higher power."

"No one would blame you for thinking that after everything you've been through, babe. All done!"

Amber cleaned away the excess blood and ink from Simone's arm. Simone admired the finished product in the mirror. A dark silhouette of tentacles, pincers, and teeth framed the words "Ordo ab Chao" in gothic font along the inside of her forearm.

"Ordo ab Chao," Simone read aloud. "Order from Chaos. I love it."

The front door of the tattoo parlor opened with a crash. A homeless man having some kind of meltdown howled and wailed in the entryway.

"Azathoth, sultan of daemons!" he shouted. "Pan's flutes and accursed drums keep it in slumber!"

Simone and Amber both jumped. Another tattoo artist at the front of the store tried to calm the man down. The man's beard and hair were long and matted. He shoved people away and knocked framed photos off the walls. Spittle erupted from his mouth as he gnashed nonsense.

"Blind idiot god!" he screamed. "We exist in its dream!"

The man's eyes fell on Simone's tattoo, and he stopped, eyes bulging. "Ordo ab Chao," he whispered. "A window to Azathoth's power!" The man fell to the floor, foaming at the mouth. His heavy coat fell open to reveal red lines on his bare chest. It looked like he'd been scratching furiously at his skin. He writhed on the floor.

When the ambulance arrived, the paramedics had to sedate him to stop his thrashing.

Amber swore, clearly rattled. "Shit. You okay?"

"Yeah, I'm fine," Simone said. She looked down at her tattoo. "Who the hell is Azathoth?"

\* \* \*

LATER THAT EVENING, alone in her bedroom, Simone wrote in her journal:

*The needle tears through, leaving ink behind. My tattoo is organized chaos. Beauty derived from destruction. A mosaic from shattered glass.*

Her forearm itched and stung from the fresh tattoo. She resisted the urge to pick at it.

Behind her, something clattered across the ground. Simone sprung to her feet and turned around. Along her wall, where many of her books stood in tall stacks, a pile of books had fallen over. Simone stepped closer to investigate.

Just a pile of books. Simone let out a sigh of relief. She was on edge after the incident in the tattoo parlor, she decided.

She set them back in an unsteady stack against the wall, sat back down to her desk and wrote in her journal again.

*When I move my piles of books, the dust creates an outline, an imprint of what was there before. When I finally come to rest, and the dust traces my outline, what will my imprint be?*

\* \* \*

THE NEXT MORNING, when Simone climbed into her car to go to class, she turned her key in the ignition. Her tattoo flared with pain. Her engine died. She turned the key in the ignition again. Nothing.

Simone spoke a few obscenities. Opening the hood of the car was a pointless gesture since she knew nothing about mechanics, but she did it anyway. Her car's battery looked rusted and corroded beyond belief. It hardly even resembled a battery anymore. It looked more like scrap metal that had been hauled from the bottom of the ocean.

Cursing her misfortune with cars, she called a tow truck and got a ride to the culinary school from a classmate. While she waited for her ride, she looked at her tattoo. The skin had swelled. Normal for a fresh tattoo. But the shape seemed different than it did the night before. Simone could have sworn the tentacles were in a different position now, wrapping farther around her wrist than she remembered.

\* \* \*

SIMONE USED a pair of kitchen shears to crack through the chicken's rib cage with a hollow crunch allowing her to remove its spine. From there, she flipped the bird over and used her hands to press down hard on its chest. This flattened out the bird with the sound of cracking bone and cartilage. This technique—spatchcocking—cuts the cooking time of roasting a whole chicken in half. Simone pierced the bird through the legs and the breasts on both sides with metal skewers to make the chicken hold its shape while it cooked. She seared the chicken in a large cast iron skillet, then moved the chicken, pan and all, to a preheated oven. While the bird finished cooking, she prepped ingredients for a pan sauce.

Simone loved to cook. Secretly, what she loved most was the *violence* of it. In the kitchen, Simone was Shiva, the destroyer. She sharpened knives and hacked vegetables apart. She seared, boiled, chopped, and sliced. Cooking is an act of creation, an act of creation that can only follow destruction. Ordo ab Chao.

Chef Pasquale, their instructor, walked by each student's cooking station and graded their performance based on taste, technique and presentation.

"Great work, Simone. Perfectly balanced."

"Thank you, chef," she said.

The instructor continued down the line. Simone let out a sigh of relief. She needed a win after the car trouble that morning. When the man with the tow truck had finally arrived, he'd asked Simone why she'd left a car to fall apart for so long. He didn't believe her when she'd said she'd driven it just the day before.

"HA!"

Simone looked over with a start. Chef Pasquale, usually a temperate and sober person, had let out an explosive laugh. All the students in the class looked at the instructor, then at each other in confusion. Chef Pasquale bent over in arrest, a smile splitting his face, eyes watering.

"HA!" Chef Pasquale bellowed again. This time it sounded somewhere between a laugh and scream.

"What did you say to him?" one student asked.

"Nothing, he was just grading me," said another student.

"AHAHAHA!" The instructor dropped his clipboard and fell to his hands and knees. He coughed and gasped for breath in between fits of laughter like someone being waterboarded.

"Something's wrong," someone said.

"What do we do?"

Chef Pasquale began to seize and thrash on the tile floor. His face reddened. A vein bulged in his forehead. His eyes widened. Despite the laugher and maniacal smile, the horror in his eyes was unmistakable.

"Call an ambulance!"

"Help me hold him down," a student said to Simone.

Simone stepped forward to help, but a biting pain in her arm made her stop. Under the plastic bandage wrapped around her forearm, her tattoo *moved*. The abstract forms of tentacles, eyestalks and chiton around the words *Ordo ab Chao* writhed in her skin.

Covering her mouth with her free hand, Simone stepped back. For a moment, instead of seeing her instructor seizing on the kitchen floor, she saw her father collapsing in the lobby of a movie theater.

"Simone!" the student shouted. "Simone, help!"

All Simone could hear was her mother screaming, "Somebody help!"

Simone looked from her tattoo to the man writhing in madness on the floor, then turned, grabbed her backpack and ran for the exit.

* * *

AFTER RUNNING FIVE CITY BLOCKS, Simone arrived at her mother's place, breathing heavily and coughing the phlegm from her lungs. Her mother's psychic practice was a hole in the wall at the far end of Center Street. While still technically part of downtown, most pedestrians on Center Street turn back before walking this far. Nestled between a pawn shop and a novelty book store, if it weren't for the large hand-painted sign outside, it would easily go unnoticed.

Outside her mother's business, she tore at the plastic wrap around her tattoo and discarded it. With a trembling hand she poked at the shapes and letters. Nothing about the tattoo seemed out of place anymore. She second-guessed herself. Did she really see her tattoo move?

For years, ever since her father passed away, her therapist had advised her to write down her thoughts and feelings as they came. Sometimes it helped. Simone opened her back-pack, sat down against the wall of the building, pulled out her journal and began to write.

*Shapes and sounds. That's all language is. Meaningless gibberish we collectively agree means something, a shared dream no one wants to wake up from at the risk of it falling apart, imploding and collapsing on itself like a tower of cards. Like the Tower of Babel.*

Her tattoo itched. Her mother's business sign came crashing down right next to her. She flinched and let out a scream.

"Ugh!" Simone growled, kicking the painted wood. "Stupid sign!"

She looked at the rotting piece of wood, which was in constant need of repair. Its bright letters and astrology symbols advertised palm readings. Simone decided she was being irrational. Sure, some weird stuff had happened since the day before, but weird stuff happens all the time. She was reading too much into it.

*This is what it means to be human,* she wrote. *We witness the cold, uncaring chaos of the universe and pretend we're at the center of it—that every coincidence must be part of a grand design. This is what it means to be human: to have an ego so big you believe your own lies. We're nothing but charlatans.*

She looked at her mother's sign once more.

*Some of us more than others.*

Simone closed her journal and leaned against the brick wall. She focused on her breathing and tried to calm herself. She saw two different people in the last twenty-four hours have some kind of mental breakdown. That's just a bad coincidence. If anything, it shows the awful state of mental health services and support in the United States. If there was a pattern, that's what it was. Nothing supernatural going on, she was sure of it.

Simone looked at her new tattoo again and shook her head. Amber was going to throw a fit if she didn't take proper care of her tattoo.

Gathering her things and re-centering, Simone stood up and entered her mother's business.

The bell above the door rang as Simone walked in. The familiar scents of incense smoke and essential oils barraged her senses. Trinkets and velvet, crystals and cards. Several generations back, Simone's family were Afro-Cuban immigrants that practiced Santeria. The kind of "fortune telling" Simone's mother did now had nothing to do with those practices, however. The crystal balls and tarot cards were what people expected to see, so that's what her mother used. There was nothing authentic about it. It was a business that capitalized on people's expectations and superstitions.

"Be right with you," chimed her mother in her fortune teller voice from the other room.

"It's just me, Mom." Simone called, putting down her backpack. "The sign fell down again."

"Not again," her mother said, emerging from a back

room. She'd already shed the fake fortune teller voice. "Don't you have class today?"

"Yeah, the teacher was, uh—" Simone thought back to Chef Pasquale's mental breakdown and shuddered. "He wasn't feeling well. Listen, Mom. My car broke down this morning. Can I borrow yours for a bit?"

"Of course."

"Great, thanks." Simone held out a hand for the keys.

"You're just gonna grab my keys and run? Why don't you sit with me for a while?"

"Please don't do that, mom." Simone rubbed her eyes.

"What? Between school and work I hardly see my own daughter anymore."

"You're using the fact that I need something from you to keep me here. That's extortion."

"Just sit down and tell me how school is going."

Begrudgingly, Simone sat down across from her mother, a phony crystal ball situated on the table between them. "School is going really well, actually—or at least it was before my teacher freaked out this morning."

"What happened?"

"I don't know. He just started laughing and couldn't stop. Someone called an ambulance, and I left. When he fell over, it uh—" Simone struggled to find the words—"it was really triggering."

"I am so glad you found a place at that culinary school. I'm sure your father is very proud."

Simone thought of the day her father died. They had gone to the movies as a family. Her father collapsed in the theater lobby. Details from that moment were frozen in her mind: the smell of popcorn, her mother screaming for help, a song from a movie trailer playing from overhead speakers. "Life was a dream" sung in an old crooner style.

Simone snapped back to the present moment. "Dad's not proud, he's dead."

"Simone!"

"Look, if it helps you to pretend he's still out there somewhere, fine. But that doesn't help me, because either way, I don't have a dad anymore. He died."

"How can you say things like that, Simone? You used to be such a sweet girl."

"Don't do that, Mom. Please! You do this every time."

"Do what?"

"You make me feel guilty for speaking my mind. You put me in a position where I either have to bottle up my feelings or I have to apologize for making you feel bad. I lose either way."

"Aren't I allowed to grieve my own way?"

"What you're doing is not grieving, Mom. It's denial."

"What you're doing isn't grieving either, Simone. It's self-destruction!"

Simone shook her head, trying to hold back her anger and steady her breath.

"Over and over again," her mom continued. "Trips to the emergency room because you've been cutting yourself or drugging yourself. If you really don't think your father's spirit is out there, then why do you seem so eager to join him?!"

"I'm not gonna listen to this." Simone picked up her things and stormed out.

"Where are you going, Simone?"

Simone didn't respond. In truth, she had no idea.

* * *

*"LIFE WAS A DREAM..."*

Her father handed her a large popcorn. "Don't eat it all before the show."

Simone gave him a mischievous look. She watched as her father's left eye drooped. The left side of his face sagged unnaturally. His cheek. The left corner of his mouth.

"Dad?" Simone asked. "You okay?"

He collapsed. His legs thrashed. Her mom screamed for help. Vomit on the carpet.

He was gone.

* * *

SIMONE CALLED Amber and asked for a ride home. Like clockwork, Amber was there. The most dependable person in Simone's crazy life.

"Hey, you okay?" Amber asked as Simone climbed into the car.

Simone didn't have the heart to answer. She just rolled down the passenger-side window and watched the city slide by. Amber didn't pry. The skin under her tattoo stung and itched.

Amber screamed and hit the breaks. Metal crunched against metal. Glass shattered. Simone looked up to see two cars that had just collided into each other in the intersection directly ahead of them. The collision missed them by a few feet. They could see the driver of one of the cars through a shattered window. Blood spurted rhythmically from the side of their head.

"Oh my god," Amber said. "What do we do?"

"Shit, Amber. I don't know. The whole fucking universe is one big car accident."

"Simone?"

"Amber, I don't have any fucks left to give. Let's just get out of here."

"Simone!"

Simone followed Amber's gaze. It was directed at her tattoo, which was, without a doubt, slowly writhing and shifting in her skin around the words, *Ordo ab Chao.*

Someone screamed. Simone and Amber looked at the same time to see a woman dressed in business attire laughing hysterically as she pulled out chunks of her own hair at the roots.

"It worked," Amber said.

"What do you mean? You can see this? Did you do this? What did you do?"

"Don't worry. We need to get to the tattoo parlor. I'll explain everything once we get there."

\* \* \*

AMBER CAME to a screeching halt right outside the tattoo parlor. Once they were both inside, Amber locked the door behind them and drew the blinds.

"Amber, what's going on?"

"I need to gather the others," she said, pulling out her phone to text a message.

"What others? Amber, why is my tattoo *moving*? Did you know about this?"

"Yeah, but we didn't think it would start this soon. All right, listen. I have this group of friends. We're on the verge of tapping into something so powerful, so cosmically significant, you'd never believe what we're gonna be capable of. And you're the key, Simone. You're gonna make it all possible."

"This is crazy, Amber."

"Is it? You've been right all along, Simone. Everything *is* meaningless. Life is nothing but a dream. A dream we haven't had any control over. Until now. Imagine being able to shape the dream of reality to what *we* want it to be. We're so close to the finish line. So many rituals, the components for your tattoo—you wouldn't believe the amount of research."

"Components? What did you put in my tattoo?"

"Don't worry about that right now. What needs to happen now is we need to cast some warding spells so the madness stops spreading. This is so exciting!"

"You should have told me about this. You had no right to make this decision for me!"

"Do you want your Dad back?"

"What?"

"You can have your Dad back, Simone. Anything you want. We can make it real with this," she said, taking Simone's arm.

"That's not possible."

"Can you explain the things that have been happening around you since I gave you this tattoo?"

Simone thought about everything: the homeless man's rant, her car falling apart, her instructor's uncontrollable laughter at culinary school.

"It...does seem like a lot of weird things all at once," she admitted. "You're not about to tell me I'm a wizard, are you?"

"No," Amber laughed. "Not exactly. I'm sorry this is happening so fast. We meant to bring you into this slowly, but we don't have a choice. We need to act now."

Amber's phone rang. She answered it.

"Hey!" she said to whoever was on the other line. "I know! We're at the shop. How soon can you get here? Okay, I will. Hail Azathoth!"

"Hail what?" Simone asked. "Amber, are you in a cult?"

"Oh, grow up. That's just a buzz-word. Come with me."

Simone followed Amber into a basement below the tattoo parlor, a room Simone didn't know existed. Amber turned on a light at the bottom of the stairs. What Simone saw made her gasp. Intricate symbols and words in a language she'd never seen before covered the walls. Where two walls met the floor in one corner of the room, the symbols and words converged into a spiral. A semicircle of candles surrounded it.

"Amber, this is freaking me out."

"Trust me, Simone."

Simone winced and took a tentative step toward the stairs.

"Hey," Amber said, holding her in place. "I know this is a lot. But how long have we been friends? You know me, right? You can trust me. This is going to change everything for the better."

Simone's tattoo writhed and itched. The spiral in the corner of the room fluctuated and swirled as if in reaction to her proximity.

"We need to hurry. Let me get changed." Amber began to take off her clothes. Under the stairs were shelves of a dozen crimson, folded robes. Amber stripped naked before donning one of these robes, complete with a red mask that covered everything but her eyes.

"Amber," Simone said, counting the sets of robes. "How many people are in your group?"

Two individuals in similar crimson garb descended the stairs.

"Hail Azathoth," they each said upon entering. Amber responded in kind to each of them.

"Let's get started. Simone, you stand here," Amber guided her closer to the spiral in the corner. As she neared the corner, Simone could feel a pull on her arm.

"This is the first step. First, we bring back your dad. Then, the universe is ours to mold. Focus on what you want it to do."

"Okay."

Simone thought of her father. She thought of his manner-isms, his jokes. She thought of his record collection. She thought of lazy Sunday afternoons listening to music together.

Amber and the other two masked cult members began to chant in another language. The spiral in the corner swirled. With a sound of cracking wood and plaster, the point where the two walls met split open. On the other side was a deep black void. The air sucked out of the room, pulling at Simone's hair.

"Focus, Simone! Think about your father!"

Simone thought of her father handing her popcorn with a drooping eyelid.

From the void came a sound, faint at first, but recog-nizable.

*Life was a dream...*

The song was slowed down, pitched lower, eerie. The tattoo in Simone's arm writhed with pain more than ever before. Simone could smell burnt popcorn.

"Simone?" a voice came from the void. It sounded distant and distorted, but familiar.

"Dad? Dad, is that you?"

"Simone," the voice said. The voice sounded like her father's, but layered with dozens of other voices pitched higher and lower than his.

An abstract humanoid shape took form in the void. Simone wanted to believe that this nebulous shape beginning to form in front of her was her father, and maybe it was, but something didn't feel right.

"Simone," the voices said in unison.

"Something's not right," Simone said over her shoulder.

"Don't stop, Simone!" Amber shouted. "You have to keep going. Picture your father. Bring him back!"

Simone focused her thoughts on her father. She thought

of how badly she wanted him back. All the pain she'd felt at his loss since he'd been gone.

A hand reached out of the void. It was like her father's hand, but wrong. Extra fingers twisted and writhed from the back of the hand and the wrist. Simone recognized her father's wedding band on one of the fingers, but chunks of hair and teeth protruded from the skin.

"Simoooone!" shouted a dozen voices from the void.

Simone screamed.

"Simone, you have to keep going!" Amber shouted.

"That thing isn't my Dad!"

Simone began to focus all her thoughts on closing the void. The swirl of letters and symbols in the wall slowed to a stop and shifted the opposite direction.

"Simone, what are you doing?"

"I'm sending that thing back."

"No!"

Simone felt hands on her. The cultists restrained her. They held her arm toward the void where an abomination of her father reached back.

"We didn't want to do it this way!" Amber shouted behind her. "Don't make us do things the hard way."

They forced a gag into Simone's mouth.

"We command a portion of Azathoth's power!" Amber shouted. "Let Simone's father be revived!"

The doppelganger of Simone's father clawed out of the void. Its head emerged. The right side of his face looked familiar, but the left side of his face sagged with five milky, blind eyes bulging from his cheeks and forehead. The creature that wore Simone's father's face opened its mouth and a dozen voices groaned forth. From its chest, a tentacle emerged, lashing out to wrap around the masked face of one of the cultists. The cultist let out a muffled scream.

"Welcome, father of Simone!" Amber exclaimed.

All Simone could think about was getting away from that void, away from the abomination she'd just released.

In a gut-lurching sense of vertigo, the floor stretched out before her. The room elongated in between her and the opening in the void, creating a tunnel between her and her father's doppelganger. The cultist in the tentacle's grasp was torn away from her, held in place next to the creature now emerging up to its waist from the void.

"Simoooooone!" the doppelganger roared with a dozen voices.

"Let the void open wider!" Amber shouted behind her.

*You don't command this power*, Simone thought. *I do.*

Simone shut her eyes and focused on what she wanted to happen.

From the void, a flurry of chains whipped out, wrapping around the creature and dragging it back into the void.

"Simone, stop!" Amber screamed. "You don't know what you're doing!"

Simone thought about holding Amber in place. The concrete floor around Amber's feet became liquid and she sank, waist deep into the floor. The last remaining cultist tackled Simone and straddled her, wrapping two meaty hands around her throat, strangling her. Simone gasped for air. Her mind raced for something that would help her. The only thing she could think of as the edges of her vision turned black was spatchcocking a chicken.

There was a sickening sound of cracking cartilage and breaking bones. Through the eyeholes of the cultist's mask, Simone saw the expression of shock. His grip slackened and Simone dragged in a gasping breath. The cultist slumped aside. Simone sat up to see a trail of blood leading from the cultist's back to the opposite side of the room where a human spine rested against the wall. Simone gagged and averted her eyes. She turned to see the doppelganger fighting against the chains that pulled it back into the void.

Lifting her arm to point at the void, Simone closed her eyes and said, "Close! And don't ever open again."

The walls converged on each other around the void, sealing the doppelganger on the opposite side.

"Simone, wait!" Amber shouted, stuck waist-deep in concrete. She pulled off her mask. "If you stop now, you'll never see your Dad again."

Simone paused, then turned to face Amber. "I know. And maybe I'll never be okay with that. But I have to accept it."

The void sealed itself shut.

\* \* \*

SIMONE SPENT the next hour painfully blacking out her tattoo with Amber's coil tattoo machine. As she emerged from the tattoo parlor, an eerie quiet settled around her. It was like stepping into a warzone. A car on fire coasted by and came to rest against the wall of a low, brick building. Glass and debris littered the sidewalk. Simone could hear someone crying nearby. Despite the chaotic aftermath of the cultists' ritual, Simone felt a deeper calm than she'd felt in a long time.

\* \* \*

"I'VE REALIZED SOMETHING," Simone said. "Even if there's nothing after this life, that doesn't make it all meaningless. I've spent all this time since Dad died thinking that nothing matters and no one is special, but maybe the fact that nothing is guaranteed or permanent makes it all the more special."

"That's the most hopeful thing I've heard you say in a long time," said Simone's mother. "I'm proud of you, baby."

"Well, there are still more of Amber's friends out there. I don't know what they wanted with me, but they're probably not done. And I don't know if shading over this tattoo did the trick. What if it's like trying to put a lid back on Pandora's box?"

"I'm sure it'll all work out."

Simone accepted a hug from her mother. Their first genuine hug in a long time.

"Thanks, Mom."

The doorbell of the psychic shop rang at the front of the store.

"Coming!" sang her mother in her fortune teller voice.

"It's all right, Mom. I'll just wait here for you."

"Are you sure?"

"Yeah, I'm fine."

"I'm proud of you, Simone," she said with a smile before walking away.

Simone sipped her tea, resisting the urge to scratch at the fresh lines of tattooed ink in her forearm. She realized, sitting there, that she'd been running for so long from fear— a specific fear that was hard to define. She turned the thought over and over in her mind, looking at it from different angles. The thing she'd been running from for a long time was the fear that everything might be okay. A fear that once she'd finally healed from losing her father she'd make it without him. But now, that prospect was less scary. She knew her father wouldn't want her to live that way. And besides, those moments she shared with her father while he was alive will always exist in the past. Never gone.

Simone sipped the dregs of her tea and stood from the table to get a refill. Stepping across the small kitchen, Simone stopped to part the door and steal a glance at whoever entered her mother's business. In a strange sight, Simone saw two large men undressing in front of her mother. Then, once the men had stripped naked, they opened a briefcase to reveal neatly folded crimson robes, which they wrapped around themselves, donning their hoods as well. Simone's eyes widened as she leaned close to hear her mother speak.

"Whenever you're ready, Simone is right through there," she said. "Hail Azathoth."

*TYLER CLARK IS A POET, a writer and a prolific home cook. His short stories have been the recipients of several awards including second place in the Return of the Night Owl contest hosted by Vocal Media in February 2022, and Honorable Mention in the Writers of the Future Contest in 2022. He lives in California where he and his wife raise a cat.*

# CASE NOTES

## JESSIE ULMER

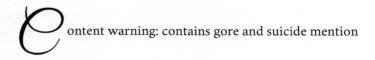 ontent warning: contains gore and suicide mention

THE SECOND TIME Alex sees Case, Case's pulling her hand out of the hole in the wall, the words *fucking dead* obliterated by her fist. Partially obliterated. The *f* and the *ad* still stand out in splattered red paint. *Fad.* It's a fad, is all. A fluke. The dead, the walking, the awful strength they seem to share. But Case is smashing her hand in and pulling her hand out—no blood dripping from her skin, and Alex is stuck to the floor, watching, just watching.

"What the fuck do you want?" Case growls and somehow, somehow, Alex cannot look away. The red paint. Case's hand. The lack of blood dripping between them.

"Nothing," Alex says, shuffling her notes between hands, trying to draw her gaze away. But it lands, instead, on Case's face. Strong. Formidable. Surprisingly soft curve of lip. Alex's gaze sticks. She cannot look away.

The third time Alex sees Case, her back is to her in

Vance's small office. The nearly shuttered windows cast jail cell bars across her skin. From her position at the door, Alex can see the rough rise of stubble gracing Case's neck, how it rounds the curve of her head, crew cut close to the skin. Alex knows some of the dead started cutting off their hair when they realized it would no longer grow. It's a myth, after all, hair and fingernails growing after death. And Case's are both whisper short.

There's no sentimentality here, no room for remembering. The sparse shadow of hair barely covers the top of Case's head where the rough edges of skin explode upwards, as if something beneath burst through, and Alex knows it had.

Alex doesn't know who Case was—before—who any of them were, but she knows Case wears her hair short and temper shorter, that she drives with a lead foot and leads, when they let her, with an iron fist. They don't always let her. Not Vance, even proactive as he is. They'd get shit for it, the agency, Vance's little pet project. His baby. And they don't want that. You don't give shit to a baby. If you can help it.

So Case is here, in the office with Alex and not out in the field. Not off where she could do some damage, leave a mark. Alex remembers splatters of red paint, the wrenching air. More of a mark. More of a mark, at least. It's Vance's fault, really. He's the one who hired them, the dead. The one who started scouting the back alleys and abandoned buildings they'd been dumped in, cleaning them up, offering for them to come aboard. There were plenty who said no. Plenty who'd rather spend their undeterminable amount of time left haunting the streets, lumbering between buildings, drawing disgusted glances from passersby. More than disgusted glances, sometimes. The dead can still be cut down, even here. Even now. But there had been plenty that had said yes, plenty that had left the alleys and cleaned the blood off their faces and come to work, and Case had been among them.

Case, who now stands tall and broad in Vance's office, back to the door. She hasn't seen Alex yet, hasn't turned her face, and Alex wonders if it's not too late to slip from the door—perhaps from the building—walk out into the street and choose a new life. One that doesn't leave her in a room with the dead. Perhaps she could sell flowers or bake bread. Perhaps her mother would finally start calling her back. It's not that her mother hates her. Alex knows what people think, knows what they whisper. It's just that she fears the stink of the dead will get stuck to her skin, be carried out into the world, infect it. Alex puts down the phone. She stops calling.

Across the way, Vance shits in his chair, noticing her, noticing how she hovers in the doorway, one hand on the latch, the other drifting towards her belt and what lays strapped there. Noticing.

"Well," he says, eyebrows raised, "in or out?" And before Alex can turn, before she can make a bid for out, Case is turning too, and her eyes are turning dark, and a scowl is spreading across her face. Too late. Too late then. Alex siddles into the room, tries to pretend she was going to all along, tries to pretend she doesn't count the mere measures of space between her arm and Case's. She doesn't tell her mother that she worries too.

From the corner of her eye, Alex almost catches Case rolling hers, but that can't be right. Do the dead still do that? Roll their eyes? Care if you stand a few feet away from them? Alex should know, should've been paying attention to the mandated training course they'd all had to watch—HR breathing down their necks until they'd taken the quizzes and filled out the right forms and gotten on with the business of understanding each other.

But that's the thing. Alex does not understand the dead. Does not understand how they walk and talk, if they breathe or do not breathe. No one does, no matter the tapes they make them watch, no matter the presentations that drone on and on, focusing more on PR and proper use of language than any of the fundamentals. Anything useful. If the rumors about the eating are true. How many shocks with a taser it takes to make one stay down. They'd had to figure that out for themselves. What kind of blood-thirsty rage pools beneath their fingers, what kind of regret. That is still unknown. It's just that they're dead, is all. It's just that they should stay dead, stay down, stay where people can mourn them and memorialize them and move on.

But that was before the rising. That was before the dead—not all of them—started pushing their fingers back up through the dirt, banging on coffin lids, rising from morgue tables—autopsy scars flashing in full relief—to roam the streets and cities. That's part of it. The roaming. What makes people so uncomfortable. The dead don't know how to stay down, don't know how to stay quiet, and there are more of them than ever these days. Clamoring at doors. Breaking down windows. Trying to get let in.

Alex shifts, surreptitiously, away from Case. She thinks it's surreptitiously. But Case snorts, which is interesting, given her probable lack of breath, and if it were anyone else, if it were a real living person, Alex would feel ashamed. But it's not. Just Case. Mess of flesh at her chin and scalp, crewcut barely covering it. Just Case with her impossible eyeroll, her lungs that do not hold air.

Somewhere, Vance is talking, somewhere, he is saying Alex's name.

"—Up on Aspen, a pack of them, roving. We've gotten calls. Lucky it came to us before the police. We're picking up traction. People are noticing. That flier campaign last August

—a stroke of genius. It's the simple things that work some-times. Well—"

He cuts himself off, waving a hand. Acknowledging and dismissing his genius both. Beside Alex, Case shifts on the balls of her feet, the word *roaming* caught between her teeth like a bullet. Alex sees the tear of flesh at the crown of her head. Not caught, then.

That's the problem, of course, with the dead coming back, to lives that can no longer hold them. Some of them try, return to houses and diner tables and play catch in the yard. But it's not the same. They sit before empty plates, throw balls so fast they break hands and sound barriers. Bring more grief to the living. So what can they do? They wash up in parks and empty buildings. Find each other. Build packs. Roam. The dead are looking, always.

When the roaming starts, there's no way to end it. No way but to put them down with how many shocks of a taser as will do it. Bullets don't work, just go straight through. It's something with the electricity, something with the shock that does it. Finally hits home. And you've got to end it. The dead clamor up and the living rear back and there's no way to traverse the space between them, no way to share air.

The dead always want what the living have.

"How many are there?" Case asks, hands clasped behind her back. Where Alex sees but Vance cannot, her fingers are clenched into fists. It's madness, Alex thinks. Letting her on the team. Letting any of them in. How are they supposed to wrangle the dead when they can't even keep them out of the offices? But then there's Vance. Vance, so enamored by his pet project. Vance, so sure it will come to fruition that he'll use any tools available, anyone who's willing, pulse or no, and Alex knows Case hasn't got one. Alex knows any blood on Case now belongs to someone else.

"About ten, maybe more." Vance waves a hand, measuring.

"Maybe less, if you don't count all the missing body parts." Ten. Not too many, enough to count off on two hands, if you're counting. If you've still got them—hands that is. Enough to worry about missing body parts. "But they've gone rouge," Vance continues, raised hand moving to his hair. "You know, raving. Causing a scene. The cul-de-sacs don't like it. Called us in." Out of Vance's view Case's grip tightens. Alex can see the crescent moons her fingernails— trimmed short—make on her skin, can almost imagine the blood rising up to meet them. Almost. Something rising.

"What's the verdict?" Case asks, before Alex can get the words out, before she can tear her eyes away from the pale stretch of Case's skin, moonrise blooming across it. Vance runs a hand through his hair, which springs back up again before his fingers have even cleared the last strands. It really is a sight. Vance's hair. What he does to try to contain it. Which is nothing. Alex should've known. Should've taken one look at his hair and declined the job. Should've called her mother back when she still had the chance, moved on to that help wanted sign at the bakery.

But it's just that. Well. It's just that Alex wanted to make a difference. Had seen the dead rise up with everyone else, faces pressed to TV screens, lawn chairs propped open then abandoned at the local cemetery—coolers left melting in the summer heat—soda cans and tuna salad forgotten as the dead came on. Not quite a show then. Not quite.

Alex had seen it all, had felt hope rise, unbidden in her gut, had stalked tombstones with faltering steps. Hoping. Just hoping. And who can blame her for that? The dead can, that's for sure, and Case, surely. Case blames her, somehow, as she does all the living, for being what she cannot. Except. Except Alex sees the mangle of flesh at Case's skin and thinks maybe there's another reason entirely.

Alex wanted to help. It's that simple. That complicated.

She watched the dead rise, watched them pour from autopsy tables and reach from graves, rise up from splattered apartment floors and thought maybe. Maybe if I do this. Maybe then. She's not the first to hope. Not the last. Not the first even to plan, to scheme, to try and make something better than what they have while they have it. That had been Vance.

Vance, tech-boy genius, earned his first million straight out of college—hadn't even bothered with graduating, that's the kind he was—Vance who could do whatever he wanted with whatever he had (millions, that's what, some startup tech that lasted the year before being sold to the highest bidder) and he had chosen this. Chosen the dead. Bought the building, hired the staff—Alex included, Case included—and got down to the business of rehabilitation. That's what he calls it. That's what they're supposed to see it as. Rounding them up. Washing them off. Getting them back to work, back into the economy. That's what life is, after all, a nine-to-five. Rented rooms in the city. They don't even need a grocery budget. Alex has heard some of the apartments don't even come with electric lighting. What do the dead care, she supposes. Nine-to-five. Apartment in the city. What's that to the grave?

And Vance, their fearless leader, tech-boy genius, he of the wild hair, he'd had reason to hope, hadn't he? Reason among the rest to wipe down faces, peer into eyes, do it again and again, apprehension cresting then cut down after every swipe.

Maybe she's still out there, we tell him. Maybe it'll be this time. This raid, this sweep, this strangling newcomer. Maybe, despite it all, she'll want to come home. We don't tell Vance this last bit. He can lie to himself, well enough, hold those pictures to his chest, run fingers across an abandoned locket, chain grimy with wear. Maybe she's not dead at all, Alex wants to say, wants to insist, wants to hope. But she, more than anyone, knows the end to this story. Some of them don't come back, after all. No matter what offering you leave on grave stones, no matter how you rake the ground with your fingers—dirt scooped then discarded, fingernails broken and bloody, until, maybe, drunk one night on cheap spirits and cheaper grief, you hit a coffin lid. Some dead stay gone. And what can you do about that?

If you're Vance you keep on, fresh with purpose, buoyed by hope. If you're Alex, you stop calling your mother, sell the apartment, thank the groundskeeper who doesn't call the cops (but it's a close thing) and move away.

Vance looks to Case, face bright, eyes hoping, bounces a little on the balls of his feet, filled with energy for the cause, even now.

"Same as always," he says. "Take those who want to come."

"And those who don't?" Case asks, hands still held tight behind her back.

Vance nods to the tasers at their hips, to Case's strong arms. "Take 'em anyway." Case does not grimace, does not let her lip raise in scowl, but it is a close thing. A tick at her temple gives her away, just a little tremor of humanity, what she has left. Vance notices. His mouth falls to a somber line.

"What else are we supposed to do with them?" he asks. His voice is not unkind, his eyes are sincere, but Case does not falter. Instead, she stands ramrod straight, chin raised just short of defiance, mess of flesh bared to the air. What else are they supposed to do with them? Alex thinks, but comes away with no answer.

So that's how it goes. Vance gives them the directions, tosses them a radio—Case catches it in strong hands, fingers nearly leaving indents on the plastic—reminds them to be careful. As if they need reminding. As if they'd listen. And then they're off.

Alex gets the keys to the van, which isn't fair but makes

her feel better, and Case scowls and they leave. Simple as that. Simple as sliding into the unmarked, unremarkable van, pulling the seatbelt across her lap with a satisfying click and slipping the key into the ignition. She does not turn to see if Case has buckled up, doesn't suppose it matters. They drive in silence, radio on the dash forgotten, words not so much as threatening to hang in the air. Alex does not want to know what music Case listens to—if she stills listens to any—does not know what to say that might bridge the silence between them, doesn't want to say anything back.

It's not like she believes the rumors—the whispers—that if you hear the dead talk you'll go their way soon. That if you hear the dead talk you're as good as them yourself. Maybe. Maybe she doesn't believe the rumors. But it's not as if Case has anything to say, not as if she's raising any words from the ground and laying them between them. She just sits in the passenger seat, arms folded, eyes on the road, picking out the flashes of movement that dart in and out of the alleyways. The shadows that are just shadows, until they're not. Alex shudders. Keeps her eyes on the road. Beside her, where Alex cannot see, Case's eyes flick to the ceiling.

Aspen is uptown, away from the hustle and bustle of the city. Away from the usual packs of roaming dead that weave in and out of the taxis and parked cars, blocking the bike paths and queuing in line at the post office—pale envelopes held in paler hands, stamps mysteriously bought and bartered. Alex wonders, even now, where the letters go. She wonders, desperately, if she will ever get one—knows Vance checks his mailbox twice daily, hoping, even now. To live in the word of the dead is an aching thing.

There is no post office on Aspen. Or rather, the closest one—Pine Street, two blocks over—keeps its door barred, a sign reading "no dead" bright in its window. It's not legal, strictly speaking. No one makes them take it down. Not in this part of town. Not where the houses rise up, shiny and new, where the HOA keeps the grass at a precise three inches, nothing more, nothing less, where lawns are watered daily and flowers pruned and preened. But people die in Aspen. People die everywhere. And now they have risen up, pushed out of the neat memorial cemetery on the corner, risen from the morgue, walked out from forgotten corner's tables and hospital beds and all places death touches. Everywhere. Death touches everywhere.

Case is the first to see them, Alex's eyes still fixed resolutely on the street. Case is the first to pick the moving limbs, those that are left, out from the scenic backdrop of trees and cream houses (HOA ordered), the first to put her hand on the wheel, Alex's fingers stuttering back, to say, in a clipped voice. "Here. We stop here." Who is Alex to argue? This is the job, after all, rounding up the dead, clearing them from lawns and post offices so the fearful civilians can go back on with their lives, forgetting, again, the dead that should be below the ground. Except they're not. Below the ground. They're lumbering forward, on the sidewalk, then in the street, then in front of the van. All writhing mass of them.

Alex can make out the vacant wash of air where limbs should be, the hands that should hold fingers, the empty socket of an eye. There, to their right, walks a man, chest agape, static organs held in place by bulging stitches and nothing more. He moves with the others, ever forward, and Alex can see the push of flesh meeting skin with each step he takes. The bulge. Carefully, she closes her eyes, swallows down something hot and sick, does not think of a familiar stone carved with a familiar name, skin soft against her arm, a smile bringing sun. Does not think.

It is moments later Alex realizes that Case is out of the car, that she, too, should be moving, that she should be taking the lead. Never let the dead get too close to their own kind, that's what they tell them. That's what Vance says, when the doors are closed, when Case and the others aren't listening. Alex fumbles with the seatbelt, fumbles with the ignition. Fumbles. She's out of the car before Case has made it to the dead, out of the car before she can see what Case will do if she gets there before her. It's all she can do not to run, all she can do not to stumble forward, to grasp Case's arm, but the thought makes her gag, bile rising once more.

She needn't have worried. At least, not about that. There are plenty of things, Alex knows, that she should worry about. But, curiously, this is not one of them. Because Alex stumbles from the car and Case is there, standing still on the pavement, not moving forward. Case is waiting for her, like anyone would, like any of the living. Case is waiting for her and Alex feels something small and unbidden rising in her chest, the beginnings of an understanding that she swallows with the bile. Small things. Small things. She swallows what she can, spits the rest out onto the street, HOA be damned, and strides to Case's side. In front of them, the dead come on. Limping, some. Walking, others. Each with skin that has gone soft and gray and fraying at the edges.

Alex knows that if one were to take her hand, if she let them, their grip would be strong enough to crush bone, to turn her hand into just another pile of flesh, useless on her body. But from where she stands in the street, the dead are fragile things, lilting forward, then falling back, unsure. Their hands, those that have them, are raised in surrender. Or something like it. Alex keeps her hand on her taser, her back to the van. She remembers red paint dripping from a hole in the wall. Her empty bed. She's seen what the dead can do. The holes they leave behind.

Now she does see Case roll her eyes, understands that the dead still can, because Case rolls her eyes and takes a step forward and the dead take a step and then they are meeting in the middle. Case and the dead. The dead and the dead. Meeting.

Alex's fingers stray to her hip, fingers firm on plastic, but before she can draw, before she can do anything, Case is reaching her hands out, palms up and flat, her own surrender —reaching her hands out and Alex can see the space between them, then the closing. Engulfed. There's a word. The dead engulf Case, swarming her as only the dead can, fingers on skin, in hair, running along arms. Through all of it Case stands, still as God, lets herself be poked and prodded, caressed and careened. It's all Alex can do to stand there, feet rooted to the spot, all she can do not to run. Not to Case. That'd be bravery and Alex only has so much. She wants to run away. Back to an apartment with flowered curtains, back to a time when laughter soaked the air and hands ran tender down cheeks, where soup bubbled on the stove and day jobs were just that, light stretching long and luxurious, back through months and years to where the dead stayed dead and the living stayed living. Living. That's what all this is about, really, what is and what isn't. What they all have lost.

Alex's feet stay rooted to the pavement and before her roils the mass of the dead. Somewhere within them, Alex knows, Case is standing calmly. Somewhere within them, Case does not hold her breath, has none to hold. There is the sound of something bleeding out. A sigh. A release. A breath pulled impossibly from empty lungs. Alex's fingers close on her taser. Somewhere, Case is in there. She tightens her grip. Somewhere, the dead stay dead. She falters. Lowers her hand. What is there but this? What is there but the dead rising? Some refusing to rise. What is there but those we love staying gone?

Then the dead ebb. It happens like that, a tide pulling out, Case left in stark relief on the land. The dead ebb and Case is there, but suddenly more pale than Alex has seen her, more pale than even the first time—blood on the walls, viscera on the carpet—more pale than any of the dead, who draw away with flushed cheeks, steady gaits, fingers that might be warm to the touch. Case falters. She swoons. The dead ebb. One minute they are there and the next they are gone, melting into yards and across streets, moving off towards the playground and the post office, feet steady, eyes sure. Alex feels the bile rise, must spit, once more, onto the pavement.

In front of her, Case stumbles. She barely finds her feet. Her lips, and Alex realizes she knows what Case's lips look like, have gone dusky against her skin, the ragged edges of flesh at the crown of her head and curve of her jaw grown darker at the edges.

Alex doesn't mean to do it. She means to get back in the car. She means to drive back to the agency, report to Vance what has happened, collect her paycheck and go home. Or perhaps she means to drive, Vance and paycheck be damned, take the van and go with whatever gas it has, however far it and her remaining cash will take her, out past the town limits, out of the city, down the shoreline until she reaches a place where the dead don't walk and no one is tasked with wrangling them. Mexico. Maybe Mexico. Do the dead still walk in Mexico? Alex isn't sure, would have to ask the man at the gas station where she would buy jerky and peanuts and whatever the $25.30 she has in her wallet would get her. Whatever that is. She means to.

But. It is a moment before Alex realizes that the sturdy curve of the wheel is not under her fingers, that her foot is not pushing the pedal to the floor, that instead she has crossed the space between her and Case, has hooked one arm around a waist that is cool to the touch but not cold, that she is hoisting the weight of a body that is still very much a body up onto her shoulder and only then moving back to the van. Only then curling her fingers around Case's arm, feeling the way the flesh pushes down but doesn't remain indented. Case's body on hers feels very much like a body indeed. Small things. Small things.

They are by the van and then they are in the van, Alex reaching over to buckle Case in. She's not sure why she does it—Case can't die twice after all, only got one shot at it (pun morbidly intended). But Alex is leaning over and buckling Case in and Case is slumping forward against the belt, body kept up by just a thin strip of fabric and suddenly, Alex is not sure that Case can't die twice. That this isn't it. Case's odd power bartered back to the dead it came from. It's not like anyone knows anything about it. It's not like anyone knows why the dead are rising, what might keep them risen. It's not like anyone truly gets back the ones they love. Right? Alex finds herself wondering as Case's head slumps into her shoulder, as Case's body lulls into the empty air before her. Case. Full name Cassandra, cut off with her hair. Dead at twenty-eight. No survivors. That's what Vance had said. That's the briefing he'd given Alex on her first day on the job, fresh and new and still hopeful—Sam's picture still folded in her wallet, fresh flowers still on her grave. That's what Vance had said when he'd tossed her the keys to the van, told her to take a taser, just in case, and sent her on her way.

The first time Alex had seen Case? Well. There's really no nice way to put it. Brain blown out on the apartment wall. Blood splattered. She hadn't even left a note. Hadn't even left a clue about who she was before becoming just another roaming dead. Who might miss her. There are those, Alex knows, no matter what Vance had said, no matter what notes had been typed out in stark relief in Case's file. Case file. Hah. They'd laughed at that, Alex and the others, until Alex had pulled up at the apartment building, opened the door and come inside. And then there had been Case. Cassandra. What was left of her brains splattered on the walls, body oozing. It had been cool by the time Alex had gotten there. Cool by the time she had spread her fingers over Case's palm, urged her to come along. Case had scowled, yes, she had scowled, and Alex had drawn back. It was the first time she had touched the dead. The first time, until now.

The skin of Case's forehead is cold under her palm. Not cool. Cold. As though ice, not nothing, flows through her veins. Case lulls her head, looking at Alex, eyes gone cloudy and blank in the dusky light of oncoming dusk.

"Don't tell Vance," she says, only it comes out a croak, comes out, "Don't tell. Vance." As though Case is struggling to breathe, struggling to push breath out through her parted teeth, only Alex knows she isn't. She's slowing down, lolling, something bartered to the crowd of dead that have already slipped away, already disappeared against the picture perfect houses and setting sun. "They just need something to keep them going, something to keep them fed." And apparently that something had been Case, apparently that something had been the light in her eyes, already fading to dusk like the street around them. Faltering. Can the dead die? Alex finds herself wondering. Is she going to have to see it all over again?

The first time Alex had seen Case, Case had been sitting upside down on the sofa, her legs thrown over the back, feet pointed and head lolling—blood and worse pooling on the carpet. She had rolled her eyes up in her ruined head and looked at Alex—really looked—and then sneered.

"What?" she had asked. "Were you expecting someone else?" And Alex had been sick. It's not that Alex hates the dead, not that she loathes their mangled appearance or strange lilting words, it's just that they know more than they're supposed to. Have seen the other side, some say, know who else might be there. And so Case's head had lolled and she had said a name that had made Alex's heart stop and then she had added, "She's not coming back." And Alex had been sick. It was not kind. It was not fair. Case was sitting there, bullet hole passing straight from her chin through her skull. Alex had stalked graves and apartment buildings, talked to priests and coroners, wrote letters and read diaries, and it had made no difference. Case was there and someone else was not.

But now. Now Case is lilting too, body hung heavy against the seat belt, skin ashen where it is still skin. Something, even now, draining out of her. Alex wonders, suddenly, if she'll have to drive home with a corpse, if she'll have to see, even now, the last of the light leave Case's eyes. Case. Fierce Case. The beginning of it all. Alex's first dead, never her last. No. Not her first dead. The first that had risen.

Alex holds a name on the tip of her tongue, remembers gentle fingers in her hair. Knows that some of the dead don't come back, keeps looking, anyway. Keeps hoping. But now the hope has left the car, drowned out by the noise of the engine idling, dragged away by the hands of the dead, who are even now nimbly navigating playgrounds, crossing lawns, padding softly into the night. What will Vance think, if she comes back with a corpse? And suddenly Alex realizes that he won't care at all. No one will. She hadn't even left a note, hadn't even left an emergency contact.

Suddenly, Alex realizes her fingers are on Case's face, suddenly she realizes they are drawing back, aimed in a slap. The blow rocks Case in her halter, but no blood rises in her cheeks. She rocks a little, to and fro, but soon the motion too is abetting, soon it looks as though nothing has moved her at all. Case is still, unmoving, and Alex feels something rise in her chest, something dark and cloying. It takes her a moment to realize it's fear, takes her a moment to realize that Case being gone is a fearful thing, no matter what Vance thinks, no matter what her mother thinks, no matter what the masses and the HOA think. Case is here. And Alex wants to keep her that way.

It is desperation that does it, desperation that makes her raise her hands, fingers trembling, and lay them on Case's face. Desperation that makes her turn Case's head, glassy eyes still open, mouth still gape. It must be. Because then Alex does the only thing she can think of, the only thing she remembers from her trainings in the field, what to do in a situation like this, breathless partner beside her. Before she can think, her head is moving, before she can think her lips are parting, before she can think. Alex parts her lips. Carefully, so carefully, she lays them over Case's own. The skin is cool and smooth. Not unpleasant. Not like she'd been told. That's her last thought, before she does it, takes the air in her lungs, the last she can offer, and breathes out. The breath moves from her lungs, slides up her throat and across her teeth, moves from her mouth into Case's.

Nothing happens. Alex sits. She breathes. Her hands do not tangle in Case's hair—there is none to tangle in—her fingers do not brush the skin of Case's chin—there is none on which her fingers could rest. She sits and she breathes and she remembers a name that used to flood her heart with joy. Which is to say, she hopes. She and Vance and everyone else at the agency. Guilty of hope. Alex sits and she breathes and she hopes. She doesn't know for what. Doesn't know what this mad exercise might bring, is on the brink of pulling away, but then. She almost doesn't notice. Almost doesn't realize the pads of her fingers—cold in the autumn air—are warming to spring. She falters, makes a little gasp, and Case's mouth moves with it, pulling forward to follow the retreating air, her hands, suddenly, at Alex's elbow. It is a breath, and then it is something else. It is a giving, and then it is a moving of mouths, Case's lips firm against her own, breath bartered and then passed back. Alex feels air that is not her own moving into her lungs, she feels a press of heat at her fingertips and when she pulls back, head spinning, thoughts reeling, it is to see a slight rose blush rising on Case's cheeks. Not so small then, these things. Not so small.

"What's happening?" Alex asks, breath caught back in her own throat. She does not realize that her fingers are still tender on Case's face, that Case's head, mangled as it is, is still cradled in her hands, doesn't see the dip of sun outside painting the night dusky violet. Her eyes are forever on Case's face. Case swallows. Case swallows. Alex feels her eyes grow wide, her fingers tighten on Case's skin, the way that Case's skin—flush and pounding—pushes back.

"I," Case starts. She catches breath. "I don't know." It comes out in a rush, an exhale, and suddenly Alex knows. She can see. Can feel it, soft on her skin. Case breathes. Just twice. In and out. That's all they get. Just twice. Just Case's skin warm, then fading against Alex's fingers. Just one swallow before Case's throat no longer needs to be cleared, just one more breath passed between them. It is enough. Somehow, impossibly, it is enough. Alex lets her fingers fall from Case's skin, feels the air pass between them.

"I won't tell Vance," she says, gaze not meeting Case's eyes, which furrow in her brow.

"About?" Case asks, voice cautious. Alex shakes her head. Doesn't speak for a moment. How can she? How can she put something so big into words? How can she contain such hope?

"I won't tell him," she says again and this time Case nods. This time, she purses her lips.

"One of us should," she says, finally, hand raised to skim the back of her head, stopping just short of the wound barely hidden in the stubble. Alex nods, considers.

"Yes," she says, finally, "but I won't." It is something. Not big. Not small either. Case looks at her, really looks, the way only the dead can, the way only those that have left and come back can understand. Carefully, she raises a hand from her lap. Carefully, she runs it through Alex's hair, stray strand now tucked behind ear. Her skin is cool against Alex's. Cool. Not cold. Small things.

The fourth time Alex sees Case, they're sitting in Vance's office. Vance is sitting too, legs propped up on the desk, family picture he hasn't been able to let go of scooted over to make room for his feet.

"Well?" he asks, barely listening. Barely paying attention to something as routine as a roundup. Not when there are other things to think of, other things to worry about, the rehomings and the work orders and the sudden over-crowding in the cities—too many bodies piling up and not enough free real estate. Well. Enough real estate. Not enough understanding landlords. He's hardly got time for them, hardly got time for a pair that came back empty handed, tasers not so much as sparking. He's got paperwork to do and a grave to visit—still one of the hopeful standing sentry in the cemetery, open graves like gaping mouths stretching around him. The only one that matters still full. He's got his own problems, after all, his own reason for being here.

Alex looks at Case. She shifts in her seat. Case is not looking back, is studying the wall, muscle jumping in her jaw, face a mess of shadows, and Alex realizes that, after everything, she doesn't believe her. After everything, she doesn't think Alex is on her side. So she does it. She looks at Vance, straightens her shoulders, and she lies.

"They were gone when we got there," she says and Case starts. It's such a small thing that Vance does not notice, but Alex is sitting with her leg pressed to Case's thigh and she feels the tick of muscle, the immediate attempt to control it. "They were gone when we got there," she says again, and

Vance looks at her funny at the repetition, but doesn't comment. Alex can tell by the look in his eyes that it's a visiting day, has seen on the shared office calendar that Vance plans to spend the rest of the day out of the office. Knows where he goes. Knows where she goes. Knows what's missing. What they can never get back. But.

Carefully, so carefully, Alex moves her hand. It is on her leg, then beside her leg, then her fingers are reaching. They are reaching and then they are not reaching. Are reaching and then they are found. Carefully, below the desk, where Vance can't see, she takes Case's hand. Her fingers in hers are cool but not cold, and as she holds them, as their fingers tangle together atop their press of legs, she can feel the temperature rising, feel the thrum of something moving beneath Case's thighs. Not small at all.

Case looks at her. Vance misses it. Then Case opens her mouth, fingers tight on Alex's, begins, at last, to speak. "There's something else," she says, "something you should know." Beneath Alex's fingers, Case's skin is warm.

*AUTHOR OF BEWILDERED, Jessie Ulmer adores the abyss—the magic and mystery that can be reached in the dark unknown. She writes soft and eerie fiction exploring themes of ability, identity, sexuality and gender. Her current projects include reluctant zombies, queer swan maidens and tender murder ghosts. She is delighted to edit for Sword & Kettle Press, and has been published in Syntax & Salt, Gingerbread House, 3Elements Review, Pins and Needles: A Journal of Contemporary Fairy Tales, The Yellow Chair Review and Washington's Best Emerging Poets Anthology. In 2019 she was nominated for a Best of the Net Award.*

# THE CARETAKER

## SCOTT BRENDEL

$\mathcal{T}$ime stood still that summer with a prickly, anxious feel, the house condemned to the silence of grief. School had been Tanner's only reprieve, but when it let out in June, he was trapped at home with nothing to do.

Tossing his comic book aside, he wandered down to the living room where his mom rattled the ice cubes in her glass. Each afternoon, she sat down with a highball—sometimes the first of many—and looked across the fields at the town cemetery with what Tanner figured was the thousand-yard stare. Something the VFW guys talked about when the soldiers—boys who'd gone to war and come back as old men —started returning from Viet Nam.

"Mom?"

She never moved, never turned, never acknowledged he was even there. Instead, she watched the cemetery as if waiting for something to happen. But nothing ever did. Hadn't, since Uncle Walt's burial in March.

Tanner fought a lump that formed in his throat as he watched the overgrown grass at the edge of the cemetery wave in the wind and the dandelion seeds drift across the fields.

After a moment that seemed to last forever, his mother reached for the bottle of rye and refilled her glass. "Go find your friends."

\* \* \*

COLLINSPORT HUDDLED beside a bend on the Erie Canal. It was a port only in the imagination of the town founder, named back in the days when barges moved freight across upstate New York. During summer, the biggest excitement in town was the twice-weekly raising of the lift bridge that allowed old Ezra Pickett to motor down the canal and visit his retired girlfriend.

"I'll bet he's dickin' her," Douglas Allen said, as they watched Pickett pass. Douglas—who preferred "the Dougster"—was a scrawny kid with ears that stuck out like the solar panels on the Viking orbiter.

"That's gross," Tommy Lamott said. "Old folks don't screw." Tommy was a short, fat kid whose parents owned a trophy store in a town too small to sponsor sports.

"Sure they do," Vic Pizello said. "What else do they do with their time?" He whipped a rock at the passing boat. It hit the side panel of the windshield and shattered it. "Shit. Let's get outta here!"

"God damn kids!" Pickett screamed, shaking the gnarled root of his fist.

\* \* \*

"WHAT DID YOU DO THAT FOR?" Tanner asked, pulling up with a stitch in his side.

"Because I wanted to," Vic said.

"Christ, Vic," the Dougster whined, ears twitching like radar on high alert. "What if he recognized us?"

"What if he did? What's he gonna do?"

Tanner wondered the same thing, worried it might get back to his mom, even as the sick thrill of the moment finally began to fade. Of the four of them, Vic was the wild one. His family had moved to Collinsport from Brooklyn for reasons unknown. On this, rumors were split. According to one, he'd been expelled from junior high for punching out the shop teacher. According to another, his father had ratted out the mob and was on someone's hit list.

"You'd kick his ass," Tommy said.

"You'd mess him up," the Dougster agreed.

Tanner said nothing while Vic pulled a pack of cigarettes from his shirt pocket, lit one and made it look cool.

"Want one?" Vic held out the pack to Tanner.

"No, thanks," Tanner said, trying to hide his surprise. "I'm trying to cut back."

The one time he'd taken a drag from a cigarette, it had nearly made him puke, and he didn't want Vic to think he was a pussy.

"I'll take one," the Dougster said.

"Did I offer you one?" The cig hanging from Vic's mouth waggled as he talked. "Tanner's my friend. You're a dickhead I put up with."

And there was the biggest surprise of the summer, Tanner thought. Vic Pizello, the only kid in eighth grade who had to shave every day, had decided Tanner was worthy of friendship.

"I'm bored." Tommy scuffed at the dirt. "What you guys wanna do?"

Vic squinted at the sun as it hovered above the horizon. "Smoke my cigarette in peace."

"There's nothing *to* do," Tommy whined, picking up a stick and whaling away at the trunk of a tree.

"Yeah, there is," Vic said, in a way that made Tanner nervous. "Tonight. After dark."

\* \* \*

TANNER CROUCHED beneath a window of Collinsport Junior High, sweat beading his forehead. It might have been the humidity, but he didn't think so. "You sure about this?"

"Yeah, I'm sure," Vic said. "I'll boost you up. You crawl through the window and let us in the back door."

"Why's it gotta be me?" Tanner asked. It didn't feel right.

Vic gestured at the other two. "Because Tommy's too fat and Dumbo can't fly."

"Why we gotta do this at all?" Tanner asked.

"Because Richards took a set of wrenches I brought to school. I'm gonna send him a message."

"You're gonna leave him a note, right? We're not gonna do anything that'll get us in trouble."

Vic's eyes seemed to sizzle. "That's right, Tanner. A love note. Now get your ass up there."

The school had no air conditioning, so Mr. Richards, the custodian, left the window above his desk propped open. Tommy helped Tanner up onto Vic's back while the Dougster stood guard. After slipping through the window, Tanner crept through the halls, half expecting Richards—or worse, his step-father—to jump out of the dark. Opening the back door, he let his friends in.

"You sure he's not here?" Tanner asked as he followed Vic back to the custodian's office.

"Nobody works after dark."

The Dougster loped along behind Vic. "This is cool."

"Yeah," Tommy said. "Feels different when nobody's here."

Tanner wanted to smack them both. School was nothing more than detention for these two morons. Vic, on the other hand, was bucking for something worse than juvie.

Shouldering past the door, Vic surveyed the workshop, which was filled with cabinets and tools. "Richards," he muttered. "Where would you keep 'em?" He started rifling the drawers of the cabinet beside the workbench.

"Hey, look!" the Dougster said. "Spray paint. I love the smell of this stuff!" He took the cap off a can of red paint and sprayed some into the air, then leaned forward and sniffed. "Cherry."

Tommy opened a cabinet filled with garden tools. "Whoa," he said, as if he'd found the treasure of the Sierra Madre. He picked up an ax.

Tanner watched him take some slow-motion swings. Tommy had been kicked out of Boy Scouts when he nearly chopped off the Scoutmaster's foot.

"Here they are." Vic lifted a case of crescent wrenches and stroked it gently.

From somewhere far down the hall, a door banged open and a baritone voice rippled through the air with an ululating cry. It was Richards, doing his Tarzan imitation.

"Holy shit," Tanner whispered. "Someone's coming!"

That started a frantic shopping spree as the boys started cramming stuff into their pockets.

"We gotta get out of here," Tanner whispered.

The Dougster ran past him and down the hall to the exit with a can in each hand, spraying streaks along the walls. Tommy followed, after taking a swing at the custodian's door with the ax.

"Hey! Who's there?" Richards bellowed.

"Vic!" Tanner said. "We gotta go! What are you doing?!"

"Leaving Richards a message," Vic said, holding his dick in one hand while he hosed down the custodian's desk.

* * *

THEY MADE it out of the school unseen only because Richards was so slow. 'Nam had left him with a limp so bad it looked like he'd tip over with every other step. They crossed the parking lot and ran into the woods, then slowed to a walk.

"That was close," Tommy said, his chest heaving. Wind sprints were not his strong suit.

"Damn right!" said the Dougster. His belt held cans of spray paint pressed to his stomach.

Tanner was pissed. "You said no one was there." He glared at Vic.

"Guess I was wrong."

"We coulda got caught."

"Who gives a crap?"

"I do!" Anger made Tanner forget himself. "All over some stupid wrenches? What's the big deal?"

Vic wheeled on him and pinned Tanner against a tree, his hand around his throat.

"The big deal? Those wrenches are mine. And Richards took 'em." Something worked in Vic's eyes. Then he let Tanner go.

Tanner rubbed his throat and picked the bark out of the hair on the back of his head. Vic deflated and looked suddenly inconsequential, something Tanner could never have imagined.

"Hey, Vic," Tommy said. "What are we gonna do with all this shit?" He held the ax like he'd just discovered it in his hands. Pruning shears and trowels sprouted from his pockets.

"We'll stash it," Vic said.

"Where?" the Dougster asked.

"There," Vic said, pointing at the cemetery beside the canal.

* * *

I<small>T MADE</small> sense on a certain level, but that didn't mean Tanner wanted to go in there. And it wasn't because he was scared. He'd read his share of *Tales from the Crypt*, but the stories were just a bunch of made-up bullshit. What bothered him was thinking about the casket of broken body parts—all they'd found of Uncle Walt in Long Dong or Duck Fuck or wherever he'd been killed—moldering beneath the earth. "Let's hide this stuff and get outta here."

"Any ideas?" Vic asked.

"Follow me."

Even in the dark, the cemetery was beautiful, its lawns manicured, the canopy of trees protecting it, vibrant with life. The headstones stood orderly and erect, the grass between them trimmed as if by hand.

"Hey, look," the Dougster said. "A little house."

"That's not a house, you dumb ass," Tanner said. "It's a mausoleum."

"A place where dead people live," Tommy explained.

Tanner shook his head, not sure who he wanted to smack first.

"Who's in that one?"

"Angus Collins, the guy who started the town. There's a statue of him beside the mausoleum." Tanner had read just about every gravestone in the cemetery on the Sunday afternoons his mother brought him to visit, so he didn't have to listen to her cry.

Tanner led them past the statue to a thicket of bushes. A secluded spot he'd found the day of Uncle Walt's service. "Dump the stuff here and cover it with those leaves."

"We'll meet at the gas station tomorrow night, then come back to divvy the stuff up," Vic said. "I'm outta here."

"What's the rush?" Tanner asked.

"I gotta get home quick."

"Why?"

"Who is Richards gonna think busted into the school?" Vic looked grim. "I gotta be home when the cops show up. So my old man knows I didn't do it."

Tanner couldn't fault the logic.

"See you tomorrow." Vic left, while Tommy and the Dougster trailed along like fish on a stringer.

Only after they were out of sight did Tanner cross the cemetery to a newer section beside the woods. The polished marble slab, flanked by a small flag, gleamed in the light of the moon. Two lines—a name and a range of dates—had been engraved in the stone. It wasn't much, but what could you say that would fit on such a small surface?

"Boy."

Tanner whirled in surprise.

A man emerged from the woods but stopped short of the moon's reach. He wore a long coat—unusual for such a hot, muggy night. "What brings you here?"

Though startled, Tanner was not afraid. He could outrun the old man if he had to. "None of your business."

"Aye, but it is. Everything that happens here—" the man raised his arms as if summoning an orchestra to its feet "—is of interest to me."

"Who are you?" Tanner asked, worried what the man might have seen.

"The one who watches over this place. The one ye'd best not cross."

The challenge brought Tanner's anger and grief to a head. "I come to pay my respects."

"Best done during day," the man said, stepping into the glow of the moon. He wore muttonchops and a three-cornered hat. Then something—a trick of the light?—made it seem like the planes of his face shifted, as if rearranging themselves.

Tanner stepped back, his anger gone, as fear found a foothold.

"Go," the man said. "And warn your friends. There'll be no mischief tolerated here."

Tanner turned and ran until he was clear of the cemetery. Only then did he look back.

The man had vanished. Fog filled the shallow bowl in which the cemetery lay. Within its folds, Tanner glimpsed movement, shadowy figures moving back and forth amidst the quiet clank of tools.

* * *

IT WAS a week before Vic met them outside the gas station, fading bruises on his face. Apparently, his father hadn't bought the story he'd told.

"Go buy a pop," Vic told Tanner.

"Why?"

Vic lit a cigarette. "To establish an alibi."

Like it had made a difference the week before. "What about you?"

Vic smirked. "They always remember me."

Tanner made a big deal over the pop machine, pretending it had stolen his dime so the guy behind the register had to help. Then he met his friends back on the street, where the four boys ducked down an alley and headed for the cemetery.

The streets of Collinsport gave way to fields of potatoes and corn where crickets filled the night with their throbbing murmur. After twenty minutes, the wrought-iron arch of the cemetery gate appeared, backlit by the swollen moon.

The warning from the old man had troubled Tanner all week. "Hey, Vic, I've been thinking."

"Yeah? There's a news flash."

"Maybe we shouldn't go in there."

"Why not?"

"Somebody might see us. Call the cops." A lame excuse, since the only house in sight was Tanner's and that was nearly a mile away. "Besides, by this time, someone probably found the stuff and took it."

Vic stopped so suddenly that Tommy and the Dougster banged into him from behind. He grabbed the front of Tanner's shirt, twisted it and pulled him close. "That better not be the case."

"It's been a week..."

"And only four of us knew about it." Vic stared at Tanner with barely suppressed rage.

What was so important about those freakin' wrenches?

"That stuff better be there," Vic said.

Tommy and the Dougster flanked Vic, nodding like bobble-head dolls.

Tanner struggled for cool. Vic could pound him into paste. "It probably is."

Vic let go of his shirt and slowly smoothed it across his shoulders and chest, which creeped Tanner out even more.

Then a horrifying thought. What if the old man in the muttonchops had stolen the stuff? Vic would think Tanner had taken it.

"Let's go," Vic said. "Lead the way."

Tanner walked on, while the other three fell in step behind him. He saw Walt's gravestone at a distance, the little flag beside it, and wondered what his uncle would have done. Probably taken on all three of them at once. Nothing had scared Walt.

"There's the place," the Dougster said, bounding past the

mausoleum to the thicket.

"Yeah!" Tommy followed.

Vic trudged along behind Tanner, watching, as if anticipating an attempt at escape.

Up ahead, the Dougster was knee-deep in leaves. "Hey. Where'd the stuff go?"

Tanner stopped, feet suddenly leaden. The old guy had stolen it.

Turning, he saw Vic behind him, hands rolled into fists. Vic's barely contained fury made the bruises on his face seem to swell.

Then Tommy's voice drifted through the air. "Here it is, you dork!"

As Vic passed him, Tanner steadied himself against the mausoleum, then walked to the thicket.

The Dougster sniffed his paints, jeopardizing what few brain cells he had left. Tommy hovered over the ax. And Vic sat beside the statue of Angus Collins, mesmerized by the wrenches.

"So what's the deal with those things?" Tanner asked.

"I told you," Vic said.

"No, you didn't. The world's full of wrenches. What's so special about these?"

The clatter of tools stopped, and Tanner knew without looking that Tommy and the Dougster listened.

"They were supposed to be a gift for my father," Vic said.

The thick-necked bastard who beat him.

"But Richards took 'em when he found me out back in the parking lot. The day before my father's birthday."

"You should have told the principal," Tanner said. "Or called the cops."

Vic lifted the biggest wrench, like it was the key that would unlock the most important door in his life. "I couldn't."

"Why not?"

Vic stood and paced, the tool dangling from his fist. "Reasons."

Tanner would not be dissuaded. "Tell me."

Tommy and the Dougster watched, wired into the moment.

"None of your business," Vic said.

"Tell me!"

"Because I stole them! AND RICHARDS STOLE THEM FROM ME!"

Vic swung the wrench like a baseball bat, as if Richards knelt before him. On the follow-through, it clipped the hand of the statue and sent shards of marble spinning into the dark.

Tanner stood rooted to the spot, horrified. Tommy clenched the ax in his hands, while the Dougster stood poised like a gunfighter ready to draw.

Vic crouched on the balls of his feet, his face twisted in a snarl, staring at the broken statue. But what did he see? Time seemed to stop, presenting a chance to change the way things might turn out.

Then the moment was lost.

"Son of a bitch!" Vic lashed out again, severing Angus Collin's arm. "Bastard!" The next blow took off the statue's head and sprayed shrapnel into the grass.

Tanner heard strangled cries of glee as Vic's rage swept Tommy and Doug into its embrace. He saw Tommy swinging the ax at the trunk of a tree. Wood chips flew but not fast enough to sate Tommy's need to kill the young maple. And the Dougster danced while he painted the mausoleum with his own tortured vision of art.

"No!" Tanner screamed. "Stop it!"

When Vic cocked the wrench again, Tanner grabbed his wrists. But Vic was too strong. He smashed his forearm across the side of Tanner's face and knocked him to the ground. Tanner looked up in time to see Angus Collin's broken leg buckle and the statue fall.

How had things gotten to this point? And how could he stop them?

Tanner pressed his hands to the ground as he prepared to stand, and that's when he felt it. A tremor. Subtle, at first, as if something moved beneath the surface. Then the ground shuddered with a sound like grinding stone. Tanner leaped to his feet.

"What was that?" Vic asked.

"I don't know," Tanner said.

"Felt like an earthquake," the Dougster said, cans of paint hanging from his hands.

Tommy stood beside the ravaged tree, sweat glistening on his face. "In Collinsport?"

Tanner saw a stone on the ground in front of him move. On an otherwise flat surface, it rolled itself over. Then again. That's when he realized it wasn't a stone but a finger from the statue of Angus Collins.

"Holy shit."

The finger rolled again, bounced, then jumped along the ground as if scurrying for cover. Until it found another fragment—the hand it had come from—and fused itself back into place.

Tanner stepped back until he heard movement behind him. Fragments of marble raced past his ankles and converged around the broken husk of the statue. The hand reassembled itself and climbed back onto its wrist. Then something banged into Tanner's leg. When he looked down, he saw the marble face of Angus Collins staring back up at him.

Wearing muttonchops and a three-cornered hat.

"Oh, my God!"

The head rolled back onto the marble shoulders, then the statue slowly healed itself and stood.

The Dougster was the first to freak. "Holy crap!" He dropped the spray paint and ran. But he didn't get far.

Angus Collins swept his arm until he pointed at the Dougster. The kid reversed course instantly as if yanked by springs. He flew backwards, arms outstretched, mouth open in surprise, until he smashed into the side of the mausoleum.

Tanner expected him to bounce off the wall and drop to the ground. But he didn't. Instead, he stuck.

The Dougster tried to peel himself off the wall, looking for the bonds that held his arms in place. When his hand started to melt, he opened his mouth to scream, but by then his throat had begun to liquefy, too. Then, before Tanner's horrified eyes, the Dougster began to sizzle and steam until all that was left was a stain in the shape of a boy.

"Dougie!" Tommy screamed, dropping the ax and wetting his pants.

Angus Collins turned.

Tommy backpedaled until he tripped and fell against the tree. Collins raised a hand and flicked a finger. The ax, suddenly granted the gift of flight, flew through the air and pinned Tommy's head to the trunk. Tommy died, eyes and mouth wide with surprise. Then roots broke through the soil, wrapped him in a sheath and slowly pulled him below ground.

Silence settled over the moon-washed glade. Then Tanner heard the grinding of stone as Angus Collins turned to Vic.

"He didn't mean it!" Tanner cried.

The statue advanced, but Vic held his ground while anger and amazement struggled for control of his face.

"I'm not afraid of you," he whispered, tightening his grip on the wrench. "You're not my father."

Vic swung the wrench like Hammerin' Hank Aaron. But Angus Collins caught it in one hand, leaving the two of them stalled in struggle.

Then the wrench lost its silvery shine where Angus Collins touched it, and a cloudy gray color seeped down its length with the brittle sound of cracking ice. Vic looked up at his hand in surprise as the color change ran through his fist and down his arm. He tried to step away but couldn't, then turned beseeching eyes to Tanner.

"Help," he said, before the change swept through his body and froze him in place.

Angus Collins drove his fist through what had once been Vic Pizello, pulverizing the fragile form into dust and rubble. Then he turned on Tanner.

Tanner backed away, but there was nowhere to go and no point in running. It hadn't helped the Dougster.

Collins towered over Tanner, reached out with the hand that had reassembled itself, then froze. When Tanner lifted his eyes to the statue's face, he saw movement, as if currents boiled beneath the surface of the stone. The face twisted and shifted as if it were alive, remade itself until suddenly it resolved into a face that he knew.

Uncle Walt.

The sorrow he'd held in for so long suddenly gave way and he fell to his knees. Tears welled in his eyes and blurred his vision. But when they finally cleared, it was Angus Collins who stood before him once more.

"You were warned, boy, and told to tell your friends," the statue said, leaning close. "With that you'll have to live."

* * *

TANNER HUDDLED INSIDE HIS JACKET. Indian summer had been swept away by the chilly gusts of October, made all the more troubling to the townsfolk since the night that three boys had gone missing.

His mother knelt beside Walt's grave and smoothed the flag that had faded over the months. Her face was gently lined now, but it had lost its worrisome pallor when she stopped drinking.

"Mom," he said, casting a wary look at the deepening gloom. "It's getting dark. We need to leave."

She rose reluctantly. "All right."

They left the cemetery and crossed the field toward their house. Harvest had stripped it of its earlier promise.

"The cemetery is always so well-tended," his mother said. "You've done a good job."

"Thanks," he said, thinking of the hours he spent in its care. Sorrow for guilt; a reasonable exchange.

"But how do you manage? There's so much to do."

"There are others who help." Penitents, he thought, looking over his shoulder at the figures rising from the ground to begin their nightly toil.

He raised his hand, and one of the figures—the only kid in eighth grade who had to shave every day—waved back.

SCOTT BRENDEL IS the author of "The Seventh Green at Lost Lakes" (in Read by Dawn, Volume 1); "The House Beneath Delgany Street" (in Subtle Edens, an anthology nominated for a British Fantasy Award); "Ataraxia" (in Day Terrors); "Groundswell of Love" (in Something Wicked); "The Eyes of Aaron Marsh" (in Paper Tape); "In the Gray Light of Dawn" (in Penumbra); "Threesome" (in Cactus Heart); and "Ghost Tour" (in What Monsters Do for Love, Volume 2).

He lives along the Front Range of the Colorado Rocky Mountains, where he is at work on a novel.

# THE ROOTED

## LMG WILSON

*L*onnmore. The letters had been carved ages past and the wood had cracked from the damp and time. Moss snaked through the grooves of the crossroad's knotted sign, which pointed down the darker fork in the road. Although Nell Hawthorn had passed the sign a dozen times before, not once had she considered the path.

But a cough crept out from the back of the covered wagon, a ragged sound, deep and wet. She put aside the reins too big for her hands and pulled back the light fabric enclosing the wagon's interior. Her father looked frail and disheveled, so unlike himself. His waistcoat was unbuttoned, kerchief abandoned, and he breathed raggedly beneath his wool great coat. Nell needn't press her chill hand to his head to know the fever still gripped him.

She swallowed, thinking of how little it took to fell her father. He was no small man, strong as an ox, quick-witted and stubborn. But a stuck wheel in the mud, a stumble in the mire and a gash in his thigh had been enough. It took him half a day to admit the wound bothered him. By the next morning, Nell could see the fever plainly on his face.

His words when he finally accepted he could not steer the cart still shook her, even a day later. "Ride straight to Wakefield. Stop for none and keep your cap low. Whatever happens, veer not from the path."

A choice now lay ahead of her. There was the road well-traveled; the trail to Wakefield. Though barely fourteen, she'd taken the road many times before and knew it to be at least a day's ride in good weather, a day and a half in the brewing storm. And if the tingle in the air could be trusted, it would be minutes before rainfall. The wagon would be soaked through, or worse, the storm could wash out the road.

In his state, her father wouldn't fair well in the damp weather. He needed rest, a warm bed and a fire.

*He will not make it to Wakefield,* she feared.

So, Nell turned the cart towards Lonnmore.

Boughs reached over to cover the path like sickly fingers. Though not all the trees had shaken clean summer's growth, the trunks passed by as columns of pitch. And shadows danced there, on the distant dimming horizon and just beyond the cart's lantern light. They drew her eyes from the road only to disappear again with another muted thud of horseshoes on dirt.

The cart strained with groans as it passed over emerging rocks and Nell guessed no one had taken the road to Lonnmore in at least a fortnight. No one would, once the snow came.

She shivered and pulled her oversized great coat closer, but despite it being thick, she wished she'd donned more layers under the black fabric. There was small comfort that her father let her dress as a boy while they traveled, for practicality he had told her. Though now she suspected caution played a part too. After all, what safety could there be for a young girl in petticoats alone on the road?

The tense storm air thickened with each tree they passed and in the familiar drone of trail sounds, she was left no real company. Nothing more than the whispers in her heart.

*He will die this night.*

*Then, you will be alone.*

The light dimmed, swallowed by darkening clouds that lowered into the forest's canopy. The storm's first crack rang out.

Nell let out a curse unbefitting a young woman and the horse whinnied with her. "Hush now, Charleston," she said to the mouthy workhorse. "And hurry."

On Nell's urging with the reins, Charleston surged forth under the gnarled branches, some low enough to scrape the top of the wagon. They clawed at the fabric barrier protecting her father from the chill and cackled in collisions with one another in the wind.

But then it came. The rain. There was no warning of a drizzle before heaps of it drowned out the forest around her. The shiver returned and slipped in under her clothes as the rain soaked through.

On she urged, hoping the storm would continue north and not west with her to the village of Lonnmore.

\* \* \*

THE WAGON RUMBLED past the tall aged fencing encircling the village, the storm Nell emerged from still at her heels. Lonnmore looked more akin to a large farm than a settlement of note; a central field where the grass had been trodden short surrounded by several stout buildings. Half looked to be homes, the others barns, each paired and evenly spaced with grazing at their backs. But not much. The forest surrounded the entire village with but a few acres between them and the fence that seemed to hang like a noose about the border.

One house stood apart, the largest of them all set directly across from the open gates of Lonnmore.

At seeing the homes, her fears of camping in the rain and of her father's fever worsening lightened from her shoulders. Nell drove the cart through the center of the village, to the house at its heart, as the rain caught up with her.

The house sat the tallest in the village at two full stories with a red peaked roof and window shutters that looked hand carved. Beyond them, she spotted lights in the windows and shapes hurrying from one building to the next in the storm's descent.

"I need help!" she shouted and her voice seemed to shake the whole village. More shapes emerged from homes, lanterns in hand, stoic figures cautiously curious from a distance.

Nell stepped off the cart and stilled Charleston, his breath ragged from their urgent pace.

But no one came close. The villagers assembled from her commotion, but none stepped up to offer help. Whispers danced between them until the doors of the central home opened. It was then that all the villagers of Lonnmore turned their attentions from her.

He stepped out and stood under the cover of the porch, thumbs tucked in the plain buckle of his belt. Though he wore simple clothing there was an air of superiority about the man, particularly in the way he stood. His head tilted high, eyes peering down from beneath his hat atop the steps. A beard, long and wild, stemmed from his chin, as it did for all the men of Lonnmore. Flecks of gray peppered the wiry nest and hid the top of his collar. Above it sat a frown. Stern. Unflinching. It paired well with his cruel blue eyes.

Two women flocked him, willowy things all fabric and bones. Their dresses were duplicates of one another in the same simple colors of the soil. The one on his right looked to be his wife if age were a measure. Though younger than the man, lines creased her face and her hands seemed ravaged by work and time. The younger, to his left, could be their daughter but Nell wasn't sure. The girl cowered beside the man at the center, masking her features.

Despite the urgency and commotion Nell had arrived with, he did not come out from under the roof of his porch. There seemed not a concerned bone in his body.

"I am Silas Colbrook, Alderman of Lonnmore." His voice cut through the air with a boom. Deep, coarse and direct. "Say why you have come, child."

"My father," Nell stepped towards the Alderman. "He suffered a wound and it worsens with fever." She looked back towards her cart where Charleston hadn't yet settled, where her father laid waiting in a dire state. "Please, he needs help."

The Alderman's eyes narrowed as she spoke until she said fever. A murmur cascaded among the villagers that had assembled until the Alderman looked about them and their voices died.

"Have you a doctor?" Nell pressed. "Or even a place to rest. The storm soaked us through and without warmth, I fear he might..." Her voice caught in her throat.

"We've no physician here," the young girl beside the Alderman spoke, her blue eyes flashing up from their bowed position.

Only then did the Alderman turn from Nell. His hand fell on his daughter's shoulder, his grip visibly tight.

"Brother Sorrinson," the Alderman called out.

A man stepped forward at the Alderman's behest. His beard was long, cloudiness fogged his eyes and the sharp lines of his features seemed to sag from his bones. He wore what all the other men did—simple clothes and a brimmed hat. Were it not for his eyes she may not have noticed him as different from the rest.

"Lisbeth, take this...*girl* to the stables," the Alderman huffed. He then regarded Nell, though his pincer grip hadn't yet released from his daughter's shoulder. "We will store your beast and cart there for the storm. Brother Sorrinson will see to your father's wound."

Despite the relief she expected to feel, Nell's shiver didn't abate. Like the rain that remained overhead, the chill thundered through her.

"Thank you, but I would stay with him," Nell said, though a quake unnerved her words.

"Once your horse is tended and you are changed, we'll see you reunited." The Alderman released Lisbeth's shoulder and the girl stepped forward.

"Follow me," Lisbeth said, her voice soft and careful.

The villagers of Lonnmore did not disperse. Four men emerged without instruction and flocked to Brother Sorrinson's side. They fetched her father from the cart while the rest of the villagers stood fixed and watching.

"You truly have no doctor?" Nell asked Lisbeth in hushed tones.

Lisbeth took up Charleston's bridle and shook her head. She remained silent.

"We've no need," Brother Sorrinson said as he pressed a hand to her father's brow. Age raked the words that left his throat as a raspy croak. "The Wildwood provides."

With a demure nod, Lisbeth guided Nell and the cart. "The Wildwood provides," she echoed.

* * *

NELL UNHITCHED Charleston under the dry canopy of the nearest barn. Workhorses stood nestled in their stalls out of the way of the wagon that nearly filled the central path. They looked apprehensive, their eyes wild and racing about, not unlike Charleston's. A part of her whispered it was the storm but the same flinching unease seemed to seep into her skin.

"You needn't worry," Lisbeth whispered as though she could see Nell's discomfort. "He will be well. My father and Brother Sorrinson will see to it."

But the fever remained present on Nell's mind. What if her father needed medicine? What if the rest wasn't enough? And his caution tugged at her, as though a pit deepened in her gut. *"Veer not from the path..."*

Nell shivered from the chill as the storm reared its head and pelted the barn roof. In the din, Lisbeth guided Charleston to a stall where he couldn't seem to calm. Even a gentle touch from Nell, one that always worked to still the massive beast, didn't quell whatever caution shook him.

Nell tried to rub the chill away when Lisbeth motioned for her to follow.

In the rain, they ran to the Alderman's house. Once under the covered porch, Nell rushed ahead without invitation to the home. Muddy boot prints marked the path to the stairs.

"They took him up?" she asked, already mounting the steps with Lisbeth protesting at her heels.

At the top of the staircase, the men who had carried her father stood. Nell startled at first, their vigil still and steadfast as their unblinking eyes watched her every move.

"My father?" she asked, expecting them to step aside.

They did not.

"Where is my father?"

"Let the child pass," the Alderman called out and the men stepped aside.

Nell's clothes dripped as she crossed the hallway to the only open door. A lantern flickered from the floor as the last of the afternoon died in the storm's rage and Brother

Sorrinson knelt over Nell's father. The Alderman stood at the foot of the bed.

"How does he fare?" Nell pressed.

Brother Sorrinson looked up but said nothing until the Alderman nodded once. "The rain's soured the fever," Sorrinson said. "He has need of rest and warmth."

Nell looked about the sparse room where there was only one bed, one chair and a small closet. Even the lantern sat on the floor by the bed and a lonely washbasin. "I will stay with him," she decided, picking a spot on the floor to stretch out a blanket.

"No. There is room down the hall where you will rest," the Alderman said. "Brother Sorrinson shall remain at his side."

"I...I would stay with my father," Nell protested.

"There is nothing more for you to do, girl," Brother Sorrinson insisted. "Let him rest."

"And you mustn't see to him as such," Alderman Colbrook's voice felt as ice, his words more a command than a suggestion. "Lisbeth," he hollered and she seemed to appear at the door. "See to her. Appropriate dry clothes, food and bed."

"Yes, father." Lisbeth tucked her hand about Nell's wrist as gently as the girl seemed capable of. "Please," she whispered to Nell, pleading with her eyes.

All the while, the Alderman's gaze remained firm and fixed on the pair of them.

Lisbeth led Nell to a room much like her father's at the end of the hall. It too was sparse of furniture, and from the closet, Lisbeth pulled out clothes. "You would do well to dress as you should," she whispered. "As a *girl*." She laid out a long nightgown on the bed. "This was mine when I was your age."

Nell frowned. "This is your room?"

Lisbeth nodded but when Nell looked around again, there seemed nothing of the girl in it. Besides the borrowed clothes.

As Nell changed into the nightgown, Lisbeth took her wet belongings, even her boots, and disappeared. In minutes, she returned with hot vegetable stew and day-old bread to sop it up.

"I thank you, but...I would like to stay by my father's side," Nell said. "I could help, tend to him through the night. I promise to stay clear of Brother Sorrinson–"

"It is not our way," Lisbeth said quickly as though repeating words that were not her own. "And you, too, have need of rest. All will be well in the morning, you will see."

Lisbeth smiled weakly before heading to the door. She paused there, looking back into the room, her brow scrunched and the smile faltering. "I will come for you in the morning but...it would be best if you stayed in this room through the night. Do not leave, no matter what you hear." The words left her as a whisper. A warning, or a threat, Nell couldn't be sure.

Then, the silence came. It weighed heavy, even with the storm pelting the shuttered windows. Like the whole of Lonnmore was sleeping, yet when she peered out the window she spied figures crossing the field. No light marked their path, only shapes in the dark.

In the hall, she heard voices and Nell crept to the door in no more than the gifted nightgown. As she opened the door, the Alderman strode into the hall from her father's room and halted at the sight of her.

"To bed with you," he ordered and Nell frowned at the instruction. She opened her mouth to protest but he spoke before she could. "All will be well in the morning."

He stood there, waiting with an oppressive glare as if he could will her to shrink from his presence.

Nell closed the door and took to the borrowed bed but she dared not blow out the candle.

\* \* \*

A THUD WOKE Nell from her fitful sleep. Her first thought was that the storm had returned, but she could hear nothing of its rumbles. Though Nell could not remember when she'd drifted to sleep, the candle on the floor had nearly melted to the wick's nub.

The thud sounded again, downstairs this time, and Nell rose from the sheets. Her boots had not been returned, nor had her clothes. In searching for them, she passed the window and stopped.

Lights flickered in the field, more than she had thought there were villagers. They trailed in a line across the short grass and moved past the Alderman's house beyond where she could see.

A part of her whispered to go back, hide under the sheets and wait for morning.

But Nell snubbed out the last of the candle.

The hall was empty and quiet and a light flickered from the crack beneath her father's bedroom door. She had no doubt Brother Sorrinson sat by her father's bedside, so lest she be spied, Nell stepped lightly.

Down the stairs she went in the dark, hunting the windows for the last of the lights passing by the Alderman's house. In the middle of the procession, a group of the shapes looked to be carrying something of weight; a beast or a man, she couldn't quite tell. Strange how it seemed the whole village moved together, their lights twinkling until snuffing out at a structure on the farthest side of the dark meadow.

Nell opened the back door and met the damp air.

That whisper returned: *Go back. Go to sleep.* Lisbeth's

warning to stay in the room echoed from the depths of her mind.

Despite the warning, a part of her yearned to see and know of what lingered off in the dark. What could make a whole village act so strangely? Why must she stay tucked up in bed?

Taking a steadying breath, her grip on the door frame loosened and Nell stepped silently onto the grass. The chill met her toes and coerced her to follow the lights.

As the last disappeared beyond the structure's door, she hurried forward. The grass grew tall about her ankles, its dew soaking through the pale nightdress until it stuck to her legs and the damp climbed higher with a brisk caress.

Upon reaching the building, she touched its side and old brick met her fingers. It was unlike the other structures, rather stout but long and old. It reached back past the border fence and clawed into the depths of the forest beyond where she could see it end.

But more curious, between the bricks, vines held the structure together. Like a soft netting, it snaked over the windows and blocked her view of inside. The villagers' lantern lights grew dim behind the vine-covered windows as if being carried farther from where they'd come in. If she meant to follow, Nell would have to track them along the edge of the brick longhouse. She'd have to go into the woods.

Dark, impossibly so, the forest stood silent just beyond the village's perimeter fence. When Nell looked back the way she'd come, the Alderman's house was no more than a flicker in the distance and the hesitation she'd felt before leaping into the dark field seemed a small hardship. Surely, traveling further would be much the same.

Nell took in a breath and slipped past the aged fence to follow the light.

* * *

SHE KEPT a grip on the wall but the brick withdrew as more of the forest enrobed the structure. The path became overgrown, the way shrouded until she wondered if even falling rain could find her.

But a patch ahead of her glowed as a beacon. It seemed as though a few bricks had given way to the forest's reclamation. As Nell approached, a hum she thought was the wilds became voices.

As a chant, they became words.

"The Wildwood provides," Alderman Colbrook said and the villagers echoed the incantation in unison.

Nell crouched down to the break in the vine lattice where the bricks had crumbled. Inside, she spied a room unlike any other; like a church without pews, villagers knelt in rows on the floor lit by their lanterns and candles and the greenery enveloping the outside of the building, lined it within. Vines, roots and growths of all kinds seemed to emerge from the walls themselves.

Behind the Alderman, an altar was erected; a stone slab half the height of a bed and on it laid the shape of a man.

On and on, the villagers called back to the Alderman with each of his proclamations, and the mantra lulled them back and forth as if in a trance.

But a rumble sounded from behind the altar and the villagers stilled.

The back wall was fractured at its center and vines lined the jagged crack in the bricks. But they had not grown over it as they had the windows. It was as though they clawed into the wall.

No, not in. *Out.* The trailing green tendrils squirmed forth of their own accord. The crack became a crevice, and then a gap in the structure. In the space the vines made, a sickly yellow light pooled out onto the stone floors backed by the flicker of the villagers' candles.

A shadow crossed the light and bent towards the gap.

As if being born, its impossible silhouette drew nearer and surged through the widening fissure. The first of its three legs thumped on the stone floor and the digits of the limb spread out as growing tendrils of root. The tree branch legs jutted irregularly from the trunk torso that almost resembled the shape of a man. Its arms, all five of them, braced the heaving form as it climbed through the seeping gap.

The whole longhouse shook and the stone cracked under its weight. The towering ceilings of the blighted church seemed to barely house the full height of it.

It had no head, not like any Nell had seen. Like that of a dead oak, thick gnarled cords of bark twisted around the top of its torso and continued to twitch and move. Its cracked bark-flesh flaked as if infested with disease. From the splitting surface, a substance oozed in that same sickly yellow glow that bathed the floor.

And with it, the stench. Rotting, festering, a sickly thing like a wound left untended filled the room on the back of sweet roses and cedar.

It had a mouth, a jagged maw that opened and spilled forth an exhale from an abyss within. Its whole shape groaned in the movement and from it creaked the sound of trees rending.

And eyes. She had not seen them at first. Its eyes were barely slits, cracks through the grain of rotting bark with the faintest slick shimmer of black beyond. They bore through the crowd of villages bent in reverence, past the candles and the offerings placed before the shrine.

It looked right to where Nell bent peeking.

She froze.

*Do not see me*, she prayed, pulse pounding in her ears. But, just as quickly as the dark eyes had found her hidden place, they glazed over and turned to the altar.

The Alderman faced the creature. Only then, as he knelt before the monstrosity, did Nell see the man on the altar.

Her father laid still, a sheen of fever slick on his brow.

Nell held her breath. Her grip on the crumbling brick tightened until the rubble came free in her palm.

"We bring to you our humble offering," Alderman Colbrook motioned to Nell's father and the villagers kneeling around him bowed in reverence. "As it was through famine, flood and fire, we offer and the Wildwood provides."

The chant returned in unison as though practiced through the ages.

The creature's boughs shuddered in response. With another lumbering step, it drew nearer to her father's motionless shape.

Nell's lips parted to cry out, to scream for it to stop. No sound left her. Her muscles did not move of her accord. She could only tremble at the sight of the creature.

The Alderman stepped forward, hands raised to the monstrous wooded beast. "We conceal that which provides. We guard that which protects," he recited.

The creature's shadow danced upon the walls in shapes not half as ghastly as its own. Bending over her father, its spindly-branched digits inched towards the altar.

"We nourish that which feeds."

Nell gasped a breath.

The creature loomed nearer her father, its eyes peering down towards his.

The Alderman frowned. "Is he not to your liking?"

The creature seemed altogether uninterested in the Alderman. It was as though he wasn't there. Instead, it ran its fingers along her father's shape. Tendrils of root slithered out from the end of its limbs until they stopped at her father's right thigh where the wound they had poorly tended to lay open in the air.

Despite the terror holding her still, Nell would not dare to blink. She watched as the creature clamped down on her father's leg and coaxed forth a soft groan. He weakly thrashed in the monster's grip.

The jagged barked lips opened and let out a hollow sound. Its croaking breath dripped of yellow sap that congealed on her father's chest.

The villagers looked up from their reverent bows, faces contorted in confusion.

"This...one?" Alderman Silas balked. "You cannot mean this man to be your—"

The creature shook and its maw creased into a deep scowling frown.

"But, it is too soon. And by rite, the next must be of Lonnmore. An outsider cannot—"

A howling groan left its mouth and the Alderman stumbled back. It took him a moment to remember his reverence and bow his head low.

The creature's mouth opened larger than any man's lips could. From its maw leaked gobs of the sickly sap, flowing like molasses from the jagged edges of its face, down through the creases in its flesh. The smell swelled and like a wave cascaded far past the villagers. Nell imagined it could even reach the gates of Lonnmore and it took all her strength not to gag and give away her hiding place.

Turning its head to the roof, the crown of boughs shuddered in a haunting cry. The walls shook, or at least the vines holding them did, and Nell flinched to cover her ears. Even the villagers shielded themselves from the sound though she doubted it did them much good. Like a screeching rend of tearing wood, it went on and on, boring itself deeper into her skull until…it simply stopped.

The creature stilled. It staggered back from her father, slouching in a sigh, and its shape uneasily slipped into the gap. The glow subsided and the creature's roots retreated into darkness.

A small murmur crept through the villagers. All eyes looked on the Alderman as he stood above Nell's father, fists clenched.

Tears slipped down her cheeks, her hands dropped from her ears, and she leaned against the stone of the cursed chapel. Strange exhaustion seeped into her whole self and she wished for nothing more than to wake from what could only be a horrific dream.

"Return him to his bed," the Alderman commanded. "See he is washed and his wounds properly tended."

"Alderman Colbrook?" Brother Sorrinson rose from the reverent flock.

Though his fists remained clenched, shaking furiously, the Alderman spoke with calm clarity. "The Wildwood has chosen its seat. He can never leave Lonnmore."

"No," Nell whispered.

The congregation stood and gathered joyously, taking brother and sister in arms. As though a burden had been lifted, they celebrated and thanked the Wildwood in prayer. All but the Alderman who scowled at Nell's father.

After a few moments of candlelight reverie, the villagers lifted her father from the altar. Without the creature's shape holding her frozen in fear, Nell rushed to her feet.

She wiped her tears away as she ran through the night, sure to get back before they returned her father to his bed. Taking two stairs at a time, the rough pine groaned under her bare toes, but she dare not spare the moments to go quietly.

Slipping into her room in the dark, she heard the first of the villagers enter the Alderman's house. Nell tiptoed to her bed and stole under the covers as they mounted the stairs.

Dim light pooled in from under the crack of her door. She listened to them carrying her father down the hall, to the hammering chorus of heavy boots that had woken her in the first place. They then descended and she sighed in relief until a set drew nearer her bedroom door.

Nell turned over in bed. She pulled the patchwork quilt over her and the damp nightgown as the door creaked open.

*Calm your breath,* she thought, trying not to tremble. No light followed the steps into the room, only the footfalls of boots.

*Be asleep.* Her fingers tightened in the sheets and she shut her eyes. Her pulse pounded between her ears as thunder.

*Do not see me.* Tears threatened to fall.

Though she could not see, Nell felt a shape lean over her. She pictured the endlessly vacant eyes of the creature in the chapel, the Wildwood beast and its sap-dripping maw.

*Oh, God, do not let it see me.*

Fingers gripped the top of the quilt and Nell fought the urge to flinch. To open her eyes. To scream. To run.

But they merely pulled the quilt higher, covering her chilled shoulder.

The shape loomed nearer. A breath tickled her hair. As though it clung to the clothes, the faint remains of the sickening sap's stench stung her nose. Roses, cedar and rot.

*Do not see me.*

They leaned back and exhaled a sigh. "You should have never come, child," the Alderman whispered before he retreated from the room.

\* \* \*

THE ALDERMAN LEFT the door ajar in his wake. Only after she heard him head downstairs did Nell open her eyes. She exhaled a trembling sigh and the breath she'd held onto for far too long.

*Get up,* she told herself but Nell remained still. Even when the sounds of the villagers subsided and the light in the corridor dimmed further, she could not bring herself to move. The paralysis of the forest trembled with her as she repeated the words over and over. *Get up. Get up.*

"Get up," she finally whispered in the dark and forced herself to step out of the bed.

Nell tiptoed across the room an inch at a time barely blinking. When she reached the door, she knew it would creak should she open it all the way. So, Nell pried it only enough to step through. The room her father had been carried to lay only a few steps away, but between her and it was the stairs. They had groaned so much under the strain of heavy steps, of men burdened by her father's weight.

The gentle murmur of voices just below begged for caution and so Nell obliged. She pressed herself against the wall and purposefully stepped across the hall. Those few steps seemed agonizing in the wait, but at seeing her father's open door, she hurried and crossed the threshold in a scurry.

His room was dark. No light had been left. Nell stepped carefully, toes prodding for obstacles ahead while fearful thoughts screamed for her to hurry. They could return at any moment. They could take him back to the creature. The creature itself could return. With each blink, she tried to erase the image of it from her mind, the yellowing tendrils, the soiled breath, but in the dark, it was as though the shadows moved.

Beside her father's bed, a cloth lay draped over the basin of water. The first time she'd entered the room, it'd not been used. They'd not cleaned his wound and barely washed the sweat from his brow. But now the water swirled in shades of pink and that sickly yellow expulsion.

"Father?" she whispered. Her voice meekly cut through the quiet.

He did not stir.

She reached his side and pressed her hand to his head. The heat of his fever had abated. Disappeared more like. A sickening thought crept into her mind, that his last breath had already left him. But as his chest rose and fell with a steady rhythm, steadier than it had when they arrived, Nell sighed in relief.

"Father, please wake." She pressed a hand to his shoulder and shook him gently.

His eyes snapped open.

Nell startled back, nearly tripping over the basin. "Oh, thank God," she whispered and collected herself to his side.

"Where am I?" he asked, his voice not so quiet.

Nell pressed a finger to her lips and looked towards the door. "Forgive me, Father. I veered from the path. We should never have come here."

He looked at her, eyes lined with confusion and something...vacant. Nell dismissed it as disorientation and instead checked his leg. The wound had been wrapped well and, as she unraveled the cloth, it looked much better than she remembered. The skin's discoloration had faded and the swelling reduced. He no longer bled. Though thin lines trailed beneath his skin like his veins had darkened, by all measures her father was healed.

"We must leave, Father. It is not safe here." Nell helped him sit up. "Can you walk?"

He looked over himself, blinking purposefully, and pressed his toes to the floor. With a steady and comfortable stride forward, he stood without wavering.

"I can." He looked down at Nell and placed a hand on her cheek. "Daughter."

Nell frowned at the stiff address. She was strained to think of the last time he'd called her such. But below them, the front door opened and closed, boots thumping on the pine floors. More of the villagers coming or going, she couldn't be sure. Nell wasn't interested in waiting to find out.

"Charleston's in a barn nearby but...we cannot let them see us leave." Nell shifted in place. How could she explain to him what she had seen? How could he believe her if she doubted herself?

He took Nell's shoulders in his hands. He met her eyes, direct, alert. In the dark, his features were nearly masked, all but the strange clarity of his gaze. "Yes. We *must* leave the village tonight."

Nell and her father searched the closet for coats and he slipped on his boots. He moved easily and needed no help in dressing. He was so much recovered from the fever that had ravaged him no more than an hour before.

She crept to the edge of the stairs and spied down to the entryway. To their luck, most of the villagers had taken their leave save for a single man.

Brother Sorrinson sat in a chair with his back to the front door. He remained positioned facing the stairs, though every few moments his eyes glazed over and he fought the need to sleep. Nell watched him for what felt like hours and came to know there was no way to get downstairs without alerting Brother Sorrinson.

Her father moved to head down when she stopped him. "They believe you to be ill. If he would see you—"

"Ask for a drink," her father said. "Lead him into the kitchen."

Nell nodded and started down the steps.

Brother Sorrinson roused with a groan and pushed up

from his seat. "It is late," he said as though it was an accusation.

"Forgive me, I-I could not sleep." Nell reached the bottom of the stairs and looked into the kitchen. It was empty, as was the hall stretching past the front door. It seemed the house was still, or sleeping, all save the Brother.

"Could...I ask for a drink?"

Brother Sorrinson looked her up and down, eyes glowering. "You have hands."

With a gulp, she fought the urge to look back at her father at the top of the stairs but instead moved to the kitchen.

Brother Sorrinson followed her in.

"I thought Lisbeth would be here," she spoke if only to fill the silence. "Are you not to tend to my father? Or, has he improved?"

"You have need of a coat to get a drink?"

Nell looked down at herself and sure enough, a stolen coat draped from her shoulders over the nightgown. "It...I was cold," she stumbled through the words, her hands trembling as she poured water from a carafe. "I...heard voices and thought—"

Brother Sorrinson stepped closer. "What did you hear, girl?"

With a swallow, she turned, not sure what to say, when a gasp left her lips instead. Her father stood behind Brother Sorrinson. Neither had heard him come down the stairs and for a man his size she thought it strange. It wasn't until her father raised his arm that Nell saw he carried a large cast iron skillet.

Her father brought it down on the back of Brother Sorrinson's head.

Nell dropped the glass and it shattered. She clasped her hand over her mouth to stifle her yelp at the sickening crunch. In a blink, Brother Sorrinson was standing and the next the elder dropped to the floor. With a twitch, blood seeped from his graying hair.

Her father dropped the pan with a thud. He did not look at Brother Sorrinson; it was as though he was not there. He showed no awareness of what had happened. He simply held out his hand over the bleeding man.

"Come. Before the others return."

Her breaths came in pulsing waves, fast as though she was running while standing still. A body lay between them. Blood pooled and mixed with the water she'd spilled.

"Daughter," he spoke but it was as though the words were the air around her and Nell felt drawn up to meet his eyes. "We must flee."

With trembling fingers, Nell took her father's hand and stepped over Brother Sorrinson.

* * *

THEY MADE it to the barn without another soul seeing them. In the dark, it wasn't hard, just as easy as it had been for her to sneak out in the first place. Charleston stirred when Nell came in and she quickly set about hooking him to the cart.

"We've no time for that," her father said sharply.

Nell moved to argue, their life was in that cart. But a harrowing shout called from beyond the barn and more voices shrieked in the night. The bustle she'd expected from the village when she'd first arrived seemed revived at the worst possible time.

As her father approached the horse, a blanket in hand, Charleston reared and whinnied. Like he was a stranger, the workhorse wouldn't let him near.

"Calm, boy, calm." Nell tried to quiet Charleston. It took longer than it should have to drape the cloth on him.

"The road in lies across from the Alderman's house, the

one we ran from. But the villagers…." Each time Nell blinked she could see Brother Sorrinson's shape draped in red on the floor. "Even if we pass them, I do not know the way through the woods. Not in the dark."

But her father seemed distracted. He riffled through their cart, grabbing a small satchel with emergency provisions, a hatchet and his old hunting knife. His silence left Nell wanting, fearful even. Like she wasn't speaking or he couldn't hear her. Or worse, like she was not there.

The shouts outside grew louder and Nell grabbed the lantern from their cart and lit it.

"We need not the light." Her father took it from her in a fast grasp and tossed it to the floor of the barn. Amidst the hay, it caught light.

He mounted Charleston despite the horse's protests.

"Show yourself!" the Alderman bellowed from outside the tall wood walls. He sounded close, as she had feared. They could not take the road now, not through the central field, not if the village had assembled.

Nell hurried to the back of the barn, to the door that spilled out into the forests around Lonnmore and opened it enough for Charleston to pass through. Her father held out his hand to help Nell up on the horse. With one pull, she was whisked from her feet by her father's surprising strength.

He did not speak or rush. There was a terrifying calm about him in his silence.

The Alderman burst through the front of the barn, torches and villagers aplenty at his side. But already the fire had taken to the hay bales. It threatened to sweep up the sides of the structure.

"You cannot leave this village," the Alderman bellowed. "You made an oath! The Pact demands you stay for the good of us all!" The focus in his wild eyes quaked Nell to her bones. But rage didn't lie there. As Nell looked back at his face, fear burned as a well-stoked fire.

"Hold fast, daughter," her father commanded and Nell turned her back to the Alderman.

With a swift kick to Charleston, they thundered forth into the dark. They fled from the clear open fields around the village, and her father led Charleston towards an unseen path. The trees whipped past their faces and, when she dared to look back, the lights grew distant.

That her father had been spared by the creature was a miracle in of itself, and that they escaped the village was more than she could have hoped for. But Nell shivered in the still night. "Where will we go?" she asked her father, burying her face in his back.

"Far from Silas Colbrook."

Nell frowned. How could he know the Alderman's name? Her father had been in a state long before she'd veered from the path. Not awake. Not seeing. She couldn't imagine he'd even know where they were.

Though few minutes had passed since they'd been in light, her eyes adjusted enough to see. Like fireflies, green and dimly shining, a trail of tendrils slithered under the skin of her father's neck. Moving, *growing*, towards his head.

Nell's breath caught in her throat. Her fingers trembled.

*Father and I are not alone.*

He looked over his shoulder to Nell, an unfamiliar smile on his lips. "Far from Lonnmore Village."

*LMG WILSON IS a speculative fiction author and voice actor with a love for genre-bending fiction. She enjoys transporting readers to strange worlds and through time while introducing them to characters that will stay with them for years to come. Using her skills as a narrator and voice actor, she brings her short stories to life on Youtube and the radio.*

*When not writing, LMG Wilson spends time at home with her husband and two cats in New Brunswick, Canada. Learn more about her work here:*

*http://lmgwilson.com/*

*https://www.youtube.com/c/lmgwilson*

# A MOTHER'S LOVE

A.R.R. ASH

*N*yrrine sat opposite her father, Mneres, in the residence above their apothecary. Upon the cracked, lopsided tabletop between them, like an unwanted guest that imposed upon the comfort and privacy of their family, lay a notice that had been pinned to the door of their shop.

"Baba..." Nyrrine started for the third time, though her father had yet to speak, and she had no notion what she intended to say. The meager dawnfare of an egg and root vegetables sat heavy in her stomach, and the scent of the food still lingered in the small room.

The notice, written in black ink with curling, immaculate lettering and stamped with the lord's sigil—a pentagram within a hexagon within a circle within a square—announced that she had been selected to bear Lord Azos a child, and she was to present herself to his tower by evening the following day.

Over the years, no less than three other women from Nyrrine's village alone had received a similar notice informing them that they had been selected as a wife for

Lord Azos. Nyrrine's own friend, Xenia, had even been made a lady of the demesne, to which Nyrrine had experienced a mingling of jealousy and happiness. Yet neither Nyrrine nor Xenia's own family had spoken to her again since her betrothal, despite her mother and father's many visits to the lord's tower. However, they claimed to have witnessed their daughter waving to them from a balcony and had received letters from her, a fact about which they were particularly proud because she could neither read nor write before taking up residence with the lord.

The food in her stomach seemed to gain extra weight, as if she had swallowed rocks, and Nyrrine thought through her own emotions before responding to her father. Part of her was flattered at the thought of the lord wanting her as the mother to his child, particularly because he had multiple wives from whom to choose. She was also terrified at the fact that none of the women's families had had any communication with them since their nuptials, other than the odd letter or view from afar.

Her father spoke into her lingering silence, "We can flee. It is not time enough to put a goodly distance between us and there, but, perhaps, we could reach Olynia and disappear among the wilderness."

Nyrrine's chest swelled in love at the knowledge that her father was willing to abandon everything they had for her. Yet she had the notion that she should be the one arguing to run. How many fathers, or mothers, would have welcomed the prestige, let alone seized the opportunity for advancement, in having a daughter bear the lord's child? "Baba, where could we go? He would surely find us."

"He can readily choose another." The hesitancy in his tone belied the statement.

Nyrrine wrinkled her nose. "He found all the men who'd raided our village. One had made it as far as Limnopolis, yet he was returned in a fortnight, his tortured body left in the middle of the village."

Nyrrine certainly felt the sinking weight of fear in her belly and in the pounding of her heart against her chest. Yet she knew excitement as well. Becoming the mother to Lord Azos's child would surely elevate her standing and, by extension, that of her father. Too, she had to admit a certain vanity at the thought of being chosen.

"It'll be all right, Baba. Besides, we don't have a choice."

* * *

MNERES ACCOMPANIED Nyrrine on the half-day's walk from their hamlet to the stone tower of Lord Azos. She wore an earthy, in color and texture, sleeved chiton, fastened at the waist with a brown cord, and comfortable sandals. Though hardly the height of courtly fashion, it was the finest she owned.

The tower stood upon a rocky hillock amid an empty field. In times past, bands of goblins or elves or dwarves or even ogres had laid siege to the tower. Yet, though Nyrrine knew no one who had witnessed the events personally, tales tell that the besiegers had all met a grisly demise. Those who still had discernable faces were frozen in a rictus of abject fright, eyes wide and lips pulled back. What was undeniable was that raids against the lands of Lord Azos had fallen off in recent years. While life among the lord's villages was difficult, their lives were far improved over those of humans who dwelled among the other races.

The tower itself was less built than it appeared to be an extension of the mound below and shaped from a spire of rock. Stairs, carved out of the hillock, led to an iron door at the base of the tower. The outer walls were rough-hewn with numerous projections and protuberances of stone, which would make its exterior easily ascended by any decent thief or would-be attacker. Yet no one of any of the villages would have dared those walls for any reward.

Nyrrine offered felicitations to her father and kissed him upon either cheek before he turned back upon the path.

No sooner had he disappeared from sight than the iron door opened with an abrupt clang and a slow grinding sound. The portal gaped open, but no one emerged. After a confused hesitation, Nyrrine started toward the stairs.

As soon as she had passed within tower, entering into an antechamber, the door swung closed with a ponderous creak. The room in which Nyrrine found herself was circular, a good thirty paces in diameter, with walls, in contrast to the uneven exterior, smoothly mortared. Evenly spaced around the circumference, at a height beyond reach, oil lamps lit the chamber. A staircase spiraling along the wall led to a landing with a closed door of red wood.

The room held no furnishings or decorations, save for waxen figures along the wall that appeared far too realistic. Nyrrine approached one and looked into its lifeless, dull gray eyes. The point of the ears marked it as an elf. Hesitantly, she extended a single finger and moved it slowly toward the figure's cheek, as if trying to sneak upon it unnoticed or as if it might snap at her finger. It did not smell of wax but of an astringent chemical, like something found in a tannery. Her finger contacted the cheek, a shiver of unease shook her body, and she jerked her hand away. It had more of a spongy consistency than waxy.

The door of the landing opened, distracting Nyrrine from her disquiet. This time, a man emerged. Garbed in a black toga and mantle, he was not tall, indeed of a height similar her own stature.

She had only ever seen Lord Azos from afar, and she'd believed his height to be a result of distance. However, viewing him now, she was struck by the virality and handsomeness of his features. Her chest constricted at the preternatural beauty.

"Welcome." In contrast to his alluring visage, his hollow voice held no warmth, despite his greeting. "Come, join me and my wives for a repast."

Nyrrine's stomach reacted at the mention of food and offered its growling response. She mounted the stairs and entered another circular chamber dominated by a long table of black wood. An ascending staircase and lighting fixtures mirrored those of the lower level. Two doorless portals opened into one side of the wall. The smell of a flowery perfume filled the room like a miasma, but, rather than freshening the air, it disguised a powerful undercurrent of something fetid. The combination was to give the impression that the fragrance was derived from rotting flowers.

Six still figures sat at the opposite side of the table. Their views were fixed ahead of them, and they made no acknowledgment of her entrance.

Nyrrine squealed in recognition of one of the figures and waved in greeting. "Xenia!"

However, when her friend did not return the greeting, made no reaction whatsoever, a weight settled into her belly. She swayed under a wave of dizziness at the strangeness of the situation, and a horrified gasp escaped her unbidden. Bile rose in her throat, and Nyrrine put a hand to her mouth while forcing down the acidic humor.

That hollow voice from an incongruous countenance startled Nyrrine, and she gave a little jump. "These are my wives. As you can see, they are in no condition to bear my child. That honor falls to you." Lord Azos gestured toward the tables. "Please, sit." The pleasantness of his tone mocked the grotesquery of the scene and turned the otherwise polite gesture into an ominous threat.

He sat at the head of the table, at the end nearest the doors, and Nyrrine took the place facing Xenia. Looking closely at her friend and the other wives, she would have sworn that they were mere upright corpses, similar to the figures in the antechamber.

"Wonderful," Azos said, as if it were an ordinary dinner party. "I hope you have your appetite."

Although he issued no command, one of his wives, with no word and an unblinking, vacant-eyed stare, rose and exited through the left door behind Azos. Her movements, while not quite as erratic as those of a stringed puppet, were not as fluid as one of normal mobility.

A bilious residue upon her tongue, Nyrrine forced calm into her thoughts—an effort that proved only partially successful. Yet her thoughts had collected sufficiently to allow her to realize that the only way she was to survive was to maintain her composure. Nyrrine forced herself to look into those black eyes.

His gaze lingered a moment upon hers.

The wife returned with a platter of spiced meats, sliced fruit, cheese and bread, and placed it before Nyrrine, then returned to her seat. The fare was a banquet compared to the wheatmeal and boiled root vegetables to which Nyrrine was accustomed. She swallowed the saliva that accumulated in her mouth at the savory smell—the taste of bile had nearly dissipated. Her stomach turned in confusion between the inviting meal and the terror, shock and disgust at the eerie strangeness of the wives' appearance and conduct and Lord Azos's own behavior.

Hunger won, and she began to eat. Lord Azos did not have a plate of food before him, rather only a glass cup—a luxury not to be found within Nyrrine's village—of a steaming yellow liquid, from which he sipped from time to time. The wives continued their silent, impassive vigil, and

Azos said not a word to her as she ate. Growing uncomfortable at the silence, Nyrrine shifted in her seat.

"Milord, perhaps you could tell me of your family."

Azos waved off the question. "They are long gone."

Nyrrine settled upon another tack. Perhaps she could appeal to his vanity. "I have heard tales of your victories that drove away the other races from the region, and that you have held your position longer than anyone currently living can recall. Perhaps you could regale me with one of your stories."

"Do you mistake me for a rhapsodist, a common storyteller?"

"No—no, of course not, milord. I merely thought we could get to know one another."

Azos's immaculate smile never wavered—to Nyrrine, it now seemed a perverse, obscene thing rather than inviting—yet his silence spoke the threat that was not stated. Finally, he gave cold voice to what the quiet had expressed, "Do you believe that I do not know all about you? About all of my subjects?"

Nyrrine shivered. It was all going terribly wrong.

Azos took a sip of his yellow liquid. He touched a hand to his face and drew away his visage.

Nyrrine started; her knee slammed against a table leg and sent a smarting pain through the bone. She inhaled sharply.

In his hand, Azos held a featureless porcelain mask, and in place of his comely aspect was a devastated countenance. It was a face more horrid than Nyrrine had seen upon lepers and plague victims. Upon one cheek, the upper layer of skin was missing, revealing the angry red beneath. A cleft split his upper lip, and his bottom lip was absent, showing blackened, cracked teeth and bleeding gums. The skin of his other cheek was barely visible beneath the accumulation of red and yellow pustules, some of which leaked openly.

Nyrrine was aware of his scrutinizing gaze upon her, and, for the first time, Azos's smile assumed a genuine quality. She cursed herself for eating so much and willed the food that churned in her stomach from rising. The nausea caused her brow to warm and a bead of cool sweat to form. However, despite the horridness of Lord Azos's features, Nyrrine found more difficulty in turning away than when he wore the mask of exquisite beauty. Her eyes merely refused to look away.

"Your response is to be expected. I assure you, this is a consequence of my magic, and any child you bear me will not inherit my...disfigurement."

His magic? Nyrrine had heard tales of dark castings that could cause the dead to walk. Nigromancy.

An heir seemed to be his sole interest at present. She would focus upon that. With a confidence she did not indeed feel, Nyrrine said, "Milord, I can guarantee you a son, one whom you can mold into your own likeness."

Azos leaned forward. "How can you promise such a thing?"

Of course, she could not. However, she had an equal chance for a son, and she would take that half chance far into the future rather than whatever fate awaited her now. Too, despite his professed omniscience regarding his subjects, Azos's behavior exhibited an utter lack of understanding of human interactions and of the manner of women. Perhaps it was something she could use to her advantage. "You are no doubt a master of your craft, milord, but we simple folk live everyday with births and deaths and, over the generations, have discovered many methods to ensure desired outcomes. As you know, milord, my own father and I are apothecaries and are well versed in the elixirs of childbirth."

Lord Azos assumed a pensive air.

Nyrrine continued, "Milord, there are concoctions that

can guarantee a son"—the beginnings of a plan that just might ensure her survival began to form—"but I require the necessary reagents."

Azos reclined in his high-backed chair, and the fingers of one hand beat a tattoo upon the tabletop. Otherwise, the silence was so absolute that Nyrrine heard only her own breath and the blood pulsing in her warm ears.

Finally, Lord Azos nodded to himself, as if having reached a conclusion. "I will hold you to your promise."

Dread, disgust and relief all competed for Nyrrine's attention.

Azos stood. "Very well. My wives shall escort you to your room. As you can see, living women hold no appeal for me. Once they attend me, I will call upon you to implant my seed."

What she believed to be a piece of meat rose in her throat, and she swallowed the gorge. Her thoughts a violent storm, she said, "Milord, if we are to ensure a son, I must drink the concoction prior to conception." Of course, she knew the claim was claptrap, though it would remove Lord Azos for some time and give her the opportunity to investigate the tower.

Azos grunted. "Hmm. What reagents do you require?"

Nyrrine fabricated a list of ingredients. "Red clover, fennel, turmeric"—that one she added because it was an extravagance that she wished to savor—"cinnamon, and cumin."

After a moment's consideration, he said, "Very well. I shall acquire the reagents. How long do you require to prepare the concoction?"

"Not long, milord. Not more than a day." She paused. "I would like to look my best for you, milord. Would you be so kind as to bring me cosmetics as well, particularly kohl?"

Azos frowned. "I have no care for your appearance."

"Of course not, milord, but you know how vain we women are."

Azos grunted in acknowledgment. "My wives will attend to you until my return. They will answer to your command" —with a look under his brows, he added—"provided it does not violate my standing instructions." He turned away and left through the doorway leading to the descending stairs.

Without a sound, four of his six wives climbed the ascending flight in their unnatural, shuffling gait.

Nyrrine turned toward the two remaining wives, one of whom was Xenia. "Xenia! What is happening here? Are you all right?"

Her friend made no response, no movement or reaction. Xenia's blank eyes never blinked and showed no recognition or, indeed, life. Mention of Lord Azos's magic returned to her, as did his words: *living women hold no appeal for me.*

"Xenia! Speak to me!"

She might as well have been speaking to a wax figure, indeed. Nyrrine's body went chill, and her heart beat as if it sought to escape its cage. She reached her hand to her friend's arm. The skin had the same cold, spongy texture as the figures below, and she detected the same disguised reek of decay. Nyrrine closed her eyes until the wave of nausea and dizziness passed.

In a visceral release, like an avalanche of emotion that threatened to crush her, mind and body, under its relentless power, the events of the day wrenched a primal scream from her. She paused briefly to breathe and sob, then continued the cathartic purge. And, so, she alternated screaming and crying, her shoulders heaving, until her throat was raw and her eyes burned.

Through it all, neither wife reacted.

Slowly, she calmed and found that, at some point, she had fallen to the floor. No child of hers would be raised by this madman among these abominations. She would take her own life before she allowed that.

Her emotional release left her exhausted, and she wanted nothing as much as to fall into thoughtless, dreamless oblivion. Yet, first, she had to make use of the lord's time away. She started toward the left portal within the dining hall, from which the *wife* had retrieved her meal, and, for the first time since the lord's departure, the two...walking corpses...stirred.

"I-I'm just going to get a snack." Nyrrine nearly laughed at the absurdity of her finding it necessary to explain herself to those two who were little more than mobile statuary.

The doorway opened upon a small kitchen with a worktable and hearth; in one corner was a scullery that had been emptied of utensils. It seemed that Lord Azos required little in the way of cookery himself and did not much entertain. She passed through a threshold to the right and entered a pantry. Again, the room contained mostly empty shelving with some scattered fruits and moldering flour. However, one item in particular caught her attention, a rack of drying leaves of the same yellowish color as the lord's drink.

Nyrrine sniffed the leaves, which had a faintly pungent odor that stung her nostrils. She touched the tip of her tongue to one and pulled away abruptly, spitting to clear her mouth of the powerfully bitter taste. The leaves were unlike anything she had seen before. Each was roughly elliptical with an undulating pattern along the long edges and a serration along the tip; cilia grew atop the face.

A jar upon a shelf held a collection of the crushed leaves. Another doorway in the pantry led directly into the dining hall. From there, she considered whether to ascend or descend. While she was certain the door below to the outside would be barred, she thought it the height of foolishness if she did not at least try.

She exited the dining hall and alighted the staircase, followed by her two escorts. As she suspected, the door would not open. Glancing about at the figures, they were all the grimmer and menacing with her new understanding, and she hurried back up the stairs.

Again in the dining hall, she said to Xenia, now with none of the affection she once held in her voice, "Show me to my room."

They ascended the stairs within the dining hall. At the landing, another door of red wood led to a hallway with plain doors along either side and another ascending staircase and landing at the far end. She could see that that door, rather than wood, was constructed of black iron. This time, she did not bother trying the door. It appeared as if the extent of her world had diminished drastically.

Her escorts took her to the first room upon her right. That single room was half the size of the entire house she shared with her father.

*Her father!* Would he even know what happened to her? Would he make pilgrimages to the tower to catch but a glimpse of her? Would the lord have false letters sent to appease him?

It was all too much. Nyrrine fell upon the four-poster bed. Her last though was of the softness of the mattress and the smoothness of the silken sheets.

* * *

WHEN NYRRINE AWOKE, she had no way to know how long she had slept, though clarity had returned to her thoughts, and her body was refreshed as if she'd slumbered for days. She gave a glance around the room.

It was undecorated but well appointed. Every table and chair, the bed, a settee, all were of sturdy, comfortable construction. If not for the two, unspeaking, unmoving reminders standing to either side of the bed—her body shook as a shiver ran through it—she might have enjoyed the luxury of her surroundings.

Nyrrine heard movement outside her chamber a moment before the door opened. Lord Azos, canvas sack in hand, stood at the threshold, and she rose quickly from the bed.

"Milord." Nyrrine gave a slight bow.

Azos threw the bag atop the bed. "Your reagents. As soon as you complete your concoction, we shall complete our transaction."

Nyrrine swallowed. "Yes, milord."

"Inform your handmaiden when it is done, and I shall know. And I trust you've persuaded yourself that escape is quite impossible." He did not allow her to respond as he turned and walked in the direction of the stairs leading to the iron door.

Nyrrine shivered again. He was somehow aware of what transpired around his unliving slaves. Had he observed her investigation of the tower?

She retrieved the sack, removed the cosmetics, and returned to the kitchen, where she emptied the contents upon the worktable. He had obtained everything she requested. How long had she been asleep?

Nyrrine glanced over her shoulder at the two silent sentinels. Their lack of expression or, indeed, of eye movement made discerning what they observed difficult. Yet she had embarked upon this farce and would have to see it through as well as ensure that she did nothing suspicious within their view.

She lit a fire within the hearth and hung a pot of water above the flame. From the scullery, she obtained a mortar and pestle and set to grinding the ingredients. When the water came to a boil, she filled a ceramic mug and added the collection of spices. Nyrrine inhaled the rising steam; the medley of cinnamon, fennel and turmeric made for a particularly pungent aroma. Inhaling to brace herself, she touched the concoction to her lips. She grimaced at the taste but forced herself to drink half.

Nyrrine turned to what remained of Xenia. "I am ready."

\* \* \*

HER BELLY HAD GROWN LARGE. Lord Azos rarely called upon her. If she needed anything, she spoke to her ever-present, silent companions. He provided her with food, clothing, cosmetics, whatever she required, though he always accompanied his largess with the looks and noises of frustration and annoyance. She was a prisoner, to be sure, but she was one with an oft-absent jailor.

In her room that had become the majority of her world, Nyrrine doubled over in pain, placing a hand beneath her distended abdomen. "Lord Azos, I require additional medicinals."

The time of birth was nearing, and, although she did experience pain, she exaggerated its severity.

After a brief period, the lord appeared at her door with a scowl of annoyance. He rarely wore his mask in her presence anymore, and he spent nearly all his time beyond the iron door partaking in...Nyrrine preferred not to imagine what sort of depravity occurred beyond its black border.

"What is it?" His tone held no trace of concern for her wellbeing.

Looking upward beneath lowered lids, she added, voice halting, "I require hemlock and a tincture of papaver for the pain of childbirth."

Lord Azos gave Nyrrine an askance glance. "Hemlock is poisonous."

"In sufficient quantity, milord." She inflected her voice to speak as if she were only reminding him of something he already knew. "But when taken in limited amount, it alleviates the abdominal pains of pregnancy."

Azos narrowed his eyes, though his clenched jaw and slight flush told Nyrrine that he was more frustrated than suspicious. "I cannot help but wonder if this whole endeavor is worth the effort. It is a wonder that the whole of the human race has not long since expired."

Nyrrine averted her eyes downward. "I am sorry, milord. I only wish to ensure that I provide you with a healthy, male heir."

Azos grunted, "Very well. I shall leave on the morrow."

\* \* \*

Again, Lord Azos had obtained the requested substances with little seeming difficulty and had returned within a day's time. He paused at her room only long enough to deliver the supplies, then left immediately for his sanctum beyond the iron door.

In the kitchen, Nyrrine was careful to position herself such that her back would obstruct the view of her silent observers and to use separate implements to grind the hemlock. The crushed hemlock she added to the tincture and, with a surreptitious glance at the two, hid the glass bottle within a fold of her chiton. She passed quickly into the pantry, where she applied the mixture of hemlock and liquid papaver to the drying leaves, as the moisture would surely be noticed upon the crushed leaves. Nyrrine had observed the frequency with which Azos consumed the bitter leaves and replenished his stock, and his supply of crushed leaves was nearly finished.

She returned the bottle with its remaining contents to her

chiton on the chance that she needed it for herself and to prevent her child from being raised under the influence of Lord Azos. However, before returning to the kitchen, she retrieved a bowl of olives—one of the few luxuries he provided her—both to assuage her hunger and to explain her presence within the pantry.

* * *

SOME DAYS LATER, Nyrrine found greater difficulty in merely levering herself out of bed. When Azos entered her room unannounced, she could not have been more surprised if the walls had started talking—surprised not that he would enter without announcement but that he would deign even visit her.

In his curt, clipped speech, he said, "We shall dine together this evening." And, just as abruptly, he was gone.

*I was wrong. I could be more surprised, after all.* Nyrrine's heart thudded, and her breath came in short rasps. Yet surprise was not the cause of her body's excitement. What possible purpose could he have in her company?

"Come, help me," she said to her unliving handmaiden.

Her onetime friend, Xenia, moved toward her, and Nyrrine used the other to pull herself from the bed. She dressed herself in a loose chiton and did not fasten the cord about the waist. From a drawer, she withdrew a jar of silvery powder, her supply of kohl, and concealed it within the folds of her tunic; the bottle containing the residual papaver and hemlock mixture she left in the drawer, her last defense at a life worse than death for her and her child.

Intent to ensure all was in readiness, she made her slow way, on swollen, aching legs, down the stairs and to the kitchen. There, Nyrrine set the water to boiling and prepared her own duskfare of fruits, vegetables and a soup of fish and legumes. In the pantry, she did observe that the jar of his yellow leaves had been replenished with those to which she had applied the tincture and hemlock.

Nyrrine moved into the dining area to await Lord Azos.

She was not long in waiting. The lord, attired in his wonted toga and mantle, all of black, descended the stairs, entered the kitchen and returned momentarily with a glass of steaming, seeping leaves.

Nyrrine suppressed a smile. "Milord."

He sat at the head of the table and placed the glass before him. "How goes the pregnancy?"

Her response caught in her throat, so unprepared was she for the question from one who seemingly cared so little for anyone around him. More than anything, his solicitousness raised her suspicion and caution. "It goes well, milord. The time is not far off when you will have a son."

Azos sipped from the glass and set it back upon the table. Nyrrine's eyes followed the path of the vessel, and she observed that the amount of liquid had indeed decreased after his draft. The smile was harder to suppress this time, and she put a hand to her face to cover her mouth.

His eyes seemed to bore into her.

Nyrrine shifted in her seat, an uncomfortable warmth rising up her neck. "Milord, when your son is born, certain herbs will enhance his feeding."

Azos took another sip. "Perhaps, but you will not be the one feeding him."

The coldness in his tone sent a chill through her. A gasp escaped Nyrrine's throat, and her heart dropped into her stomach. "Milord?" Her voice was little more than a squeak.

"Did you believe I did not know about your intent to poison my herbs?" He sipped again, staring pointedly at her. "I had prepared a separate batch."

Nyrrine was paralyzed, frozen by his glacial voice. She

thought to deny the accusation, but her tongue would not move. She knew it was pointless. He knew.

Taking her silence as her answer, he reached into a pocket and withdrew the bottle she'd left in her drawer. "There will be no escape for you."

Nyrrine's head fell, followed by tears.

"The gestation is near complete. I will allow the birth to occur, then attend to your punishment at my leisure."

Two sets of hands grabbed Nyrrine by the arms and pulled her roughly to her feet. Exhibiting a strength belied by their petite frames, her two escorts dragged her up the stairs in an unbreakable grip to prevent her from leaping to her death.

\* \* \*

FOR DAYS, Nyrrine remained confined to her chamber. Her water had soaked the mattress and the pains were coming with frequency. The two unliving servants looked on, incapable of distress or concern. She moaned and sweated, her breathing ragged. She vowed to herself that, if she had to kill it with her own hands after its birth, her child would not be raised by that monster.

The door to her room flung open, and Lord Azos stumbled in. He smelled strongly of vomit, residue upon his toga and chin and at the corners of his mouth, and his limbs moved spasmodically, as if they could not come to agreement. "What...what did you do to me?"

He fell to the floor, retched. Moaning and crying out in counterpoint to Nyrrine's own pain, his body convulsed.

Nyrrine felt the stretch and rip of her child's emerging skull, and she screamed.

\* \* \*

NYRRINE LAY EXHAUSTED, her son in her arms, the still body of Lord Azos upon the floor. Through it all, neither *wife* so much as twitched, and they yet remained frozen within the same position.

Lord Azos had previously ordered them to attend her. Had his instructions changed?

"Fetch me water." As Xenia moved toward the door, she added, "Not from the kitchen. From the cistern."

As with so many men in the position of Lord Azos, he underestimated those he considered his lessers, particularly women. Her father was a skilled apothecary, and he had taught her much. The kohl she had asked Azos to bring her contained significant amounts of lead. She never intended to apply it to herself, and Azos, oblivious to living women, had not noticed her lack of adornment. Instead, she had saved the powder and emptied it all into his water before that last meal. One last contingency on the chance he discovered the contaminated herbs.

The baby slept, and Nyrrine settled against the headboard. Content, she sighed and beheld the child's peaceful expression. "My Mneris."

*A.R.R. Ash is a lifelong fan of both science fiction and fantasy, though he typically focuses his talents on writing dark fantasy, particularly grimdark. His first independently published novel, The Moroi Hunters, is available digitally and in print through LMPBooks.com/store. He has had short stories appear in several anthologies, including Socially Distant: The Quarantales, Hidden Villains, and Hidden Villains: Arise, also by Inkd Publishing.*

*He has received a Silver Honorable Mention and five Honorable Mentions from the L. Ron Hubbard's Writers of the Future Contest. Xy: Descent, the first book of his The First Godling trilogy, is undergoing editing, and he is nearing completion on The*

*Tribe of Fangs*, a prequel novel to *The Moroi Hunters* in which the origin of everyone's favorite vampyre queen is revealed.

In other trivia, his favorite dishes are burgers and sushi (but not together), his favorite series is *Dune*, though *The Expanse* by James S. A. Corey is making a run for the title, and he enjoys DMing for his niece and nephew. When on the other side of the screen, he usually plays as a wizard or sorcerer or some kind of magic-user. His sense of humor is decidedly an acquired taste. You can learn more about A.R.R. Ash, including watching his interview with Cursed Dragon Ship Publishing, and contact him at *LMPBooks.com.*

# THE VALRAKI TEMPLE

## KEVIN A DAVIS

"It leaves only blood behind. Whole families and their babes—all gone." Jax's dire emphasis did little to pull my focus from the scraggly line of people ahead.

Only the damnable aroma of roasting nuts from a vendor's cart gnawed on my attention as it riled my empty stomach, which is why we were in line to spend the day unloading a gnomish caravan in trade for a single fist-sized tephis cake. We'd waited two hours and I feared they'd close the queue before we reached the signup table.

"Erin, are you listening?" Jax had a dour expression for an Edael; our people used to smile more.

"I was, until you put me to sleep." I shook my head grinning, then turned to him. "Bounties to hunt a supposed Raka murdering farmers outside the city." I focused on his yellow eyes so he'd know I was paying attention. "Did you want to go flying about the countryside hunting a demon? I don't have the energy to walk there, let alone fly. We need food."

"A year's larder for the Raka's head." He murmured the comment.

After we'd arrived at this cursed land, Jax had lost his

family, both wife and son. I'd lost mine as a younger woman, before we'd left on the ill-fated Great Fleet. Our race had made one desperate attempt to flee from our enemies across the western ocean, only to be stranded in a foreign world and as likely fated to extinction. We were broken remnants. I shouldn't have mentioned flying; during the wars, he'd lost too much of his top right wing to get off the ground. "I'm sorry." I nodded down the line to the merchant's table. "Only four ahead of us."

The gnomish merchant, humans they called themselves, had hired one of our own to interview the workers. A smart move as few of us could leave the memories of the wars behind us enough to stomach the creatures. The interviewer had set up a wooden bench under an Earth maple tree already turned a vibrant red in readiness for the winter. We lined up on brown grass along the edge of a wide street of Astarin to avoid the muddy ruts the wagons left. This part of the town had few of the gnomes touring or plying their cloths.

Another hired worker left the table, nibbling a walnut sized ball of sweet tephis cake, the payment for signing on. My stomach twisted at the thought of the hearty whey bread made of local seed and corn, and flavored with nectar and honey. It had been three days now and no work.

"Sorry," the interviewer yelled from his table.

The Edael in line sparked into life with curses and threats. The man in front of me sobbed and I fought not to join him. Perhaps Jax had the way of it, be miserable about everything and nothing disappointed you. It was too late to find any open work today. The sun had risen, splashing against the wooden roofs and treetops. I would forage the over-picked countryside again with the others. Winter would be upon us soon and I might not survive another.

"Hoy, hoy. We've got a list for you." An older Edael with

wrinkled copper skin climbed up on the table the interviewer had vacated. He had a rapt audience immediately. "Just down by the three mills. You'll see the table. Daily food if we accept you. Hurry now."

Four of the able Edael took to the air, while Jax and two more wounded veterans raced into the street. I could have flown, but that would have left Jax behind. Astarin had the lazy swirling streets of all Edael towns. As a group, we turned into the first eastward forking of the road.

The mills were downslope from the town toward the farms that trailed north from Astarin. The grass had some green left and the runners ahead kicked up a fresh scent of growth. Close to some old gnomish building that had been overtaken by vines, three people had set up a white pavilion and table. Two larger tents and two wagons waited farther to the left. The pavilion appeared to be of gnomish cloth, a finer weave than we Edael could presently achieve.

There were five in line when we arrived and I'd burnt too much energy just getting here to be disappointed again. Jax panted as we slowed to join the others.

The woman doing the interviews had a pleasant smile, but I shivered when I caught her words. "...the Raka. What is your military experience?"

My blood chilled. A bundle of wooden spears leaned against a stand at the end of the table. A platter of tephis cakes sat beside her. Behind her, two male Edael listened as closely to the responses as she did.

"Wooden spears against a Raka?" Might as well have us hunt a tentacled Valraki.

"What?" asked Jax. His hearing was as poor as a gnome's.

"You got your wish. This is a line for Raka hunting." I focused on the plate of food. They were large enough cakes to keep me in line.

"Wooden spears won't work. Silver sung to a fine edge is your only chance." Jax frowned. "I killed two, you know."

His comment turned me from my reverent gaze of food. I'd never asked if he'd fought before the Great Fleet. Our conversations hinged on his morose despair and whatever snarky remarks I had the energy to come up with, which wasn't much lately. I couldn't shake the rising dread enough to say anything witty. "With silver."

"Song-hardened silver," he corrected.

I'd known little about the war with the Raka and Ichor, except that my family had died trying to stop them. We were supposed to leave death behind us, though we hadn't expected to find the gnomes, a new enemy. My lips tightened. Jax and I certainly wouldn't have any hardened silver.

Talking with Jax and peering at the cakes, I missed most of the questions from the interviewer. However, I caught the last answers of the candidate in front of me. "Empath and Glass maker." A glass maker was rare and if the Edael were in a civilized state, he would not want for work.

The interviewer handed him a cake. "Blue tent." She gestured toward the rack of spears, then the tents and wagons where the others had gone. No one had been turned away.

I stepped forward, my throat tight and my pulse racing. I didn't want to find this Raka. However, I could smell the sweet tephis cake.

The interviewer forced a smile. "Name?"

"Erin."

As she wrote in a red ledger, she asked, "Can you work with a human?"

I frowned. My stomach churned. "With a gnome, or for one?" I asked.

When she looked up, her smile was gone. "Human. With and for a human. Will that be a problem?"

I wanted to scream that it would, of course it would. "No."

A bitter smile flashed on her face. "What is your military experience?"

"Scout for Favrian on the southern coastline."

"No combat? Do you have any weapons?" Her eyes darted across my stained tunic and baggy leggings. Her companions studied me.

"No weapons. I had to kill a gnome—human once. A guard. He caught me without illusion." I still had those nightmares.

She paused, then continued. "Skills?"

"Soother, coercion, illusion." I could hear my pulse thud with each word. If I failed the interview I'd be going to the river to look for edible water grass.

She reached for a cake. "Green tent."

I fought not to lunge for my food and offered a palm calmly. Resisting the temptation, I held the solid square in my hand while I retrieved a useless spear. Flashing a smile at Jax, I ambled toward the green tent, hoping he'd be assigned with me. It was only then that I took a bite. Sweet and hearty tephis cake is more satisfying than any Earth plant could ever aspire to be.

Dawdling, I waited for Jax as I neared the two tents. He had a rare grin as he ate and jogged toward me. "They must plan on us dying," he said. "This is a huge piece."

I nodded in agreement—to the latter statement—then carefully placed my remaining half in my left tunic pocket. Halving my food had gotten me through many a dry spell. "You really believe there is a Raka here on Earth?" I had ignored the possibility when the rumors started two weeks ago, now I would have to face them.

Jax ate furiously, talking between bites. "A patrol three days ago. Fully armed. Died at their camp in the hills to the west. Bloody mess, but no bodies. This is the work of a Raka."

We entered the green tent and found ten people sitting on benches inside. The sour odor of sweat tainted an otherwise pleasant aroma of autumn wine. A lightly fermented blend of fruits, which everyone seemed to have a mug of. I hadn't tasted a cup for a decade. People smiled and shook their heads in amusement when I focused on the barrel and mugs in the corner.

A woman with white hair as thick as mine raised her mug. "Grab a sweet moment while you can. You know this can't last."

Jax finished the last of his tephis cake and stumbled toward the barrel. "We are surely going to die."

The woman laughed. "Truth. But I will die with a smile."

I followed Jax slowly. Most of the faces were contemplative, but not sour. Food and wine were rarities.

A Raka on Earth had seemed impossible, but what else would bring out this kind of generosity? After tasting the tephis cake, my anxiety had diminished, but the dread lingered on.

"You think it is real?" I asked the woman.

She sipped and smiled. "Twenty-nine missing, according to the rumors. Our people are too few not to miss them."

The others sunk into their cups or nodded. One man with a thick wooden gauge in his upper earlobe studied me. "I knew Mariel and Tendil; I worked for them during their harvest. Growers who could pull two crops, maybe three a summer. They fought for their farm during the gnome wars. Lost their son three days after the landing. They wouldn't have gone easily. Put up a fight, they would."

I waited on Jax to fill his mug. "How could they be here?" I asked.

"Who says the darkness didn't come with us, or was

already here?" He snorted. "They just need a body coaxed close enough to the black dominion. With our misery, how hard is that?"

I'd heard the stories of Raka possessing unwitting mourners who let themselves become besieged by grief. Most hosts had been captured and drugged into blind submission. I stared down into the dark pit of the wine barrel. Many of us were worn and miserable. The one hope we'd had among the savage gnomes had been the absence of the darkness.

I grabbed a mug with a sigh and leaned in to scoop a ladle of the dark liquid at the barrel's depths. The sweet smell drowned out my concerns.

By my second cup, I barely grimaced when a sweaty, tan gnome popped into the tent. "Let's go. We've got hours." He butchered our language, but the meaning was clear. I'd heard horses being walked up to the wagons and knew our time was short. "You'll be fed and watered at close." He might have been tall for his race, but we all stood at least a head higher than him.

I wondered at the last statement, but had no intention of asking him. The man with the gauge in his ear chuckled. "Daily meals, they said. Maybe they intend to fatten us up and feed us to the Raka so it's sated when they try and kill it." He raised his wooden spear as if proof.

If a gnome, a human, led this hunt, that might just be the case. One thing I learned from scouting and spying on them during the wars was they had no qualms about lying or even betraying their own. I stepped out of the tent, shivering even as the sun warmed my skin.

Twenty of us were piling into two wagons, so I stuck with Jax and we squeezed in at the front. The sky showed no sign of rain. It would be a bumpy, but not wet trip. "Where do you suppose the people from the other tent go?" I asked Jax.

"Don't care," he said.

I frowned. They had no wagons; there had only been two and we were using them. There were four grubby humans loading us and checking the harnesses, but none of them looking to the other tent. Someone inside had gone a little heavy on the wine and sang one of the old songs from home. My eyes dropped to the wood slats and ignored the music.

Two humans climbed up onto the bench seat. Dark, greasy hair covered their stunted ears. "Another load of smelly fae." They likely didn't know that many of us had learned their language. The tone had been low and muttered. They rarely called us fae in town, but I'd heard them refer to us by the term.

I straightened and noticed two other Edael, the older man with the gauge and a woman my age, who peered at the drivers.

"Another?" the older man asked me.

"That's what I heard." I turned to Jax. "This isn't their first load of us they've taken on the wagons."

He snorted. "If they think I'll try and poke a Raka with a stick, they've got another thought coming. I'll hop right out of there. Sung silver or farewell."

The older man gestured an agreement. "Thinking the same. They'll give the human the real weapon and expect our deaths to distract it."

"Save them a month of meals." Jax coughed. "Serve me right."

There were ten of us in the wagon, and with quiet conversation, the news spread. Some dismissed it, but most thought we might be heading out as fodder for the demon. No one jumped out and left. The food and wine had been too promising.

We traveled west with the higher hills ahead as the sun reached midmorning above us. Colored or leafless trees dotted the slopes, broken by an occasional gray rock or decaying gnome ruins. The horses strained bringing us uphill toward a dull burgundy tent, and we all twisted to get a glimpse of the portly human standing in front. At first, he was no more than a rotund silhouette against a blue sky and mottled brush.

Wind tugged at the corners of his open jacket and a matching black cape. Held in his hand, a silver tipped spear rested on its butt against the ground near his right foot; a sword scabbard hung at his hip and I imagined a weapon, which would be silver as well. He smiled broadly as if pleased to see us arrive. A wide-brimmed hat sat on short black hair framing a pale face. His lips were too red for a gnome.

Three more of his kind guarded the slope behind his tent.

"A cave." I gestured to a low opening among dead brush and exposed rock. Our people preferred the open air to stone.

"Welcome. Hurrah." Shorter than most of his kind, the human waddled with an arrogant but congenial flourish. The wagons pulled to a stop before him. "Thank you all for joining us. We have tracked the vile demon here, and together we will destroy it."

My hand tightened on the wooden haft. Where had the people from the other tent gone?

"Noble volunteers, you will search for our quarry with your sharp ears and eyes. Draw it out and bring it to me." He hefted his spear. "We will end its reign of terror today!"

At least he did not hide the fact that we were nearly unarmed and what our true task would be. I drew a tight breath and glanced at the cave mouth; I was not the only one among our group to show some concern.

"Rally, rally." He lifted his spear higher, and my breath

caught. He wore a black metal gun strapped under his armpit.

By agreement, none of the gnomish weapons were allowed on our lands. The metal of those bullets had poisoned many of my people. Anger flushed inside.

"Get them out and feed them," he said to our drivers. Leisurely, he ambled toward the cave.

"Up and out." The drivers began to climb down and we rose as a group. "We've got more food in the tent."

"He has a gun," I whispered to Jax.

The older man with the gauge snorted. "That's what you're going to worry about? A Raka potentially cornered in a cave sounds more dangerous to me."

Lips pressed tight, I jumped to the ground. None of this sounded like a safe venture to me, but if they fed us for a month on two cakes a day, I could survive twice that long. If we lived, I might survive the winter. I'd take the risk. The gun I considered more of an affront to our people, than a danger to myself.

Jax moved quickly to join the throng at the tent.

"In a hurry to get inside that cave?" I asked.

"Ready to fill my belly. This is my first job in a week, and if it's my last, I intend to be full."

The air in the tent hung heavy with built up heat and the scent of sweet food. I sampled two bites of the tephis cake before I added it to the half portion still in my pocket.

The Raka I had come to consider a real possibility. If the gnome got himself killed by it, our people would be running for their lives. Even if I had more than a wooden spear, I'd be one of them.

We trailed out as a group, most finishing their cakes. The gnomish drivers were brusque and pressed us to hurry. "There's torches in the bucket. Only one in three light up on the brazier."

I led Jax toward a barrel of acrid pitch torches. "We need to be careful."

He chuckled. "Now you tell me."

The woman in front of me lit her torch, so I left mine cold. With my hands occupied, it almost felt comforting. A false solace that brought a chill as soon as I looked to the dark cave entrance.

"My name is Gregor Abbott and we are about to kill the first Raka demon ever on Earth. Search every crevice, hunt down every noise. Use those marvelous golden eyes of yours to see in the depths." He sounded excited, as if he'd written a new song and wanted all the world to know of it. My people had battled the Raka for centuries, and lost. "Lead forth my good people." He gestured with a bow.

"What happened to the others?" I asked.

He frowned scanning the crowd until he locked on my face and grew a scowl. "What others?" he asked. "We are the first."

"The driver said we were another load of fae."

His eyes flicked angrily back at the other gnomes outside the tent. "They misspoke. We have sent trackers to search, but never a team such as yourself."

I glanced at my companions, not believing him, but I was not an empath. A moment passed as none of the others showed any sign of sensing him. Were none of us were empaths? First one, then more of us headed for the mouth of the cave.

The one in the recruiting line who had named himself an empath had been sent to the other tent.

I passed Gregor, ignoring his fixed gaze. There was no malice, but he noticed me and I would have rather he didn't.

The top of the opening hung so low that the first of us had to hold their torch ahead of themselves. I passed easily under it, but it felt ready to drop and crush me. The space beyond tightened into a black curve that forced us to proceed in pairs. The air stunk of rot and mold. Spider webs dragged into our white hair. Insects scurried out of our torchlight.

I had walked ten steps when the cave echoed a scrape from somewhere in its bowels. The woman in the lead paused and we all slowed. The conversation behind me stopped. I heard only my pulse in my ears. There were four ahead of me, and the bulk of the twenty behind me. I imagined Gregor at the far end.

"Go on," someone said lightly ahead.

I eased my grip on the rough stave of the torch. The hewn edges had left dents in my skin. Jax had fallen a step behind me. We walked in silence until the voices of those behind rose.

"Even with a silver blade, a Raka does not fall with one stroke," Jax said behind me.

A younger voice followed with some excitement. "You've seen one? Killed one?"

"Yes. In the wars. They are as short as a gnome, but square in shape, not like that one." He had probably been referring to Gregor, but I didn't turn. "Their noses are flat and mouths wide. They have teeth sharp enough, and jaws strong enough, to snap through that spear. Hairless, they have skin as thick as the soles of your feet."

The hall ahead widened and the ceiling arched higher so that our torches left the rock dark and shadowed. I had heard these same descriptions of Raka from my parents.

"I've seen them sliced open at the neck, pouring out their last blood, and still rip apart the soldier that just killed them. They are hateful of us." Jax sounded bitter.

A new voice farther back spoke. "I hear they take on our form if they choose."

Jax growled out a chuckle. "That would be a Valraki, and

they possess our bodies, but can change back and forth into their true forms. The Raka serve them."

My mother had died at the hands of a Valraki. My father had been killed by a Raka in the same battle. My brother had come home with what remained of their bodies, and I'd forced the story from him. Every gory detail. It was the last time I'd seen him.

"They really eat flesh, right?" someone asked Jax.

"Unfortunately, yes. They tend to like the softer organs, unless they're very hungry."

"This one is eating the whole body. Three or four at a time." It sickened me how excited the person's voice was.

"Yeah, that's disturbing." Jax sighed. "How one ended up here is what bothers me. After all these decades we've been stranded in this cursed land. No sign of them, until now."

The sides of the hall had spread far enough that our torches didn't let us see the walls. The woman in front of me veered left to search. A rat scurried at her approach. Just as happy not to be in the front, I followed her, and Jax came with us.

We'd been weaving around smaller stone outcroppings, but along the wall gray rock bulged and creviced so that we had to poke into darker corners to avoid leaving an opening behind us. Other groups pressed outward lighting all but the roof of a wide cavern. Even with it dimly lit, I felt like something waited and watched us.

Gregor stood in the center of us, and again his eyes found me. None of his gnomes had accompanied us.

Long white hair strands hung in a snag of rock. I wet my lips and spoke. "Over here."

The woman obliged, bringing her torch. At my feet, the gray rock had been stained black. I knelt and caught the faint stench of dried blood. "Someone died here." My pulse had lulled and now took up a quicker beat.

"Indeed." Jax studied the stone. "Blood here, by the hair. I'd guess thrown and bled out. Then..." Other than a dark stain and hair, there was nothing left.

"Sniff him out, my troopers." Gregor's voice caused us to jump. "Onward."

He wouldn't care about our find. We traced along the wall, even though others had already checked.

"I think there were Edael before us," I said. "And that was one of them."

Jax narrowed his eyes. "Why would Gregor lie? How is he alive?"

I glanced back at the gnome. "Maybe he didn't come in here with them. How would he know what it takes to kill a Raka?"

"Ask one of us?" Jax frowned. "But why?"

I'd wondered the same. "Gnomes come here as tourists and merchants, for sex or to let our magic rub off on them. Never to protect us."

"A trophy then. They kill wildlife for sport." Jax stopped short at a scream ahead.

I dropped my spear point to aim at the noise. In that direction, one group moved toward the other. There appeared to be no panic or attacking Raka. A man pulled up from a crevice where he'd stepped into a hole. The room had gone silent.

"Let's move forward," Jax said. "Let me light my torch, yours is guttering."

With his brighter flame beside her dimming torch, I could see a patch of darkness on the ground ahead of us. Small rocks, the size of my head appeared to have tumbled from the wall. The stain spread out among them. "Blood?" I gestured toward the spot.

Jax's torch behind me, I left shadows drifting among the rocks. The darkened ground bled under two of the stones.

"I wonder how many died in here?" Jax muttered.

"All of them, I would guess." One of the rocks tilted higher off the ground than the other. I lifted it.

A broken knife lay underneath; a wood wrapped hilt had been shattered under the stone. Splinters obliterated any hint of the delicately carved designs. The silver blade had been snapped at the guard from the impact. Someone had smashed this weapon, intentionally breaking it, right here. I picked up the tip of the blade, the edge sharp, but wavy in spots from the strike. I saw no sign of blood. "They never got to use it."

"Raka are fast, and that little knife would have to hit the right spot from the start. If we find one of the demons, throw it at it and run." He tilted his head. "Still, nice find."

Even a small piece of silver would trade for a week's worth of food. Gingerly, I tucked the blade in my empty tunic pocket. When Jax gestured questioningly to the small piece of silver left among the splintered grip, I nodded.

We both stood when someone called out ahead. They were deep in the cavern and more voices joined the first. I could see a torch at the far wall. "Did we hit a dead end?" I asked.

"I doubt it." Jax motioned me forward.

A number of the groups had two torches lit, one bright and one failing. We passed Gregor who stood in the center appearing curious, but not stepping forward. Perhaps this was where the others had been attacked. There could be more signs of blood and death in the cave; we had only worked one side. The floor sloped down and I walked carefully through the rubble of a broken stone. The ceiling above had become a black gaping maw.

A design covered the farthest end of the cavern, and I saw no obvious exit. Shadow faded as more of us brought torches closer to the back. The pattern on the wall was a motif constructed of white sticks and spheres. Those groups closest had stopped a fair distance from it, murmuring among themselves. The intricate arrangement formed the top two-thirds of a circle, which rose twice the height of any of us. There were gaps at the top, as if it were unfinished.

"No," whispered Jax.

I glanced from him to the construction. "What?"

The woman with us peered at Jax. "Do you know what it is?"

Jax winced and his copper skin blanched. "I saw one—in a Raka temple. That's a summoning arch for a Valraki."

I peered at the design, searching for Raka lettering. Some people had studied the Raka in our last city; I had stayed to my music and shunned any knowledge of them. My eyes could see clearly now. The pattern consisted of bones. Skulls formed the white spheres. They acted as joints between the long leg bones of my people. Whether true or imagination, the scent of death filled my nostrils. "We should leave," I said. Turning, I found us among the back line, and Gregor had moved close behind us. His face was lit with joy or pride and my stomach turned.

I scanned the bowl where the cavern ended and found a few dark crevices between outcroppings of rock where there might be an exit. Perhaps there was more than one Raka, and they had built this temple, just to summon one of their masters. They could have hidden during the wars, building up this altar, taking our bones leisurely while we were losing so many.

"Behold the glory!" Gregor boomed. He no longer held his spear aloft, just his hands. The small trio near him lit his beaming face with torchlight. "We have come to this new world!"

I frowned and stepped slowly away from the gnome, to the side rather than back toward the temple's altar. "We should leave." I repeated in a whisper, but Jax already circled with me.

Gregor knocked off his hat and opened his mouth wide to take in a deep breath. His head tilted back and his pupils and irises dwindled leaving blanch white eyeballs. The human standing before us bulged even fatter and his clothes squirmed.

Those closest to him dropped their torches and backed away, deeper into the temple's hall. Those of us farther away all moved to the sides. Once I had put some distance between Gregor and his gun, I'd head for the exit. From the careful movements of the others, I was not alone in my plan. Those closer to the summoning alter would have farther to run. I hated that I counted it toward my survival.

When Gregor's skull elongated and his pale pallor darkened, Jax stumbled. The gnome's clothes ripped and sloughed off as he grew in height. From his bottom lip, a beard of wormlike tentacles grew and unrolled down, dangling to his chest. The gnomish weapon I had feared landed on the floor with a dull thud beside his scabbard and clothes.

His body bare, Gregor's arms began to divide themselves. Each finger peeled a snake-like length up his arm. It coiled at his shoulder, rolled over to the back, then peeled more flesh midway down his side. Wriggling like blind worms, they stretched out and grew thicker. Each acted on its own accord, probing into the air.

I dropped my unlit torch, but held firm to my useless spear, and yanked Jax up.

Gregor had grown as tall as any of us. His frame stretched thin, he had a muscular torso, but squat legs. Claws grew out of the bony remains of his arms. His new tentacles stretched against the ground, coiling and winding as they grew in length.

Jax barely shuffled, even as I pushed him. "A Valraki." He uttered the words in a horror that chilled me.

The creature that had been Gregor lashed out a tentacle and smacked into the two closest people. As he did so, I could make out thin leathery wings rising off his back. Those he'd attacked skittered to the ground and a second tentacle already reached out for an ankle. Screams broke out around the room, echoing off cold stone walls. I let go of Jax and began to run, forcing myself to aim for the side rather than run straight for the opening.

The third member of the party closest to him stabbed at a tentacle with their spear. A dreadful fear rose like icy water along my shoulders. We had always assumed the Raka and Valraki were left behind when we escaped on the Great Fleet. It appeared they were here in these cursed lands. We were doomed.

I chanced a quick glance around, hoping I would not find Raka attacking as well. The torches had been dropped and shadows raced between them. A flame lit the unfinished summoning altar waiting for its bones.

A handful of us dashed for the exit, some on foot and others on wing. Perhaps they hoped Gregor too distracted to catch them. Screams erupted from one man as a tentacle lashed around his torso. Another died quietly in flight as one of the Valraki's limbs lashed around his throat and snapped his neck.

A man sobbed as he was dragged to the creature. I couldn't help but watch and would have taken to the air if I did not believe it would make me a target. Jax had been left behind me, but I recognized his cry when a tentacle slapped against him. The sickening thud forced me to turn.

I crouched as I neared the edge of the cavern. Jax lay in a heap at the wall. One of his wings folded irrevocably. He didn't move.

More than half our number was already down and Gregor held two more in the air. Groans and sobbing replaced the screams. The Valraki's tentacles snapped from one victim to the next. Trembling, I stepped back between two stones and focused on forming an illusion. My skills in magic were weak and useless except when I'd been a scout. I knew nothing about these creatures and could only hope illusion would work on him.

I would be a shadow among the stones. My hands shook and I shoved them in my tunic pockets. The sharp point of the broken blade stabbed my thumb, but I didn't cry out. I stared at the gray floor ahead of me and focused on a warm blanket of black covering me. The torches discarded in the cavern were guttering—flickering and spitting their way into death like my people. The sounds of pain continued. Low and moaning, or sharp cries as the Valraki attacked. Rough rock bit into my shoulders on each side of my wings. I refused to lift my gaze.

I imagined the tentacle snapping into my too-wide crevice, but it hadn't come yet. Out in the cavern, a groan would spike into a cry, then squelch or snap into silence as the Valraki finished the wounded. One by one they were being snuffed out. My breath started to quicken, and I forced it slower.

Gregor began to laugh between deaths. Deep in timbre but with a gravel rumble throughout and a gnashing snap at the end. I hated the food I'd eaten earlier as it roiled in my stomach, threatening to expose me with a retch.

The last moan yelped, and the cavern was silent. Darkness faded in around me. I could not risk hoping that I would survive.

When Gregor spoke, I jerked hard enough to tear my back on rock. His unnatural voice echoed, gravel against stone. "Do you know what it takes, beyond bones, to summon my daughter to this plane?" The Valraki appeared to be talking to the score of corpses strewn about the cave. "A live vessel. Bruised and battered doesn't matter, just alive. Once the bones are placed, then the vessel is offered as the gate."

I shook uncontrollably, but held my illusion. My hand bled inside the tunic of my pockets, soaking through to leggings and hip. I refused to flinch, though I was sure he stared directly at me. I would not survive if I ran.

"This foolish vessel I wear called to me willingly. Another, to my brother." He scraped out a chuckle. "I'm the ambitious one."

His footstep scraped on stone. Throughout the massacre of my people, Gregor had not stepped from where he transformed. A second footfall scuffed as if he flicked a stone or body away from his path. He snapped a spear with his languid pace.

I knew he walked toward me.

"I would have my daughter with me. Your life will have purpose."

I lifted my gaze. My comrades surprised me. Two spears poked out of his side, and a third pinned through one of his tentacles. They had tried. I'd abandoned Jax, and done nothing but hide. I would pay for my cowardice. Was the gnome still conscious inside the Valraki? Would I be?

"Come out, my treasure."

I gripped the silver blade, not because I could hope to stab the creature, but because I could take from it what I had already lost, my life. The will to draw it across my throat rose with a snarl.

I dropped my illusion and stepped forward. As I pulled the broken blade from my pocket, a tentacle snapped around my upper arms. Soft yet strong, it slipped behind my wings, wrapped across my chest, and peeled me away from the crevice. I would have cried out, but it crushed the air in my lungs.

He lifted me easily. His wings outstretched, they framed his odd shaped head. His overly large eyes studied me. "Yes, you will do nicely."

I struggled as I rose higher, enough to finally see the roof and the icicle-like stone dripping from the ceiling. Teeth bared, I stabbed the silver blade into his tentacle. I could hope he'd drop me and end this all.

"Oh that bitter taste. I know it well. Where did you find silver? You would need more than that little pin to harm me." His grating tone held annoyance.

He flipped me with a lurch and my heel caught a rock. Then my body plummeted toward the Valraki's face. My stomach might have finally let loose if I were not bound so tight. I would pass out soon. What would I be when I woke?

Gregor dangled me overhead so that my hair nearly touched his face. "This is going to hurt. I need to scrape a little of your flesh inside me, so that we are connected. Just an ear, I think."

As he opened an impossibly wide mouth, rows of gray pointed teeth lined a curved maw, which could fit my head. From the blood stains, I wouldn't be the first. A black tongue flickered deep in the throat.

One of my tephis cakes tumbled out of my pocket, landing nearly wedged in the Valraki's throat. Hot fetid breath exhaled as his mouth snapped shut. Gregor grunted and swallowed, glaring. "Nasty. Let's wash it down with a couple ears." His voice echoed and slurred in my head as I approached unconsciousness. He tilted me sideways and once again opened wide.

I flicked the blade tip, aiming for the throat. Had I been able to breathe, I would have made a last snide comment.

Through fading eyes, I saw the silver tip wedge at the flesh of the throat before the jaw snapped shut.

Gregor convulsed and choked. The tentacle tightened with an audible crack in my ribs. I started to black out as he gagged and howled. When I was slammed into the stone floor, the sounds of his pain faded in my ringing ears.

The tentacle still held me when I woke, but it merely wrapped limply around my torso. The cavern was all but black except for a torch flickering about a dozen paces away. The Valraki lay between, a motionless silhouette with a wing elbowed into the air. I shivered and pulled off the dead limb, finding my right side screaming in dull pain. I could breathe. I was alive.

Staggering, I rose and shuffled off the appendage. My next two steps backed me away from the monster, then I drew a deep breath and began to circle it, aiming for the dim torch.

The Valraki didn't move as I stumbled across the rock-strewn floor. My foot rolled on an arm and I pressed forward. I might find my way out without a torch, but I wanted the comfort of it more than ever. Part of me screamed that the Valraki couldn't be killed, but it was dead.

I gathered the torch, then a fresh one. Each step I glanced back at its bulk.

Jax's head had been smashed. He had died with a full belly.

No one else had survived. I found some fresh spark still alive inside me when I came across Gregor's sword. It was real, just not silver. I was alone, each of my companions had been crushed or twisted, like Jax.

The elaborate hilt of the sword had enough iron or steel exposed that it burned my hand. With a scavenged tunic wrapped around the grip, I brought it to my quarry. If the Valraki lived, I would know soon enough.

A black, oily slick of blood pooled at the gaping mouth of the Valraki. Its razor teeth reflected flickering flames. I piled three freshly lit torches against its long fleshy body for light, ignoring the reek of its searing flesh. Folded leather wings forced me to approach from the front and my eyes flicked again to the maw near my left foot.

Raising the sword overhead, I gritted my teeth against the pain of broken ribs, then hacked down into the dull gray skin of the Valraki's neck. It bit deep, about a hand's width. Sliding the blade out, the creature didn't flinch, and no fresh blood flowed.

I'd survived, but lost a friend. I took another hack, deeper, but not to any bone.

The almost finished temple I could hope the military would dispose of. The next cut dug into something harder at the back of the neck.

I could do nothing about the Valraki's brother, again, the military would have to be on the lookout. On the next swing, the sword stuck and I leveraged a foot on a loose mass of tentacles to rock it back out. A torch sizzled against a soft tentacle.

I hadn't lost all my tephis bread. Once I knew the torches would last long enough to get me out, I could take a break and eat. The blade stuck in bone and flesh again, deeper this time.

I eased it out and lifted the weapon overhead with aching limbs. Once this damnable head was freed, I'd eat for a year.

*KEVIN A DAVIS is a fantasy author with two published series set in modern settings; the Khimmer Chronicles featuring the lively assassin Ahnjii, and the AngelSong series centering around the indominable Haddie. A multitude of his short stories of have been published in anthologies. Residing in north Florida, he attends* conventions throughout the year either as a vendor, speaker, or a fan. His newest series, the DRC Files, features the curly and curvy Kristen, a witch with exceptional skill in magic, as the new agent in a secret team that tracks down the worst to seep through the realms.

Visit his website at www.KevinArthurDavis.com,

on FB www.facebook.com/KevinArthurDavis,

or Twitter https://twitter.com/KevinADavisUF

or Instagram https://www.instagram.com/kevinarthurdavisauthor/

# SAMIAM

## EMILY CARVELLI

*E*veryone went inside in 2020, but some people didn't come back out.

Sam was one of them. Sam hadn't been *out* in a while.

He didn't have a great reason for it. No monster lurking outside the door, no end-of-the-world nonsense. It didn't even start all at once. With the lockdown, his job moved fully remote. He set up a nice little home office and wore comfy clothes all day. He started getting groceries delivered. Everyone did. He could lounge around all day and never leave the comfort of his seven-hundred-square-foot apartment. It was great.

Time passed and the world went back to normal. But Sam didn't.

Maybe he wasn't trying hard enough. But sometimes he would get right up to the door, hand on the knob, ready to go out, *hungry* to go out, before he would lose control of his heartbeat. With hands shaking and weak legs, he'd have to go lay down and focus on breathing right. By the time he got back to equilibrium, going out was about the farthest thing from his mind.

You know, you don't really realize how hard it is to see people until you stop being the one to show up. Sam's friends invited him to events for a while. He got consistent Facebook invites and texts. Once the quarantine lifted, everyone was searching for that human contact again. But, over the course of weeks and months, the invites stopped coming in. And after a while, his friends stopped visiting. Sam texted them constantly to keep the friendships alive, hoping each meme and "good morning" would act as a breath of life in their relationships. But eventually, they stopped responding there, too.

By then, his seven-hundred-square-foot haven felt more like a prison than an oasis. Gray walls closing in on him. The sickly sweet, rotting smell of the garbage he let pile up to avoid the trek to the dumpster downstairs was suffocating. White plastic bags fit to bursting with takeout containers and ramen cups. From the ceiling, an airplane he crafted out of used Mountain Dew bottles hung as a decoration, attracting flies with its sticky residue.

The worst of it all was the silence though. Not that it was *silent* silent. The passing trains and the cars honking were loud, but they failed to really fill the bone-crushing *silence*. The way the walls and garbage swallowed up his own voice, making the room feel cavernous and empty. The way Sam could go an entire day without hearing another living being. Without speaking. When the silence got particularly loud, he would play a stream of videos, podcasts and movies. Anything with voices.

Online was his only real connection to the outside world. Group forums and game chats. He messaged people whose real names he would never learn, whose faces he would never see. A man in the desert seeking a mirage of human contact. Texting day in and day out to try and ignore the glaring absence of another body to share his space with.

.   .   .

> SAMIAM: How's it going today, everybody? Good I hope!

    > Chaddad79: Oh, it's definitely going...

    > iamT0e: its goooood

    > Thickumsx: great for me! powers still out but it should be back soon

    > SamIam: Dang! I hope you're safe!

    > Thickumsx: thanks (。>﹏<。)

    > rancid6969: you can come stay with me thickums <3

    > [Thickumsx is typing]

WHEN SAM first moved into his apartment, it was a steal. Cheap on account of the location and there being no elevator. The platform for the Blue Line was just below his apartment window, close enough to rattle the pane as it lumbers by. Every twenty minutes or so, the train chug-a-chugged into the platform, all squealing brakes and rattling metal.

Sam's kitchen window had a perfect view of the Blue Line platform. Every morning, Sam's alarm blared at 6 a.m. He'd peel himself out of his duvet and make himself breakfast. A frozen breakfast burrito. Every morning. He had a nice setup. A high-top table and chair pushed right up against the window, just high enough that he could comfortably look down at the train platform without having to crane his neck. It should be the right height—he bought it for that exact purpose. And every morning, he watched the people there.

Sam and the early morning commuters always drank their coffees together, bleary-eyed and regretting the early hour. When the school kids crowded the platform, their rambunctious voices would carry straight into Sam's open window. He might even laugh along if he caught a good joke, though always quietly and to himself. The commuters and students are nice. A large group of voices to fill Sam's apartment with the sounds of chatter. Loud enough that, if he closed his eyes, he could almost imagine himself down there. With them.

Sam saw breakups and people exchanging numbers. He saw people huddling together in the harsh winters and sharing mugs of cocoa. He saw acts of kindness and malice. Had the opportunity to see families grow, watch their toddlers age until they got their own school uniforms. He'd seen all the microcosms of life from his window and felt almost as if he himself experienced all the highs and lows of the people he'd grown to know from watching.

But, if 2020 taught the world anything, it's that things can change drastically without a moment's notice.

And damn if it didn't happen again.

It started with just a few shapeless spots. Dark marks on walls that could be mistaken for a trick of the light or dirt. Blurry and unfocused dark smudges. More like a figure seen at a distance in the fog than anything concrete. They stood, silent and unmoving. Watching, almost.

The spots stayed outside as far as Sam could tell. Not that he looked in-depth. Once the public really started talking about the marks though, he couldn't help the way his eyes would sometimes linger on those always-present dark places in the home. The neglected corners: under the bed, in his closet. The places the sun just failed to reach. But the spots stayed outside, from what he could tell. Any knowledge he had about them, he pulled from his view of the Blue Line platform and his forums.

> RANCID6969: yall seeing this?
> iamT0e: Seeing what?

> rancid6969: the news, my brother in christ! the weird shit going on

> SamIam: Shadow demons were not on my bingo list lol

> Thickumsx: (O_O)

> Chaddad79: What do you think it is?

> Thickumsx: ¯\\_(ツ)_/¯

> rancid6969: Welp, im not planning to go outside. Yall try and report back <3

> iamT0e: Pass

> Thickumsx: Pass

> SamIam: Hard pass

OVER TIME, the forms got clearer. They turned into distinct shadowy figures, like shadow puppets, projected onto the walls from somewhere unseen. As if someone spun the lens on a camera to sharpen the focus, those fuzzy blobs took shape. The shapes the shadows took, however, were just a bit *off*. They were the shapes you'd find if you showed someone who had never seen a human before a picture of one, just for a moment, and then asked them to draw it from memory. Arms too long, necks too wide, fingers trailing behind them as they glided from one spot to the next. The shadows moved as if through water, slow and heavy, but with a graceful floating quality. It evoked a certain eerie sickness to look at. The queasiness in your stomach when you see something uncanny. But soon, even the *off* bits disappeared. Soon, they were identical to us. Like Peter Pan's shadow in the cartoon. Fully independent human silhouettes. And the too-long arms and trailing fingers were left forgotten in the past, a bad rumor too bizarre to be worth remembering.

Some shades were smaller than the others, romping on the platform not unlike the students Sam watched. There were larger ones trudging along. Shadows rolled past in wheelchairs, walked following four-legged shadows on leads. Thousands of disembodied silhouettes going through the motions of life.

And as the shadows filled the streets with their daily tasks, the people Sam relied on didn't. The commuters and the students went back online. Only a few places required their workers to brave the outdoors with the unknown figures, leaving the streets and the train platform virtually abandoned. The tones of chatting coming from Sam's window dried up and he filled the silence more and more with the artificial voices of newscasters and the tapping of his fingers on the keyboard.

~"Do not leave your homes until further notice. At this time, we have no news about what is causing the anomalies or if they are safe."~

> RANCID6969: i stg theres one in my room!!!
   > SamIam: One what?
   > iamT0e: A roach
   > rancid6969: one of the shadow people
   > Chaddad79: Why don't you pull the other one?
   > SamIam: No way!

~"Just another outcome from the lazy leadership we've had in Washington."~

> RANCID6969: im srs, she showed up this morning
   > Thickumsx: bye ৬\( ◁ )৯

> Chaddad79: Are you safe? Is it doing anything?
> iamT0e: Ow ow, its a she?


~"The question is, what will we do about it, and are you and your children safe?"~


> RANCID6969: hell yea brother its a she
　　> rancid6969: she hot too
　　> rancid6969: she walks around nekkid
　　> rancid6969: ⌒(˭̡̞ ̡̡ᴘ˭̡̞)
　　> iamT0e: wait how do I get one again?
　　> Thickumsx: (•` _ ´•)


~"Turn now to Psalms 23:4 and read along with me. 'Even though I walk through the valley of the shadow of death, I will fear no evil, for you are with me.' He is with us in these trying times, ladies and gentlemen. I beg you to remember Him and fear no evil."~


The religious few took to the figures like they had been long foretold. "These are the end times," they said, "demons are walking among us!" While most people hid away inside, a new figure took up residence outside the Blue Line platform. He pinned American flags to his dirty, rumpled clothing and carried a cardboard sign written on in thick black marker.

"The Demons Follow Me" the sign read, "Shadows Probe Me Daily."

Oddly enough, he was one of the first to go missing.

\* \* \*

*SHE* APPEARED WITHOUT WARNING.

One morning, Sam woke up and just felt *off.* Lying in bed with his face towards the wall, he had that *feeling.* When you just know you're not alone in a room. The way you can feel the space being taken up, even if you don't see who's taking it up yet. He stalled, staring at the wall and hiding under the blanket. If he couldn't see it, it didn't exist.

Unfortunately, Sam was an adult, with a job, who needed to start his day or risk clocking in late. He hid the bottom half of his face under his blanket and rolled over inch by inch. Like the sun peaking over the horizon, the room revealed itself just as slowly. The empty ceiling, his meager wall art, and then *Her.* She was so out of place in his dingy room, so unexpected, he froze. He blinked. And blinked again, eyebrows furrowed.

There, where there used to be a blank wall next to his closet, stood the silhouette of a woman. She reached into the space of the closet and moved as if rifling through clothes. Sam's face grew warm. She was definitely a woman. The light gray of the walls hugged tightly to her curves, high-lighting just how shapely she was. Well endowed, he couldn't help but notice. She slipped into a shirt, modeled it in front of the large panel mirrors the apartment came with, then tossed it onto the floor and tried another. The cycle repeated until she finally settled on an outfit.

Sam, captivated, crawled out of bed. Hunched and care-ful, like he was approaching a skittish animal, he tiptoed across the floor, eyes never leaving Her. Afraid to blink, as if blinking would make her disappear, leaving him alone and looking like an idiot with just an empty gray wall. She moved to the floor, sat cross-legged, and started doing what he could only assume was applying makeup in front of the mirror.

Sam got closer and knelt on the floor next to her shape.

He brushed his fingertips across her face. Nothing. She was cool and smooth, no difference between the gray of the wall and her inky darkness. She didn't react. Didn't flinch or acknowledge the touch. He watched her brush a little here and draw a little there until she finished, and then, he watched her make breakfast. He watched her eat breakfast, do her hair, play with a phone and walk out the door. It wasn't until she left that Sam realized he watched her the entire morning. He forgot to have his coffee date with the few remaining Blue Line commuters. He forgot to check his messages. He failed to clock in entirely. Oddly enough, the thought didn't disappoint him.

He only hoped she would come back soon.


> CHADDAD79: Did you hear about the disappearances? Has anyone heard from Rancid?

> SamIam: no sorry

> Chaddad79: He's been offline for a week. That's not like him...

> Thickumsx: boy is busy with his shadow girlfriend

> SamIam: anyone know his irl number?

> Thickumsx: I wouldn't exchange numbers with rancid if you paid me

> iamT0e: i would do anythign for the right price ✧(｡•̀ᴗ-)✧

> Thickumsx: maybe he died :(

> iamT0e: press f to pay respects

> Thickumsx: f

> SamIam: F

> Chaddad79: This isn't funny, something serious could have happened.

> Chaddad79: I'm worried.

> iamT0e: daddy chill

> iamT0e: im sure he's fine!

SHE DID, come back, that is. And Sam found a new regular pastime. In the mornings, he watched her get ready for work and start her day. On the weekends she usually laid about. He would laze with her, finding himself reluctant to leave the room when she occupied it.

Sometimes, she ran errands and he'd get to see her on the stage of the Blue Line platform. On those days, Sam would watch her train depart and then sit by the door to wait for her return like a dog with its owner. He missed her immediately. A hungry, gaping emptiness grew inside him without Her there. He didn't bother with his radio or forums, fearing she might enter when he stepped away. In those moments, Sam wanted more than ever to try the doorknob. He might have tried, too, if he only knew where she went.

In Sam's head, a voice that sounded a lot like his own yelled at him that this reaction wasn't *right*. But that voice got quieter and quieter by the day, replaced instead with a constant stream of thoughts about Her. How beautiful she was. How kind she was. How he felt so full with Her around. So happy and with purpose. How could this be *wrong* when that gaping loneliness in his chest was swallowed up and filled by Her, moving his focus away from the empty corners and the trash heaps and the silence; and narrowing his focus onto Her. Vignetting his reality to *Her*.

> CHADDAD79: theres one in my house
> iamT0e: damn you too
> iamT0e: scale of 1 to 10 how hot is she?
> Chaddad79: not a she
> iamT0e: :/

> Chaddad79: it isnt just anyone

> Chaddad79: i swear to gd i knw him

> Chaddad79: i swear its my son

> iamT0e: how does your son feel about his shadow lol

> Chaddad79: my son died

> Chaddad79: 3 years ago

> Chaddad79: im not crazy

> Chaddad79: id recognize him anywhere. im not crazy thats him

> iamT0e: dude

> Thickumsx: i'm so sorry, are you ok?

> Chaddad79: idk

> Chaddad79: do yall think the shadows are the dead

> Chaddad79: like in heaven?

> [multiple people are typing]


THE MORE SAM watched Her the more he could almost believe she watched him back. Moments where she would stop moving, facing him. Moments where he would wake up to her silhouette stretched across the wall above his bed. But just as quickly as he convinced himself she was watching; she would move on. Sometimes when it happened, he would try and speak with Her.

"Can you see me," he'd ask. "Can you hear me?"

But she never responded. Sam wasn't disappointed, though. He didn't need a reaction. He felt fulfilled just by lying prostrate before his silent, unseeing and unhearing god. In the mornings, he watched Her get ready for work. In the evenings, he watched Her relax. They ate dinner together at the table. He had to push his bed to a different wall to get it done, but at night they slept together. He talked to Her for hours every day. Face pressed up against the wall in reverence. If he could just press his body a little closer, if he could just touch more, maybe she would feel his warmth and devotion through the wall separating them. Maybe she would hear his prayers. Maybe he would slip right through.

He didn't shower. Every second away from Her was time wasted. He found himself skipping meals, but he didn't need to eat anymore. He was filled with Her. He was losing time. He could never remember falling asleep on the floor, but more and more often he found himself waking up crammed into the crevice where the trim meets the flooring.

Sam wondered if this is what love felt like...he believed it was. Because he loved Her. He loved Her with all his heart. With his whole being. She was everything.

> THICKUMSX: I think chaddad was right
> > Thickumsx: theyre angels maybe
> > Thickumsx: something better
> > Thickumsx: have you met yours yet
> > Thickumsx: theyre perfect
> > {Thickumsx left chat}

SAM ONCE HEARD that if you met your doppelganger, you wouldn't recognize them because you've only ever seen yourself mirrored in a reflection. That's bullshit. He knew the minute he laid eyes on *It*.

She wasn't on the wall beside Sam that morning. He rolled out of bed, eyes immediately scanning the room for Her. At first, he almost mistook *It* for *Her*. For only a moment though, because when he really took It in, It was so obviously not Her.

The new shadow was the same height as Sam. The figure's arms were held away from its body, frozen. It styled its hair like him and carried its weight in its midsection like him. It was like his own shadow peeled itself off the floor and set up against the wall.

But more than just *looking* like Sam, it *felt* like him, too. Like the shadow was an extension of him. There was a red string of fate tied from Sam's heart to the matching silhouette frozen on his wall. He could tell with some intrinsic certainty that it was *his.*

At that moment, she entered. Sam couldn't tear his eyes away from his shadow, but in his peripheral vision he watched Her glide across the room. Her feet didn't touch the floor and Her form was fuzzy, blackness trailing behind Her in smoky wisps. If he looked closer, he might have noticed her arms were a little too long, or her neck too wide. He might have noticed the way her fingers lengthened in the wispy shadows and sharpened to points. He might have noticed if he looked closer. But he didn't.

She stepped behind It, and Sam pressed his hand up against her, feeling the cold drywall on his sweaty palms. Sam panted. The woman Sam had grown to love, to worship, draped her arm over his shadow's shoulders. Though eyeless, Sam could feel her heavy gaze searing into him. He could feel she was smiling. Smiling at him.

"Come here, Sam," her smile said. "Join us over here."

"It's better over here" his empty silhouette echoed. "We're with Her over here."

"Step up Sam, just step right though" he could hear Her whisper. And he could see it. He needed to go through. And he knew how he could. Sam knew, if he stepped up, if he pressed his palms into the palms of the shadow, pressed his face up against the outline of his head on the wall, he knew he would slide right through. He knew the plaster would be as good as tissue paper—that it would part for him like the Red Sea.

It was a passageway, one shaped and made just for *him.* It

was *his*. And in the end, it didn't take much convincing. Sam would cram himself into a much smaller passage for the opportunity to meet Her. But she made him his own passage, stretching onward into blackness and leading him to Her.

\* \* \*

SAM DOESN'T KNOW what's behind the shadows, and he doesn't care. He's going to step right through. And even though he will be walking through shadows, he isn't afraid. Because he will be with Her. She who rescued him. She, who hasn't left him alone since they finally made contact, continuously wheedling Sam, prompting him towards his personal exit. All things end, and so too will his time on this Earth. He needs to enter. And he will enter. Just like, he thinks, so many others must have done before him.

> SAMIAM: idk how many are left here, but I'm logging off now.
   > SamIam: it's been great getting to know you all
   > SamIam: See you on the other side
   > {SamIam left chat}

*EMILY CARVELLI WAS BORN and raised in Chicago, Illinois. As a lifelong lover of reading, horror, and reading horror, Emily is inspired to write the types of stories she's always loved. SamIam will be one of her first forays into having her fiction published.*

# TUCKERIZATIONS

Thanks to the patrons and authors who helped us Tuckerize a few stories.

Amber Tolman becomes Amber in Tyler Clark's story *Life Was a Dream* and we hope you enjoy her part in this story.

Steve Stratton plays a sheriff in *Potashe Preserve* by CE Albanese.

Ed Weisbart gets a theater named after him in L.A. Selby's *Only One of Many*.

Erin Nickerson becomes the cryptid protagonist embroiled in the disaster of *The Valraki Temple* by Kevin A Davis.

# ACKNOWLEDGMENTS

*Behind the Shadows* came to life as we realized how popular some of the horror stories were from our Hidden Villains anthologies. We reached out to Sara Jordan-Heintz for her in-depth knowledge of Horror and her editing skills. Thank you, Sara.

Inkd Publishing would like to thank Heather Lewis, April Davis, Tony Cioffi, Heather Norris, and Kevin Davis for their relentless hours helping Sara read through all those stories. They brought the best to you.

Producing anthologies offers writers a chance to expose their craft and readers an opportunity to find new favorites. We would like to thank our Kickstarter supporters for helping to make these publications possible.

Please join us in thanking the following backers for helping to make this anthology possible.

Kickstarter Patrons:

Michael Axe, Tracy Hughes, The Creative Fund by BackerKit, Zack Fissel, Ryan, Sara Jordan-Heintz, Tiffany, April Davis, Michael Feir, crystalbrier, AJ Benson, Paul Trinies, Jennifer Perry, Duchele Lazzaro, LA Selby, Alex, Steve Stratton, Bailey Meeker, Jared Nelson, Klikke Sietel, Tim Lewis, Ed Weisbart, Ryan Pote, Nelson Truong, Angelia Whatley, Derek, WritersConnX, Erin Nickerson, Stewie, bkstrq, Ashley Funkhouser, Allison Charlesworth, linda selby, Conor Neilson, Howard Blakeslee, Kira Lemons, Ashleigh Floyd, Alyssa Walker, Kyle Monson, Danny Reznor, Amber Tolman, Ronald L Weston, David 'slick' Sellers, Edward

Shafer, Paul Clark, Kari Blocker, MaryAnn Selvidge Shuman, Giusy Rippa, Andrew Foxx, Serge Burack, Michael Nastasi II, Ronald Miller, Austin Hofeman, Smilesallday2, Emily Rousell, Frank Lewis, Richard O'Shea, Caroline Coriell, and Melanie Briggs

Please visit us at InkdPub.com